“Like café [illegible] anet serves up a delicious story to be savored and shared. Too much wine, a charming Frenchman, and a stolen ring spell disaster for über-organized Chloe Turner. *Je t'aime Kissed in Paris*!”

—**Lauren Clark**, author of *Dancing Naked in Dixie* and *Stay Tuned*

“This madcap romantic comedy is full of thrills and adventure, and it is the first novel in many years that interrupted my sleep and left me craving for more.”

—**Komal Mansoor** of *The Review Girl*

“From my patio, I could smell the melted cheese and chocolate on the streets of Annecy. I envisioned a vineyard outside of Lyon, and the scent of lavender and rosemary was real…if only for a moment. *Kissed in Paris* by Juliette Sobanet is the best way to travel to Paris without a passport.”

—**Peggy Randall-Martin**, author of *Backwater*

“*Kissed in Paris* is the perfect balance of fun, romance, and adventure. Sobanet had me laughing out loud, but she also had me in tears. Her easy voice and pacing made the book fly by. You know a book is a great read when you do more cardio at the gym just to keep reading it. Can't wait to see what's next from Sobanet.”

—**Rachel Kall**, author of *Legally Undercover*

"Ms. Sobanet's descriptions of French pastries and wine will place hints of lavender and butter on the tip of your tongue and leave you longing for a skimpy red dress to wear while gallivanting around the Alps with a handsome, chain-smoking stranger."

—**Jennie Shaw** of *Well Shut the Front Door*

"I loved, loved, loved this story! *Kissed in Paris* is a fabulous, fast-paced romance that I would highly recommend. I can't wait to read Juliette Sobanet's next novel!"

—**Candy Morton** of *So Little Time*

PRAISE FOR

SLEEPING WITH PARIS

"This fun, fast-paced debut novel by Sobanet is the kind of story you want to pick up at the end of the day with a glass of wine and let the rest of the world fall away."

—**Sophie Moss**, author of *The Selkie Spell*

"This book was a breath of fresh Parisian air, full of butter croissants, fine wines, and the rush of life one can only feel in the streets of Paris. Juliette Sobanet is an amazing author who knows how to tell a real story, one that makes you angry, sad, giddy, and feeling a bit sexy too. *Sleeping with Paris* has become my favorite read of 2012."

—**Thomas Amo**, author of *An Apple for Zoe*

"This story of a twenty-something grad student in Paris trying to mend her broken heart while 'dating like a man' may sound like one you've read before. But, trust me, it's not. Just as *West Side Story* was a new telling of *Romeo and Juliet*, *Sleeping with Paris* is a fresh approach to this tale. This book had me wiggling in my seat, laughing out loud, and itching to book a trip to Paris!"

—**Stana Warren**, avid reader and Francophile

"A fun read about a heartbroken American newcomer to the City of Love…and how she manages to overcome her hurt (and various other obstacles along the way!). If you love Paris, you'll definitely enjoy this. I did!"

—**Talli Roland,** author of *Build a Man*

"You remember the Calgon jingle 'Take Me Away'? *Sleeping with Paris* does exactly that. It makes you want to pour yourself a glass of wine (or eat some delicious chocolate), dive into the book, and leave your cares and worries behind. I haven't read a chick lit novel in a while that was this romantic and entertaining."

—**Amy Bromberg** of *Chick Lit Central*

"Anyone who loves the story of a strong woman finding herself and her heart is going to be absolutely enamored with this book."

—**Michelle Bell** of *Michelle's Book Nook*

KISSED IN PARIS

ALSO BY JULIETTE SOBANET

Sleeping with Paris

Dancing with Paris

Midnight Train to Paris

JULIETTE SOBANET

The characters and events portrayed in this book are fictitious. Any similarity to real persons, living or dead, is coincidental and not intended by the author.

Published by Montlake Romance
PO Box 400818
Las Vegas, NV 89140

ISBN-13: 9781477805909
ISBN-10: 1477805907

Dedication

To Alison, Karen, Marion, Tracy,

Sharon, Mary, and Tara.

You are the most fabulous

friends and critique partners

a girl could ever ask for.

May your wildest writing

dreams come true.

PROLOGUE

From: Angela Kelly
To: Chloe Turner
Sent: Thursday, August 25 at 1:00 a.m.
Subject: Pack your bags. The City of Love awaits.

Chloe,

Have come down with a deathly contagious flu and cannot take Paris trip. You will have to go in my place as there is no way I can be all Frenchy and sophisticated when I'm running to the bathroom every five minutes. Am stating right off the bat what a wretched boss I am for asking you to do this a week before your wedding, but you've worked for me long enough. You know I can be an unapologetic bitch, and I know you will get the job done. It's what you always do.

Flight leaves today at 6 p.m., landing at Charles de Gaulle early tomorrow morning. Language instructor conference runs Friday and Saturday, and flight home is Sunday morning, leaving you plenty of time to prep for wedding. You're staying at swanky Hôtel Plaza Athénée off the Champs-Élysées. Do it up. Just don't do *any of those gorgeous French men. Paul probably wouldn't like that too much. Plus, even though I'm not one for weddings, am actually looking forward to yours…that is, if I'm still invited.*

Angela Kelly
Kelly and Rain Premier Event Planning
Washington, DC

From: Chloe Turner
To: Sophie Turner
Sent: Thursday, August 25 at 1:03 a.m.
Subject: Change of plans

Hey, Soph,

Am trying not to flip out about this, but just heard from my crazy boss, Angela. She is sick and is sending me to Paris on business…tonight. Okay, I'm officially flipping out. How can she do this? I'm getting married in nine days. NINE days! I cannot go to Paris this weekend! It's not an option. Plus, you're flying in on Saturday, and I am not leaving you and Paul alone in the same house when I'm not here to mediate. We all know how much the two of you love each other. I'm going to write Angela and tell her I'm not going to Paris. It's out of the question. Please don't worry Dad, Lily, or Magali with any of this.

Love you,
Chloe

P.S. In the rare event that I do go to Paris, send me your flight info so I can move your flight to Monday. Just in case. I'm not going, though. I'm not.

From: Sophie Turner
To: Chloe Turner
Sent: Thursday, August 25 at 1:07 a.m.
Subject: Paris? WTF?

Chloe,

How can Angela ask you to travel to Paris when the wedding is next weekend? Your job is insane. And so is your boss. Seriously. But she's just insane enough to fire you if you don't go. And if you do *go, Paul is going to throw a royal fit (which will make next week so. much. fun.). It's no secret he wants you to quit your job and be a stay-at-home wife (which, by the way, could actually be a good thing—when was the last time you chilled out for five minutes?). Point is, though, going to Paris on business this weekend will only fuel Paul's fire…and if you don't go to Paris, well, you'll probably* be *fired.*

Good luck, sis. Glad I'm not in your shoes.

xxx,
Soph

P.S. I resent the fact that you don't trust me to get along with Paul. Even though I would like him much better without that giant stick up his ass, it's not like I'm going to be a bitch to him the week of your wedding. Nevertheless, I'll accept your offer to change my ticket to Monday. And I'm only doing that because I don't want Mr. Polo Shirt Khaki Pants Paul (and I mean that in the most loving way possible) to feel uncomfortable with your hippy California sister invading his home. Forwarding flight information to you now "just in case" you go to Paris. Ha.

From: Angela Kelly
To: Chloe Turner
Sent: Thursday, August 25 at 1:09 a.m.
Subject: Bonjour?

Chloe,

Am certain reason you haven't responded yet is that you are packing your bags for Paris. Obviously, no need to remind you that both your bonus and your career are riding on the perfect execution of this event. First international conference for Kelly and Rain. Can't blow it.

Angela Kelly
Kelly and Rain Premier Event Planning
Washington, DC

P.S. Really need to deep-clean the tile in my bathroom. But barely have energy to tap this e-mail into phone, let alone scrub grungy tiles. Please respond so I can go back to lying on cold, dirty tile with eyes closed. Phone screen is making me dizzy.

From: Lily Turner
To: "Big sis" Chloe Turner
CC: "Lil sis" Magali Turner
Sent: Thursday, August 25 at 1:11 a.m.
Subject: Oh la la

Hey, big sis,

What's this news about you jetting off to Paris a week before the wedding? Not having cold feet, are you? Can you bring me back a few bottles of French wine? And maybe a sexy French lover to go with? Or better yet, can you fly us all over together so we can throw you a real *bachelorette party at some wild underground Parisian club? The stuffy dinner we had at Paul's mom's house with all of his prim and proper cousins hardly counts as a bachelorette party. I mean, Magali is almost eighteen, she can handle the strippers. Right, Mags?*

luv,
Lil

From: Chloe Turner
To: Sophie Turner
Sent: Thursday, August 25 at 1:14 a.m.
Subject: Re: Paris? WTF?

Sophie,

I specifically asked you not *to tell the girls about the possible Paris trip. Can you ever keep your mouth shut? And for the record, Paul knows how much I love being an event planner, and he would never ask me to quit my job just because of a last-minute business trip. I'm sure he won't be excited about it, but then again, neither am I.*

Thanks for your never-ending support,
Chloe

From: Magali Turner
To: Chloe Turner
CC: Lily Turner
Sent: Thursday, August 25 at 1:16 a.m.
Subject: Re: Oh la la

Sistas!

We're going to Paris? OMG! This is so exciting! I don't know about the French strippers, though. Sounds kind of nasty. Does Dad know about Paris? Or about the strippers? What about Paul? And the wedding? Will we be back in time?

Mags

From: Sophie Turner
To: Chloe Turner
Sent: Thursday, August 25 at 1:18 a.m.
Subject: Re: Paris? WTF?

Chloe,

First of all, Paul will definitely want you to quit your job if you tell him you're going to Paris. That is a fact. Secondly, as if Dad, Lil, and Mags wouldn't have found out you were in Paris for the weekend. You know they'll be calling you all weekend long with questions about the wedding, and they're going to flip when they find out you're not home. Among other pressing matrimonial issues, Dad is having problems with the tux place and apparently Lily's dress still isn't short enough.

Soph

P.S. Remember how much Mom loved France? Bet if she were here, she would be jealous of your Paris trip. I miss her.

From: Chloe Turner
To: Sophie Turner
Sent: Thursday, August 25 at 1:21 a.m.
Subject: Re: Paris? WTF?

Sophie,

You could've at least waited until morning to tell the girls. They're already e-mailing me about hijacking my trip and turning it into a stripper-filled bachelorette party. I thought the dinner we had at Paul's mom's was okay…wasn't it?

I'll handle Dad's tux issue, and Lily's bridesmaid dress is already too short in my opinion. Do not let her alter it any more. Please.

Chloe

P.S. I never understood why Mom was so in love with the French. I wish she were here to take the Paris trip for me. I miss her too.

From: Chloe Turner
To: Lily Turner, Magali Turner
Sent: Thursday, August 25 at 1:25 a.m.
Subject: Re: Oh la la

Girls,

I may be taking a short trip to Paris for business. I do not have cold feet and there will not be any French strippers involved. Please refrain from using the word stripper *with Dad or Paul while I'm away (if I even go), or ever, for that matter. I'm getting married in nine days. Remember?? Love you both, and I'll see you next week.*

xoxo,
Chloe

P.S. Lil—Sophie told me you aren't happy with the length of your bridesmaid dress. Too bad. If you make it any shorter, the guests will mistake you *for the stripper.*

From: Angela Kelly
To: Chloe Turner
Sent: Thursday, August 25 at 1:30 a.m.
Subject: Think chocolate croissants, wine that flows like rivers, and hot French men with tight asses!

Chloe,

The Eiffel Tower is calling your name…and so am I. Why haven't you responded? I know *you sleep with your iPhone.*

Your sick-as-a-dog boss,
Angela

From: Chloe Turner
To: Angela Kelly
Sent: Thursday, August 25 at 1:34 a.m.
Subject: Re: Think chocolate croissants, wine that flows like rivers, and hot French men with tight asses!

~~*Angela,*~~

~~*Sending me to Paris a week before my wedding is completely out of the question. Paul is going to be irate, my dad and sisters need me home this weekend, and I…oh, screw it. Who am I kidding? I can't lose this job.*~~

Angela,

I'm packing my bags as we speak. And just for the record, I don't think I'll be paying much attention to the "tight asses" while I'm in Paris. In case you forgot, I'm getting married next weekend.

Feel better,
Chloe

ONE

"*You are in Paris, the City of Love. You must not be so controlled. Here, have another glass. I promise you, it will not hurt.*"

I jolted upright in bed, the man's deep, seductive voice echoing through my mind.

And just as quickly as I'd popped up, the pounding in my skull knocked me back down again. I groaned as I rolled to my side and squinted at the light pouring in through the wispy white drapes in the hotel room.

Why did that voice seem so real? And why did I feel like I'd been run over by a train? And why couldn't this lavish hotel have invested just a little extra money in black-out blinds for their guests?

Squeezing my eyes closed once more, I willed the room to stop spinning around me. *Did I drink last night at the hotel bar?* All I remembered ordering was a sparkling water. Plus, I never drank when I was away from Paul. I never drank at all, actually. And I certainly wouldn't have started while away on business in Paris, the night before I was set to fly home, no less.

I rubbed my throbbing forehead, and as my stomach cramped, I thought of Angela's deathly contagious flu. Oh, God. I must've caught it. How would I fly home in this state? Please don't let it be the flu. I can't handle that right now. I have to be healthy this week. I'm getting married in—

"*My name is Claude.*"

I jerked back up to a sitting position, my eyes now wide open, my breath caught somewhere between my seizing stomach and my spinning head.

Why was that voice lodged in my head? And who was *Claude*?

Jagged snippets of memories scissored their way through the cobwebs in my brain, refusing to form a cohesive picture.

A crisp black suit. Deep-indigo eyes. Chiseled cheekbones and slick black hair.

"*Let us have just one more drink in your room. I am having so much fun with you. I never want this night to end.*"

I could still hear his thick French accent ringing in my ears, feel his warm hand as it wrapped around mine and led me down the hallway of the fancy hotel.

One last memory taunted me. I remembered tripping and ramming my shoulder into the doorway…as I'd let the suave French man into my hotel room.

"Oh là là, ma chérie. *You must be careful. We have a long night ahead of us,* non?"

"No," I said out loud, shaking the images from my mind. "*No,*" I repeated. "It was all just a dream. A vivid, awful dream. Get it together, Chloe."

But when my right shoulder began throbbing, I peered down before I could stop myself and spotted a swirl of black and blue.

Oh, God. What had I done?

Slowly, I turned my head toward the other side of the bed, dreading what—or *who*—I might find.

The sight of crumpled white bed linens coupled with a firm dent in the fluffy pillow confirmed my worst fear.

I hadn't slept alone.

The intoxicating scent of aftershave emanated from the crisp white sheets, making my stomach lurch. I stumbled out of bed and nearly slipped on the creamy marble floor in the bathroom as I lunged for the sink, filled my hands with cold water, and splashed it over my steaming face to combat the nausea.

And the guilt.

How could I have brought that man into my hotel room? What had I done with him? And where in the hell was he now?

I lifted my bloodshot eyes to the mirror and gasped when I spotted my black bra and underwear fitting snugly over my pale skin, no sign of the business suit I'd been wearing the day before.

This time I lunged for the toilet.

After confirming in the worst possible way that I had most definitely drunk more than one glass of red wine at the hotel bar last night, I wrapped my shivering body in a towel and forced myself back up to the sink to brush my teeth.

I scrubbed my tongue, my gums, and every crevice of my mouth until it was raw, hoping to rid myself of the guilt and the questions that threatened to swallow me whole.

What had really happened last night? Why had I agreed to drink wine with some random French man at the bar? How could I have brought him up to my room? And worse, what had I done with him to end up in my underwear?

Tossing my toothbrush back onto the bathroom counter, I ignored the pounding behind my eyes and tried to recall *what* exactly had happened the night before.

When I couldn't put another memory into clear focus, my thumb automatically reached for my left ring finger to twist my engagement band around—a nervous habit I'd picked up ever since Paul had proposed last year.

But the minute I felt bare skin where my ring normally would've been, the hairs on the back of my neck stood up.

Where was my ring? I never took it off. Not even to shower.

The fluffy bath towel slipped off my scantily clad body as I raced out of the bathroom and over to the dresser, where I would've left my purse. But my sparkly ring wasn't there. And neither was my purse.

I tore apart the gorgeous hotel room, yanking the covers and the pillows off the bed, opening every drawer, every closet, peering in every crevice. But in the end, all I found were crystal chandeliers, empty glasses with remnants of red wine settling in the bottom, my tall black heels—one by the bathroom, one by the closet—and a slinky red dress that most definitely did *not* belong to me.

No suitcase. No purse. No phone. No diamond ring.

And no passport.

It was gone. It was all gone.

I sank onto the king-size bed, the room now spinning even more fiercely than before, last night's drinks threatening to make one more trip through my stomach, when another image flashed through my brain.

Claude's tall, dark-haired silhouette stood over the bed, his firm hand stroking my hair.

"*Yes,* chérie, *go to bed now. I will see you in the morning...*"

I'll see you in the morning, all right. After I've taken all of your possessions.

I buried my head in my hands as panic seized my chest. What had I done? I had a flight to catch. And more important, my wedding to Paul was in six days. *Six days.* How was I going to get home without a passport? And how would I explain this to him? He wouldn't even believe me. I was always under control. I didn't drink. I worked to the point of exhaustion. And in the eight years we'd been together, I'd never even contemplated cheating on Paul.

Plain and simple, Chloe Turner did not do things like this. Ever.

A screeching sound made me jump from the bed.

It was the hotel phone. Maybe someone had caught that lying, stealing French man on his way out the door.

"Hello?"

"Chloe, I've been trying to reach you on your cell, but it seems to be turned off. Are you okay?"

I cringed as my breath once again failed me.

"Hi, Paul. I...I'm fine. Everything's fine."

TWO

"I was starting to get worried. You never turn your cell off. Did the battery die or something?"

What was I supposed to tell him?

"Chloe, are you still there?"

Just spit it out. Paul is my fiancé. I can't possibly lie about something this serious.

But the dent in the pillow. Me waking up in my underwear. My ring. My passport. Oh, God.

"My phone was stolen," I blurted.

"What? How?" Paul's voice rose about three octaves, making the dread in my stomach turn sour.

"It...it was my fault. We were having dinner last night near the conference site, and I...I left it out on the table, and when I remembered and came back, it was gone." My cheeks blazed with heat. I'd never lied to Paul before. I'd never done anything I'd *had* to lie about. Not in all the years we'd been together since college. But I couldn't possibly tell him what had *really* happened...not until I figured it out for myself.

"Jeez, Chloe. It's bad enough that you agreed to do this business trip a week before our wedding, but now your phone? What a disaster."

I glanced around the empty hotel room, then down at my half-naked body, realizing Paul was clueless as to just what a life-altering disaster this had become.

"So, how are things at home?" I asked him, desperate to change the subject.

"Nuts. Your sisters have been calling nonstop with wedding demands, and I guess Sophie is flying in tomorrow. Did you know that? Why does she need to come so early?"

This couldn't really be happening right now. I had to get home.

"She's the maid of honor, Paul...and she's my *sister*. She's coming early to help out."

"Well, I still don't understand why your sisters have to play such a big role in our wedding. You're an event planner, for God's sake. You can obviously handle this without their input. Even your dad has been calling me with questions I don't know the answers to. You know the long hours I've been putting into the firm lately, and I don't have the time to deal with his anxiety over every last detail of his flight arrangements and his tux fitting. I can't believe Angela asked you to take this trip. And even worse, that you agreed. Is this job really worth it to you?"

"We've already discussed this, Pa—"

"Never mind. What's done is done. We can talk about your job when you get home tonight."

My lips froze, paralyzed at the gravity of the situation.

"Chloe? Are you there?"

I snapped back to reality. I couldn't let Paul know that something was wrong. He was already freaking out about the wedding coming up and my crazy family overwhelming him. I would work everything out. I would go straight to the US embassy and they would help me get home. And as for whatever I'd done with Claude...I could only hope that somehow, some way, it would turn out to be a horrible misunderstanding. Surely, even in my drunkest state, I wouldn't have actually had *relations* with some French man I'd just met when I'm about to walk down the aisle in less than a week?

"Chloe?" Paul's voice shot impatiently over the line.

"Sorry, I think the jet lag is still wearing on me. I better run, though. I need to eat some breakfast and get ready to head to the airport." I peered over at the clock. It was eight a.m. My flight left at one o'clock.

"I'll be waiting."

"Bye, Paul."

I listened for Paul to say good-bye, but instead was met with a blaring dial tone.

How could I have let this happen? How could I have gotten so drunk that I couldn't remember what I'd done with this French guy? Or how I'd ended up in my underwear? I couldn't worry about that right now, though. I had to focus on getting home.

With no other choice in apparel, I slipped the mysterious short red dress over my head, threw on my three-inch black heels, and snatched the room key off the nightstand—at least *Claude* had left me that. I ran down the hallway and busted through the closing elevator doors to find a woman in a large red hat and a light-blue sundress giving me the once-over before lowering her eyebrows and turning her back to me.

Oh, God. She probably thinks I'm a prostitute.

What a nightmare.

As the elevator let me out on the ground floor, I ignored the heavy stares that trailed me while I charged around the corner toward the front desk of the Hôtel Plaza Athénée. Amid the bouquets of fresh white calla lilies, the tall, creamy pillars, and the Louvre-worthy art on display, two police officers loomed over the desk, speaking with hotel management.

I dashed toward them but stopped abruptly when I spotted the taller, black-haired officer revealing a large photo to the manager.

I strained to see the glossy picture as it tilted in my direction.

My breath caught in my throat when I made out a woman with long, wavy, auburn hair, holding a glass of red wine and laughing.

It was me…from the night before.

Why did they have a picture of me?

"La femme s'appelle Chloe Turner."

My heart slammed in my chest. Even with his strong French accent, there was no mistake that the police officer had just said my name.

Before I had a chance to process any of this, the hotel manager met my eyes and nodded in my direction. The police officers swiveled around, then after a quick sideways glance at each other, they marched over to me.

The taller officer flashed his badge as his beady eyes combed the length of my body...and the short length of this stupid red dress. "I am Officer Laroche, and this is my partner, Officer Fournier." He gestured to his shorter, lighter-haired counterpart. "Please follow us, Mademoiselle Turner. We need to ask you a few questions." They took off down the hallway without giving me a chance to respond.

How did they know my name? And why did I suddenly feel like I was the one in trouble? No, that was ridiculous. They were obviously here to help me and to bust this Claude guy. I just needed to tell them everything that had happened...well, everything I could remember, that is, and they would certainly help me get some kind of emergency passport and make it to my flight on time.

I followed the officers into a secluded office at the end of the hallway, where they gestured for me to have a seat opposite them. Just as I was opening my mouth to explain what had happened, they slid two photos across the desk.

There I was again. My cheeks flushed, my long, unruly hair let down. But I wasn't alone. Claude's arm draped loosely around my shoulders in one photo, and his lips pressed against my cheek in the other.

I felt bile rising in my throat as I realized I couldn't remember either of those moments actually taking place. But what startled me even more was the distant, off-centered look in my own green eyes in each of the photos. I barely recognized myself.

How many glasses of wine did he get me to drink?

Officer Fournier spoke first. "Tell us how you know this man."

Tearing my eyes from the photos, I met the officers' stern glares. "I met Claude last night at the hotel bar. He must've convinced me to drink a lot, which I never do, because I don't remember exactly what happened. But I woke up this morning, and all of my things were gone. My passport, my wallet, my luggage, my clothes. He even took my engagement ring, and then he left me this awful skimpy red dress. I would never wear this. I would never normally even talk to someone like him. I don't know what happened, and I really need your help. I have a flight to catch in a couple hours, and—"

Officer Laroche held his hand up to quiet me. "Yes, we know. You are getting married this weekend. And please, do not bore us with your *histoire triste*. We have heard it before—the red dress, the memory loss, all of it. Just tell us the *truth* about how you know Claude Dubois."

Don't bore them with my sad story? What? And how did they know my wedding was this weekend? And the red dress? Had Claude done this to other women too?

Gripping the sides of my chair, I forced myself to keep calm. "I'm telling you the truth, Officers. I met this man last night at the hotel bar, and he stole all of my things. You do believe me, don't you?"

They didn't respond. Instead Officer Laroche slid a piece of paper across the desk. "Can you explain this to us, Mademoiselle Turner?"

I peered down to find a bank statement snapshot with both Paul's name and mine listed at the top. It was a statement for our joint checking and savings accounts. How did they get this? Before I had a chance to ask them, I noticed two highlighted transfers—one for $13,000 and another for $20,000. My stomach clenched as I focused and refocused on those numbers, wishing my eyes were playing tricks on me.

But they weren't. Those transfers had been made out of our account. Without my knowledge. And certainly without Paul's.

My hands trembled underneath the desk as I shot pleading looks at the officers. "This is insane. He must've tapped into our account. He stole my purse, which had my debit card inside, so somehow he must've used that to access our funds. You have to help me figure this out and get this money back."

Officer Fournier tapped his long, skinny finger against the paper. "Not so fast, Mademoiselle Turner. You may want to take a closer look, because if what you are saying is true, that Monsieur Dubois *just* stole your things last night, then why were these transfers made close to forty-eight hours ago?"

"What? That can't be..." I started, but my voice strangled in my throat when I saw that the date for the transfers was in fact two days earlier.

"I'm sorry," I said, my breath quickening, my stomach feeling so nauseated I could've been sick right there on the desk. "I don't understand what's going on. I didn't make these transfers. All I know is that I have to get home today. And I have to get that money back. I'm getting married this weekend, and we can't afford to lose that kind of money!"

Officer Laroche stood abruptly. "I am afraid you will not be going home today, Mademoiselle Turner. You are under investigation for fraud, and you will not be permitted to leave the country until the investigation is complete."

My eyes jetted frantically back and forth between the two officers, willing one of them to tell me that this was all a huge misunderstanding. A cruel joke they played on unsuspecting foreigners. But they said nothing.

I couldn't let them do this to me. I had to get home today.

"You're making a huge mistake!" I blurted as I grabbed one of the photos and shook it in their faces, unable to control myself for a moment longer. "This man, this *con artist, he* is the one who came in here, got me drunk, stole my things, and somehow messed with my checking account! You have to believe me. What could I possibly have to do with any kind of fraud?"

The officers raised their eyebrows at each other before turning to face me again.

"*Calmez-vous, Mademoiselle Turner,*" said Officer Fournier, the sting in his voice making me flinch.

"I'm sorry. It's just that I don't think you understand what's really going on here. I have nothing to do with any of this, and I *have* to get home today."

"We understand your urgency, Mademoiselle Turner. But *you* clearly do not understand the mess you are now involved in. And if you are innocent, as you *claim* to be, then of course you will have nothing to worry about. Either way, I think you will find it in your best interest to cooperate with us and to refrain from making a scene. For now, you must follow us to the station for further questioning."

The smugness in his voice made me want to scream.

"I need to speak with my lawyer before answering any more of your questions," I said.

Officer Laroche turned around, a creepy grin spreading across his thin lips. "Your fiancé is a lawyer, no?"

My gut clenched. How did he know that?

"How would *he* feel about the fact that you allowed Monsieur Dubois up to your hotel room last night?" He let out an obnoxious snort, then turned and filed through the door with Officer Fournier.

My mind raced as I followed the officers back into the hallway, wondering what in the hell was going on and how I'd gone from being an event planner on a last-minute business trip in Paris to a suspect wanted for fraud. We passed by the women's restroom on our way back to the lobby, and I realized I needed a minute alone to think this through. To figure out what I was going to do, who I was going to call, and how I was going to get out of this mess.

"Excuse me, Officers," I said in the calmest voice I could muster. "I need to use the restroom."

They shared another questioning glance.

"Please, I'll only be a minute. I'm not feeling well."

Officer Laroche nodded. "*D'accord.* But I will have to accompany you."

Accompany me? To the restroom?

I opened my mouth to tell him to stop treating me like a criminal, but the severe look in his black eyes made me stop. Instead, I kept quiet as Officer Fournier set off through the lobby and Officer Laroche escorted me back down the hallway of the elegant hotel, my head suddenly so dizzy I wondered if I would pass out before I even made it to the stall.

"I will wait outside the door," announced my new babysitter.

Thank God. I needed to be alone.

The pristine marble bathroom smelled of roses and honey, but the wary-eyed reflection staring back at me in the mirror, along with the scant red dress strung over my shaking body, reminded me that life was *anything* but honey and roses right now.

I leaned over the sink and ran my hands under the cool water, trying to decipher a way out of this unimaginable situation.

My mind glazed over with fear, refusing to cooperate. Refusing to do anything but worry.

How in the *hell* was I under investigation for fraud? Why didn't they believe me? How was I going to explain any of this to Pa—?

The bathroom door burst open and Officer Laroche fell through it, crashing onto the floor with a grunt. I stifled a scream as a rugged man with a full head of messy chestnut hair and an unshaven face tackled Officer Laroche, punched him in the face, and knocked him out cold. He removed Officer Laroche's gun from the holster, tucked it into his jeans, then lifted his deep-brown eyes to mine.

"Who are you?" I screeched, backing myself up against the wall.

He reached into his back pocket and whipped out a shiny badge.

"Julien Moreau. I am an undercover agent assigned to the case of a certain Claude Dubois. Judging by the *minuscule* red dress you are wearing at eight o'clock in the morning and the police escort waiting outside the bathroom door, I see you have met him. No?"

"Yes...but why—"

"I know you are innocent, Chloe. I can help you get your passport back, but we have to get out of here before he wakes up." Julien reached for my hand. "Come."

A million questions zipped through my dazed head as Julien peeked outside the door, then swiftly led me down the hallway, past a lush arrangement of red roses and around the corner, where we were alone.

I pulled my hand from his grip. "How do you know my name? And why did you just knock him—"

"Shhh!" Julien covered my mouth with his hand, his face only inches from mine. "If you don't leave this hotel with me right now, the police are going to arrest you. Claude's operation has infiltrated the police. He has someone working for him on the inside, which is why you must *not* follow Officer Laroche and Officer Fournier to the station." Julien let his hand slide from my mouth, his body still hovering all too close to mine.

"But they said—"

"What they *said* does not matter. I have been on this case for months now, and trust me—Claude could not arrange the types of scams he pulls off and get away with it *every* time without using someone on the inside. If you go with them, you will *not* make it home in time for your wedding. I am one step away from arresting Claude, and I know exactly where he is headed next. If you come with me, we will get your passport back, and you can go home without any trouble. But we must leave now."

"How did you know I'm engaged? And where are you going to take me? And how do I know for sure—"

"If you do not want to be accused of fraud and held in France against your will, you'll have to trust me."

I took a closer look at the man who was asking me to place my trust in him. He wore a coal-gray T-shirt paired with dark jeans and scuffed black boots, and there was an intensity in his eyes that made my stomach flutter…but then again, that was probably from all of the red wine Claude had fed me the night before.

"You don't seriously expect me to evade the police and run off with you, do you? I mean, you just knocked out that officer and stole his gun," I hissed.

Instead of answering me, Julien peered over my shoulder, took my face in his hands, and planted his lips on mine. I vaguely heard

Officer Fournier's harsh voice echoing down the hallway as Julien pressed his warm chest into me and pushed me up against a marble pillar. He held me there in a deep, long kiss, his moist lips brushing over mine, his cool, masculine scent engulfing me and nearly drowning out the sound of the restroom door banging open and shut.

By the time he pulled his lips away, I'd completely lost the ability to speak. Or to breathe.

"I rank higher than the police," Julien whispered, his warm breath tickling my neck. He shot a pointed gaze down the hallway, where the officer's tense voice rose. "And if you don't come with me, your fiancé *will* find out what you have done. You think it is a mistake that Claude chose you, the cautious American with a hefty bank account and a wedding next week? Your life will be in ruins faster than you can blink. I have seen it happen to many women before you."

I locked eyes with the man who'd just kissed me, trying to concentrate on his words, but instead wondering why I hadn't felt the urge to push him off me and run away.

"They just took the elevator," Julien continued, completely unfazed by my dropped jaw or my inability to form a coherent response. "We have only two minutes before they will realize you are not in your room and come back down looking for you. This is your only chance." His big brown gaze intensified as he slid his hand over mine and squeezed it. "Follow me and act natural."

In that split second, it was as if some other girl had swooped in and inhabited my body. I felt as if I was watching myself in slow motion—my hand resting inside Julien's, my legs following him underneath the crystal chandeliers and through the lobby, and my dazed eyes looking on as he smiled at the doorman on our way out of the Hôtel Plaza Athénée.

As we emerged onto the fancy Parisian avenue, the late-summer humidity clung to my skin like a leech and snapped me out of my trance. I yanked my hand free of his grasp. "Who do you think you are? I'm engaged! You can't just kiss me like that. You don't even know me."

A smirk passed over his full lips. "You didn't seem to have any problem doing that with Claude last night, no? And besides, it was the only way to make you stop talking. *Allez, viens.* We don't have much time."

Julien took my hand again and led me down Avenue Montaigne toward a miniature, sleek black car.

"Get in," he ordered as he unlocked the passenger door.

"Okay, just hold on a second. I can see that you clearly know who I am and that you know this Claude character I met last night. But how do I know *you're* not in on this whole thing with him? *You* could be the insider he's working with, for all I know. I have a flight to catch today, and I'm getting married this Saturday. I need to go to the embassy right now. They can help me there. I'm not going anywhere with you."

I spun around on my heel and scoured the street for a cab, trying to push the memory of Julien's warm kiss out of my dizzy head.

"Suit yourself." Julien leaned against the car and folded his arms over his broad chest. "But you must know, the embassy will not be able to protect you. Your name *and* your bank account are now tied to illegal activity, and it could be weeks or even months before you will be cleared to leave the country. In fact, the last girl Claude scammed—a beautiful Brazilian woman—is *still* under investigation. But, if you come with me, we will take a short drive to where Claude is, I will arrest him, you will get your passport back, your name will be cleared from this mess, *and* you could still make your flight. *Simple, n'est-ce pas?*"

I shook my head at him, my stomach still woozy and my legs wobbly from the night's events. And, if I was being honest with myself...from his kiss. "I'm not getting in that car with you."He shrugged, letting out a low laugh before nodding back toward the hotel. "It's now or never."

I swiveled around to find my two favorite police officers exiting the hotel.

"*C'est elle!*" Officer Fournier shouted before they took off in my direction.

I hadn't taken French in years, but I understood enough to know they weren't charging at me to tell me they'd made a mistake and that they believed I was innocent. Or to help me get my passport back and make it home in time for my wedding.

Julien was already in the driver's seat when I jumped into the passenger's side.

He sped down the tree-lined boulevard, took a right on Avenue Georges V, then turned left onto the crowded Champs-Élysées. He glanced my way, shooting me a disarming grin.

"Now do you believe me?"

THREE

"Where are you taking me?" I peeked around my seat to make sure the police weren't following us, my heart threatening to pound right through my chest.

Julien shifted the car into gear, causing it to jolt forward as we sped past swarms of tourists lugging their heavy shopping bags while they meandered up the sunlit Champs-Élysées.

"We are going to Giverny. It is where Claude Monet lived. You know Monet?"

"Yes, I know who Monet is. What does that have to do with anything? How far away is this place?"

"Only one hour. And with me driving, it will be less."

I gripped the door handle as Julien raced around the Arc de Triomphe and zoomed through a red light.

"And you're sure that Claude is there? In Giverny?" I asked.

Julien balanced the steering wheel with his knee as he used one hand to roll down the window and the other to grab a cigarette from the pack in the center console. "So many questions. It seems you have trust issues, no?"

"Well, excuse me for asking questions, but I'm riding in a car with a French maniac who just accosted me in the lobby of a five-star hotel less than a week before my wedding, which I may not even make it to now that some other maniac French man has stolen my passport. Not to mention the fact that the police are chasing me! I think I'm entitled to a few questions."

He popped the cigarette between his grinning lips, once again letting go of the steering wheel to light it. "Yes, I guess so."

My stomach churned at the smell of cigarette smoke billowing past my face. "Do all French police officers drive like this? And what is it with French people and smoking? Has France not received the lung-cancer memo?"

"First of all, I am not a police officer. I am an undercover government agent. And secondly, has America not received the 'live your life and have fun while you can' memo?" He shook his head, puffing another cloud of smoke into the tiny car. "It seems not."

"If having fun in France means drinking poisonous French wine that makes you forget what you did the night before and getting all of your things stolen, then yes, I believe I've received the memo."

Julien actually refrained from racing through the next red light, instead glancing over at me, the smile wiped clean from his face. "You are not the only one who needs to find Claude, you know. After following this dirty *voleur* for months now, and seeing woman after woman in your situation, I will not stop until I put him in prison. You have my word."

"What is a *voleur*?"

Julien shifted in his seat, an odd flicker passing through his gaze. "A thief."

"Speaking of thieves, what do you know about my bank account being tied to illegal activity?"

Julien ignored my question and removed the gun from his jeans.

"What are you doing?" I screeched.

"I do not need to carry two guns. I only stole this one because I did not want to risk the officer using it on us." Julien rested his arm on my bare knee while he tossed the gun into the glove compartment. After closing it up, he reached into the backseat, where he rifled inside a plastic bag.

A greasy croissant wrapped in tissue paper emerged, the strong scent of butter and fluffy bread almost drowning out the cigarette smoke. He dropped it into my lap. "Eat this. It will help you calm down."

I gazed down at the pastry when suddenly another scene from the night before flashed through my head. I could see Claude, his chiseled cheekbones and his jet-black, slick hair, feeding me an olive. I could almost taste the bitter juice rolling around in my mouth. Then he'd picked up a glass of red wine and tipped it past my lips, the blackberry current sloshing down my throat and into my stomach.

"*It tastes good, does it not?*"

Ugh. My stomach gurgled. I glanced over at Julien, the skinny cigarette dangling from his lips, his muscular forearm shifting gears, his brown eyes fixed on the winding Parisian boulevard ahead. When I noticed the way his cheekbones cut straight through his jawline and reached all the way down to his full lips, the gurgle in my stomach turned to a flutter.

Oh, my God. Who cared about his damn cheekbones? What was I doing? How had all of this happened in less than a day? I should've been on my way to the airport. Flying home to greet my sister as she arrived in DC the next day. Finalizing my wedding plans. And preparing to marry Paul—my stable, no-nonsense fiancé who would never dream of smoking a cigarette or running a red light or eating a fattening pastry for breakfast.

"You look a little pale," Julien cut into my thoughts.

I gripped at my aching stomach. "It's just…this situation is out of control."

I tried to take a breath but suddenly felt as if no air was coming in or going out. What was I doing? How could I have climbed into the car with this man? What if he wasn't telling me the truth? What if he wasn't really an undercover agent? I had to get out of here.

"You need to breathe. Are you okay?" he asked, his deep voice ringing loudly in my ears.

I leaned my head back on the headrest and squeezed my eyes closed. A wave of heat made its way through my stomach and up to my stinging face. Sharp pains ripped through my chest as I struggled to suck the air into my heaving lungs.

Julien's hand enclosed mine, and I felt the car come to an abrupt stop, my ears now ringing even louder, blackness closing in around me.

"Chloe, look at me. Chloe, open your eyes," he said firmly.

I blinked my eyes open and peeked up at Julien, hoping he wasn't going to hurt me. Hoping I hadn't made a huge mistake in choosing to trust him. Clearly I'd already made a catastrophic decision in trusting Claude the night before.

"You can trust me," he said, keeping his gaze fixed on mine. "I know you are confused, but it will all be over soon. I have seen Claude do this many times before, with women just like you, and I do not want you to get hurt. We are driving to Giverny, we will find Claude and get your passport, and you can leave France. I promise."

My sharp breaths slowed down as I focused on his eyes. I didn't know this man from a hole in the wall, but for some strange reason I believed him.

Julien reached down for the croissant in my lap. "*Mangez*," he said. "You had a lot to drink last night, and if you do not eat, you will be sick."

I didn't say a word as I picked up the croissant, tore off a piece of the flaky pastry, and tucked it into my mouth.

My breathing relaxed further as the chewy bread made its way into my stomach and soaked up some of the alcohol that was still swishing around in there, making me feel nauseous.

"Better?" he asked as he put the car back into gear.

I nodded as I gazed out the window and noticed row after row of gray apartment buildings, their black balconies all in a line, bunches of purple and white flowers trickling over the sides. The charming scene zooming past reminded me of a postcard of Paris my mom used to keep tucked in her bedroom mirror. After she died, my dad had stashed the postcard away in the basement, just as he'd done with the rest of her things.

Finishing the last bite of my croissant, I pushed the memories of my mom and her boxed-up life out of my mind. Now wasn't the time to think about her. I had a few more pressing questions that, unfortunately, she wouldn't be able to answer for me.

"Does Claude usually...take *advantage* of the women he steals from?" I asked.

"You mean, does he have sex with them?" Julien said, not missing a beat.

I nodded, swallowing the lump in my throat.

"No, sex is not in Claude's game plan. That complicates things too much, and all he is after is your money."

"So you're saying he doesn't do *anything* with the women except get them drunk to the point of passing out before stealing their things?"

"No, I said that he doesn't have sex with them. That doesn't mean he won't do *other* things. You did wake up in your underwear, no?"

I clasped my hands together in my lap, my knuckles turning white. "Yes," I said through gritted teeth.

"With the exception of sex, Claude will do whatever he needs to do to get you to drink a lot, take off your clothes, and pass out. If that involves kissing you or—"

"I get it," I said firmly. I didn't want to hear what else I may have done with Claude last night prior to the point of passing out in my underwear.

"Don't be so worried," Julien said. "Trust me, Claude does not have sex with the women he steals from."

"How can you be so sure?" I asked.

Julien's eyes bored into the road ahead, his jaw clenching. "I have been on the case for some time now, remember? I know how Claude operates. Stealing your money and taking your possessions are his main goals. Sex would mess up that plan."

"What kind of despicable human being does something like this? Seriously, didn't his parents teach him anything?" I huffed.

Julien responded by revving up the gas and screeching the tiny car around a corner.

How had I gotten myself into this mess?

I glanced at the clock to find that it was already nine o'clock. Only four hours left until my flight took off. If we arrived in Giverny before ten, found my passport, and Julien drove me back to the airport, I could potentially make it there by eleven thirty or twelve at the *earliest.*

Even if I did make it to my flight on time, how would I explain to Paul that a massive amount of money had disappeared from our account, that all of my things were missing, and that I was wearing a skimpy red dress? And how on earth would I tell him that the beautiful, two-carat diamond engagement ring he'd given me was gone? I couldn't bear to think about it.

"Is there any chance we'll get my engagement ring back?" I asked Julien.

He shook his head. "*C'est possible*...but it is likely that he has already sold it."

"But he couldn't have been gone for more than a few hours by now."

"That is all it takes. Claude is a professional con man. He's very good at what he does."

"How do you even know that we'll be able to get my passport back, then?"

"Because he usually holds on to that for a day or two."

"If you know so much about how Claude does all of this, why haven't you caught him yet?"

Julien paused before turning sharply down another skinny, cobblestoned street. "Like I told you in the hotel, we believe Claude has a mouse on the inside."

"A mouse?"

Julien sighed. "Not an actual mouse. It is an expression in English, no? When someone is working on the inside, feeding information to—"

"Oh, you mean a *mole.*"

"Mole, mouse—it is basically the same animal, no? *Merde*," Julien muttered under his breath. "Anyway, there is no other explanation for how he has escaped us so many times. That is why I was assigned to the case. But you do not need to worry about all of this. Once you have your passport in your hands, you can fly home and never return to this smoke-infested, poisonous wine country ever again."

Thank God for that. I looked at Julien in his dark jeans, his rugged five o'clock shadow, and his slim gray T-shirt. He couldn't have been more different from Paul if he tried. Paul always had a smooth, shaven face to go with his neatly trimmed black hair, and even on the weekends he wore clean, ironed polo shirts and perfectly tailored khaki pants.

"So, what were you doing in Paris?" Julien rolled the window down farther and stuck his hand out to catch the humid breeze.

"I was here on a business trip."

"What kind of business?"

"I'm an event planner."

He nodded, his lips curving into a knowing grin. "I see."

"What do you mean by that?"

"That explains why Claude chose you. He selects women who are used to being in control. The cautious ones in their prude business suits with their rich fiancés, diamond rings, and prestigious careers. The ones who have a lot to lose. Because once you give these women—the women like *you*—a few glasses of wine, all of that pent-up energy and desire comes pouring out, and the control you are used to having, it vanishes into thin air. I am right, no?"

I crossed my arms over my chest and fought the urge to smack Julien across the face. I didn't want to think any more about what may or may not have happened with Claude the night before.

"You don't know what you're talking about," I said.

He threw me a sideways glance. "I think I know exactly what I'm talking about."

"I thought you were an undercover agent, not a therapist," I shot back.

He laughed. "Sometimes I have to think like a therapist to get into the mind of the thief, you know. To anticipate his next move."

"So is that how you knew *I* was the woman Claude had duped this morning in the hotel?"

"Besides the signature red dress that Claude leaves for his ladies and the police officer glued to your side, there are not many women in the Hôtel Plaza Athénée looking...euh...well, as you looked."

I narrowed my eyes at him before glancing at myself in the side-view mirror. Black, smudgy makeup circled my bloodshot eyes, and my long, auburn hair—which I normally kept pulled back into a clean bun—was fluffed up in an unruly mess around my shoulders.

As I sat in Julien's tiny French car, which zipped at an impossible speed down the highway, the sights of Paris now barely visible in the rearview mirror, I wished I could take a shower, brush my teeth again, and change into a pair of my own clean clothes. Then I would curl up in my king-size bed underneath our crisp, four-hundred-thread-count Egyptian cotton sheets, with Paul lying next to me, stroking my hair and telling me that this was all just a bad dream.

Julien flicked his cigarette out the window, then took a swig from a half-empty water bottle. "Thirsty?"

I stared at it, wondering where his mouth had been, and decided that no matter how thirsty I was, I could wait. Granted, I'd already come into contact with his lips once today...but at least this time I had a choice.

"No, thanks."

"Suit yourself," he said, taking another drink.

"Can I borrow your phone?" I asked. "I need to call my credit-card companies to put a hold on my accounts."

"Sorry, no phone."

"You're on the job and you don't have a cell phone? Are you kidding me? How are you keeping in touch with the police department to know where Claude is headed next?"

"I am an undercover agent, remember? I am not in touch with the police; my connections are much higher. But that is not for you to worry about."

"If your connections are higher than the police, then *why* are we running from them?"

"Correction, *you* are running from the police."

"Whatever. Why didn't you just flash your shiny badge at them and tell them you were in charge now?"

"Because only one other person knows who I am and what I am doing."

"What? Are you saying that if the police catch us, you won't be protected?"

Julien nodded. "This is the type of assignment that is…how do you say it in English?" Julien scratched his chin. "Ah, *unsanctioned.* This is the word, no?"

"You mean illegal?"

Julien hesitated. "No, it is not *illegal.* It is simply the only way this can work. In order for me to find Claude, no one except for my boss must know I am on the case. Otherwise the mouse—or the *mole*—will tell him, and the operation will be ruined."

"So if the police catch us, what would happen to you?"

"Same as what would happen to you: I would go to jail. But that, *chérie*, is not going to happen because as you saw in the hotel, I am good at what I do. Evading those *imbécile* policemen will not be a problem."

I buried my forehead in my hands. "Oh, God."

"Back to your original concern—your credit cards. Claude is not concerned with them. It is the debit card—the checking account—that he is after."

"Why would he take everything, then? I mean, couldn't he at least have left me *something*? I can't even buy myself a phone card, and I have to get in touch with my bank."

"A thief is not concerned with your well-being, Chloe."

"Clearly."

Julien took another swig of water. "Claude has already tapped into your account, so there is no point in calling your bank. They will soon place a hold on the account for suspicious activity, if they haven't already."

That meant there was no way Paul wouldn't get wind of this. As soon as he tried to use the debit card and was denied, he would find out about the hold. Unless I could get home first and run damage control. I had to get on that flight.

"Back to what you just said about the debit card," I said, trying to calm the desperation that was seeping back up through my chest. "How could Claude use that to access my account if he doesn't have my PIN?"

"Did you use your debit card at an ATM at all while you were in Paris?"

"I used it once. I took money out to buy a new purse for myself. Which, by the way, Claude stole."

"*Et voilà.* You have your answer."

"What? You mean Claude was watching me?"

"Was there anyone standing behind you waiting to use the machine?"

"I don't know. I wasn't paying attention."

"I told you, Claude knows what he's doing. He's done this so many times he could do it in his sleep."

"What a sick man," I spat, wishing I could see Claude again just so I could smack him across the face and tell him what a disgusting human being he was.

I crossed my arms over my chest for the millionth time that day and gazed out at the rolling green hills as they whizzed by. Never in a million years would I have imagined I would be in a smoke-infested, miniature car with an undercover French detective, racing through the French countryside to find my passport, asking questions about how some slick con man stole my PIN.

"Do you come to France a lot for business?" Julien asked.

"This is my first time. I wasn't even supposed to be here, actually. My boss was slated to make this trip, but she got sick at the last minute and sent me."

"Then it must've been fate."

"In that case, fate and I are *not* on speaking terms."

FOUR

A half hour later, after Julien had made four illegal passes on the skinny country roads that led to Giverny, he pulled into an open field and parked the car.

"We are here," he announced before throwing his most recent cigarette out the window and climbing out of the car.

I breathed a sigh of relief as the fresh country air filled my lungs and replaced all of the smoke I had just inhaled.

"Follow me." Julien slipped on a pair of dark sunglasses as he took off across the field.

I struggled to keep up with him, my three-inch heels sticking into the muddy ground with each step. "Could you slow it down? I didn't exactly get a chance to change into a more comfortable pair of shoes for our country outing, with Claude stealing my entire suitcase and all."

Julien didn't slow his pace. "We have to hurry if we want to get your passport. Claude may already be gone."

"How do you know for sure where he is? You don't even have a phone."

Julien shook his head and mumbled something under his breath, not breaking his brisk stride.

As my right heel lodged into the ground, I bent over to yank it out, trying not to let the tiny dress give Julien a show. "Why are you helping me, anyway? I mean, if you're after Claude, why didn't you just let the police take me? You must be getting something out of all of this. You don't even know me."

Julien stopped at the edge of the field and pushed his sunglasses down his nose, revealing his penetrating brown eyes. "What? You would rather be at the police station in Paris being accused of a crime you did not commit? If you don't want me to help you, just say the word, and I will arrange for your trip back to Paris. I am sure Officer Laroche and Officer Fournier will be very happy to see you again."

"No, I'd rather not go back to the police station. The only place I need to go is to the airport."

"Well, then. *On y va.*" He pushed his sunglasses back up his nose and walked out onto a small country road lined with lush, green trees and skinny, black lampposts. Two gray-haired women strolled down the path, gift bags in hand, and when their gazes landed on me and Julien, their eyebrows furrowed in disapproval.

"People are staring at me," I whispered as I tried to keep up with his quick stride, crossing my arms over my chest to hide the inappropriate, low-cut neckline of the skimpy red dress.

Julien chuckled. "Well, you are not exactly dressed for a walk in Giverny."

I tried to run my hands through my hair to calm it down, but the humidity was making it poof up like a cotton ball. It was beyond help. I just needed to get my passport and get the hell out of here. I didn't even want to imagine what was going to happen if I didn't step off that plane tonight in DC. Paul would be worried sick, not to mention irate. My sisters would go nuts, and my dad, my poor dad, would have to run damage control. And he never did that. I was the one who always had things under control so that he'd never even know if there was a fire that needed to be put out.

Despite the heels of my shoes now rubbing massive blisters in the backs of my feet, I picked up my pace. If trusting Julien was the only way to get my passport back and fly home before those police officers found me and kept me in France for God knows what crime, then I would just have to trust him.

After passing another group of happy vacationing tourists, Julien made a sharp turn down a long, dirt driveway, which led to a beige cottage with clunky brown shutters and red rosebushes climbing up the walls.

As I followed him down the dirt path, my stomach churned again. God, I hoped this would work.

"Do you speak French?" Julien asked.

"I took it years ago in college…but I don't really remember much. Why?"

He turned to me as we reached the door, his gaze hardening. "Because I don't want you to say a word in there. Just let me do the talking."

Julien tried the door handle, but when it didn't open, he stood back a few feet, lifted his black boot into the air, and kicked the door open.

Something told me this wasn't going to be a peaceful exchange of goods.

Beads of sweat dripped down my neck and slid underneath the thin red dress as I followed Julien inside a tiny, clean kitchen that smelled of coffee beans and honey. A half-eaten baguette and an open jar of Nutella sat on the table, begging to be eaten. For a split second, I wished this was my vacation cottage. I wished I could take a huge glass of water from the sink, scoop a big spoonful of Nutella onto that bread, and forget about this whole mess. Then take a hot shower and lie down in bed with the sound of the birds chirping outside, lulling me to sleep.

Before my daydream got too carried away, Julien was already in the next room. I crept through the doorway, my ears perking up at the sound of a scratchy voice coming from around the corner.

"*Salut, Julien.*"

A short, balding man in a long-sleeved, black-collared shirt appeared on a staircase across the room. That definitely was *not* Claude.

Julien's body immediately tensed up. He narrowed his eyes and began barking in French.

I struggled to understand as the little bit of French I'd taken in college wormed its way back into my brain, but all I could get out of his rant was the word *où*, which meant "where." Before I could figure out the rest, the man with the shiny bald spot on his head shouted something completely incomprehensible in French. Well, completely incomprehensible to *me*, at least.

Julien must've understood him perfectly—and he must not have liked it one bit—because he charged across the room, flew up the stairs, and punched the guy straight in the jaw.

I backed up against the doorway and covered my mouth to stifle my scream. Julien leaned over the man, grabbed him by the collar, and kneed him in the groin. The man moaned loudly and curled into a ball as Julien let go of him and continued grilling him in French.

The man hesitated, then finally yelped out a response. Julien flared his nostrils and huffed out a loud breath before turning to me.

"Let's go. Claude is not here."

I peered over Julien's shoulder at the man on the stairs, who was still hunched over, groaning and rubbing his jaw. He lifted his eyes to meet mine, and for a brief second I actually felt bad for him.

What had I gotten myself into?

Julien stormed out of the cottage, his black boots scuffing along the dirt path as he mumbled what I assumed to be French obscenities under his breath.

"What the hell was that?" I asked.

"I had to do that to find out what I needed to know."

"So where's Claude?"

"Claude is gone."

"What about my passport?"

"It is with Claude."

"Well, where the hell is he?"

"He knows the police are after him, so he is on his way to Annecy."

I struggled to keep up with Julien as he turned back down the wooded path.

"Where is Annecy? Can we get there in time to find my passport and make my flight?"

Julien shook his head. "No, it is several hours from here. You are not going to make your flight, Chloe. I am sorry." He ran his hands through his messy hair as a bead of sweat ran down his cheekbone and under his chin.

The panic I'd been swallowing for the past hour overcame me as I realized that I was completely screwed.

"But I'm getting married! In six days!" I shouted, not caring about all the jolly tourists passing by.

Julien didn't respond. Instead, he kept walking.

"Didn't you hear me? I said I'm getting married in less than a week. My fiancé will be waiting for me at the airport tonight and you don't even own a phone that I can use to call him and tell him I won't be there. My sister is flying in tomorrow, and we have a million things to do before the wedding. I *have* to make that flight."

"Maybe you should've thought of all of this before you accepted a drink from Claude last night."

I stopped along the dirt path and leaned against one of the lampposts to catch my breath. "Why did I trust you? What was I thinking? If I would've just stayed in Paris with the police, I could've explained to them *again* that I hadn't done anything illegal, that Claude had stolen my things and my money, and one of them would've believed me. I mean, all they would have to do is pull up my spotless record and see that there is no way I would *ever* be involved in illegal activity. But now here I am, watching you beat up innocent men in country cottages. And I'm no closer to the airport, the US embassy, or to getting my passport back."

"That man in the cottage was *not* innocent," Julien said, still barreling down the path.

"Well, if you're really some kind of government agent, why didn't you arrest him? And how did he know your name?"

"It seems that you keep forgetting I am *undercover*, which means I have to *act* as if I am one of them. Haven't you ever watched any of those crime shows back in the—" Julien's eyes widened as he muttered under his breath. "*Merde.*" He grabbed my arm and pulled me down another dirt path behind a pack of tourists.

"What is it?"

"Don't turn around," he hissed through his teeth. "The police have followed us here. They must've gotten my plate numbers and trailed us from Paris."

I swiveled my head to the side to see Officer Laroche and Officer Fournier holding my photo and talking to a man in a pair of brown trousers with green suspenders stretching over his potbelly.

"I told you not to look," Julien scolded. "Here, put these on." He shoved his sunglasses into my hands and herded me farther into the crowd of tourists.

"I'm not putting these on. I'm not doing this anymore. I'm going to go talk to them and demand that they take me to the US embassy. I haven't done anything wrong, so I'm sure it's all a big misunderstanding, and once they find Claude—the *real* criminal—they'll know I'm telling the truth."

Julien tightened his grip on my arm as we stayed sandwiched in between two fanny pack–clad Korean women and a group of high school–age French kids.

"Don't you understand? They are not looking for Claude at the moment. They are looking for *you*. And if they get a hold of you, you will not be going to the embassy to get a new passport," Julien said, his whisper ringing with agitation. "Remember, Claude is a scam artist. He takes rich women's belongings, taps into their bank accounts, ties some of the money to illegal activity, making it look as if *the woman* is responsible. Meanwhile, he steals the rest and wires it into an offshore account. So the police will not believe anything you are saying until they run a full investigation. And by the time they are finished, Claude will be long gone with your money and your passport, and you will have missed your wedding."

I wondered if Paul had gotten wind of the whopping $33,000 that Claude had already transferred out of our account. My stomach clenched just thinking about it. He was going to flip out. And he would flip out even more if he found out that all of this was happening because I'd allowed some strange French man into my hotel room. Continuing the lies was unbearable, unimaginable. But even so, I couldn't tell Paul about bringing Claude into my room. Not if I still wanted him to marry me in six days.

"So if I can't go back to the police, what am I supposed to do now?" I asked.

Julien peered over his shoulder as he continued to whisper in my ear. "You will come with me to Annecy. We will be there by tonight, we will get your passport, and you can fly home tomorrow. But if you choose to go back to the police, you are on your own."

I suddenly envisioned myself sitting alone in a cold, cement jail cell while scary police officers yelled at me in French and Paul waited for me at the airport, peeking at his watch every five seconds, wondering where I could be. Then I thought of Paul getting a call from the police telling him I'd been seduced by a French con artist who'd taken all my things.

The wedding would be canceled. My life would be in ruins, just as Julien had warned.

I had to go to Annecy to find my passport. What other choice did I have?

"So, can we leave for Annecy right now?" I asked.

"Yes, but first, we have to get away from those officers." Julien held my hand as we picked up our pace, weaving through the mob of picture-happy tourists. "Follow me."

We squeezed through a wall of chatty English women, and once we'd made it to the other side, Julien pulled me off the path and around a giant willow tree facing a gorgeous green pond. He gathered me into his chest, then reached around and tucked my hair down the back of the dress.

"What are—"

"Shhh," he whispered. "They will be passing by here any minute. We can't take any chances that they will see your hair or this bright-red dress. You need to get closer to me."

Julien wrapped his arms around my waist and pressed my back firmly into the tree, completely covering me with his body. "Don't move," he whispered as his warm, scruffy cheek pressed into mine. I closed my eyes and prayed that the police wouldn't see us. The cool scent of Julien's cologne calmed my nerves but also made me remember his kiss from earlier this morning. I squeezed my eyes tighter and tried to conjure up Paul's standard scent—the same Tommy Hilfiger aftershave he'd been wearing since we first met in college—but I couldn't.

Julien gripped my waist a little tighter. "It's okay, they are almost gone."

I opened my eyes, only then realizing that I was shaking.

"*Allez, viens.* We must go the other way." Julien slid his hand from my waist and intertwined his fingers with mine.

I guiltily swiped the image of Paul's face from my mind, comforting myself with the hope that I would be flying home to him the next day, and that I would never again be in such close quarters with another man.

But as Julien gripped my hand and led me the opposite way around the lush, flowery pathway, my stomach remained unsettled, my heart still flickering inside my chest.

We rounded the pond, and it was only when I noticed the green arched bridge stretching across the water lily–covered water that I realized where we were. *This* was the famous water lily pond in Monet's paintings.

"It is beautiful, is it not?" Julien said, leading me past a group of Italian high schoolers and farther away from the police officers.

"It's gorgeous. Too bad I'm not here on vacation to really enjoy it."

Julien's shoulders relaxed as he let out a nervous laugh, the skin around his eyes crinkling the slightest bit. "You will never forget your trip to Giverny, though, will you?"

I slipped my hand underneath my hair, shaking it free from the red dress. "No, I will never forget this."

After making it through the swarms of tourists who were shooting their tiny digital cameras at the blossoming gardens behind Monet's house, Julien led me toward a massive black tour bus parked at the end of the dirt road.

"Where are you going?" I asked him. "This isn't the way to your car."

"We have to leave the car here. The police have the license plate number, remember?" Julien took a step onto the bus and turned to face me. "You coming?"

"What other choice do I have?" I filed onto the air-conditioned bus behind him, hoping again that the man I was following was really worth my trust.

FIVE

Julien sauntered down the aisle toward the back of the empty bus, not seeming the least bit concerned with the fact that we were now on a random tour bus and had no clue where it was headed.

I'd no more than taken my seat and wiped a bead of sweat off my brow when a large group of men and women bounded onto the bus and filled up the rows, laughing and chatting as they coupled up and sat down.

"What if the bus is full?" I whispered to Julien. "And what if someone notices that we weren't on the bus before? And what if we have to pay for a spot? I don't exactly have any money on me, you know. And, just a side note, where in the hell is this bus going?"

Julien sighed, and I could've sworn he was holding in a laugh. "Relax. The bus is going to Paris, and we will take a train from there down to Annecy. Besides, even if they find out we are imposters, do you really believe they are going to kick us off the bus in the middle of nowhere?"

"Um…yeah, actually. I think that's exactly what is going to happen."

"I promise you, if that happens, I will find another way to get to Paris. If you haven't noticed yet, I am quite resourceful."

"How are you so sure this bus is going to Paris, anyway?"

Just as Julien opened his mouth to speak, a tall blonde woman who couldn't have been older than thirty yelled from the front of the bus, "Welcome back! What did all of you newlyweds think of Giverny?"

Cheers erupted from the passengers as they passed around bottles of Bordeaux and poured massive quantities into red, plastic cups.

Newlyweds? Could this day get any worse?

A woman with short black hair and razor-straight bangs handed me two cups across the aisle.

"Here you go," she said with a smile as the man next to her thrust the wine bottle in my direction.

"Thanks, but I don't really drink," I told them.

Julien reached across my chest and grabbed the cups and the wine. "My little Chloe here is just joking. She would *love* a drink."

My little Chloe?

As Julien poured us each a tall cup of red wine—which I had absolutely no intention of drinking—the woman with the black hair reached her hand across the aisle.

"I'm Liz, and this is my husband, Jack." She smiled lovingly at him as a high-pitched giggle squeaked from her lips. "It still feels so crazy to say my *husband*. I love it!"

I glanced over at Julien, the short brown stubble on his face already a shade darker than it was just a few hours ago, his muscular forearms pouring the cup of wine down his throat like it was a glass of water.

Was I going to have to act like *he* was my husband?

"So what made you two decide to do the newlywed romance tour of France?" Liz asked as she took a sip of her wine and rubbed her hand over her husband's thigh.

Julien was mid-sip and didn't seem to be stopping anytime soon. I yanked the cup out of his hand, spilling red wine all over his jeans.

"Why *did* we choose the newlywed romance tour, *sweetie*?" I asked him.

Julien smiled over at me before taking my hand. I tried to pull away from his grasp but he squeezed my fingers so tightly I thought the bones would break.

"Well, we just got married, you see, and my little Chloe has not traveled much. In fact, she has never been away from home and—"

"That's not true," I cut in. "I've traveled all over the US for work, and—"

"Yes, *chérie*, but you have not traveled very often for pleasure. Am I right?" He shot me an annoying grin, which made a dimple appear in his right cheek.

When I didn't answer him, Liz kept talking. "We haven't traveled much either. Not together, anyway. And we've never been anywhere as beautiful or as romantic as France. I just couldn't believe it when I found this tour. I mean, who knew there would actually be a tour bus taking newlyweds to the most romantic sites in France? It couldn't be more perfect."

"Mmm," I mumbled, plastering a smile across my face. "Perfect."

The red wine swirling in my cup made me yearn for a glass of water. I hadn't had anything to drink all day, and I wasn't about to have even an ounce of that wine—not after the mess it had gotten me into.

"So how did you two meet?" Jack asked, sliding his arm around his wife and pulling her slim frame into his chest.

Julien took my hand in both of his before speaking. "I met my dear Chloe at a nude beach on the Côte d'Azur. As soon as I saw her, it was love at first sight."

I freed my hand from his grasp, immediately feeling my cheeks go up in flames. A nude beach? Was he serious?

Julien tilted his face toward mine, the corners of his mouth curving upward. "Oh, *chérie*, do not be so embarrassed." He turned back to Liz and Jack and continued talking as I envisioned pushing him off the bus.

"Chloe does not like it when I tell this story, but I cannot help myself. She was so beautiful, just lying there in the sun, her br—"

I reached down and pinched Julien's arm so hard he squealed.

"I think that's enough for now." I released my death pinch and prayed the bus ride would end soon.

Liz's eyes widened as she let out another screeching giggle. "I've always wanted to try out a nude beach, but I've never had the courage. Isn't it scary being totally…you know, naked?"

"Oh no. It is not embarrassing at all," Julien responded in a serious tone. "There is nothing more freeing, actually. Don't you think so, *chérie*?"

I shoved my cup of wine into Julien's hands and crossed my arms over my chest, unwilling to partake in this ridiculous conversation for even another second. I'd agreed to follow him to get my passport back so that I could fly home. I had not agreed to pretend to be someone I was not. And *I* would never be caught dead at a nude beach.

Ignoring Julien, I turned to Liz. I had to find out if this bus was going to Paris. "So, have you two ever been to Paris before?"

"No, never." She leaned even closer to Jack, nuzzling her head into his shoulder. "I can't believe we're going to be there in less than an hour. I really wish we had more than two days to spend there. I mean, how are we going to see all the sights in such a short period of time?"

Oh, thank God. We would be in Paris soon, then we'd take the train to Annecy, find Claude, get my passport back, and I would fly home. It would all work out. It had to.

Thankfully, Liz stopped making small talk and instead focused her energy on her new husband. And after Julien's little nude-beach stunt, I refused to talk to him or look at him for the rest of the trip.

I missed Paul. Normal, stable, clean-cut Paul, who would never, ever dream of letting the words *nude beach* pass through his lips.

I had no idea how I would even begin to explain any of this to him, though, and the thought of lying to him again made me queasy. But as long as I made it home within the next few days, I would figure it out. And I would never take another trip to France, ever again.

The Newlywed Torture Bus pulled up in front of the Luxembourg gardens in Paris about forty-five minutes later. I was never so happy to leave the company of a bunch of happy, drunk, lovesick Americans.

The minute we stepped foot onto the crowded Boulevard Saint-Michel with its miniature cars buzzing up and down the street, honking their horns and zipping through red lights, Julien grabbed my hand and pulled me toward a cab.

"*Gare de Lyon, s'il vous plaît,*" he told the driver as we slid into the sticky leather seat.

The cab sped off through the city, winding through the cobblestoned streets like a runaway train. I searched for my seat belt but came up empty, so I gripped the door handle instead. What was with the drivers here? They were completely out of control.

From his side of the cab, Julien eyed me with an annoying smirk on his face.

"What?" I said.

"Are you always like this?"

"Like what?"

"So controlled. So worried."

"No, I'm not normally worried like this. In my *normal* life at home, where I have a stable job and a fiancé, I'm not racing around with undercover agents and evading the police in a slutty red dress. So no, I'm not usually like this, but these aren't exactly normal circumstances. Though for you, I suppose they are." I glared at him.

Julien sighed, wiping the smirk from his lips. "I am sorry. I did not mean to offend you. All I am trying to do is help you get home."

"I still don't fully understand *why* you're trying to help me, though. If busting Claude is your main objective, and if no one else is supposed to know about you, why would you want me tagging along for the ride? And come to think of it, if you rank higher than the police, as you *said*, and you know I'm innocent, why can't you just send me to whatever government agency you work for so they can set me up with a passport while you hunt for Claude?"

"Again with all of the questions."

"And again, I'm going to need answers. Especially if you expect me to get on that train with you."

"*Merde*," he muttered under his breath.

"What was that?"

"It was nothing." Julien scooted closer to me, his jeans pressing up against my bare leg. "The reason you cannot go home so easily is because I am the *only* person who knows you are innocent. And in fact, I am under strict orders *not* to help you."

"What do you mean?"

"In the past, many of the women who appeared to be victims were actually working *with* Claude. They were working the system together. Claude would wire the woman's money into an offshore account. The woman would run to the police crying about it and get her bank to refund the money since it was ruled as fraud. Then she and Claude would split the money. Once the police started to figure this out, they kept an eye out for Claude and for any of his red-dress women who *claimed* to be one of his victims. So even my people will not believe you, and they will be required to run a full investigation on you before allowing you to leave the country. I am the only one who can keep you safe, Chloe. You have no other choice but to come with me."

I searched Julien's eyes, my mind struggling to grasp everything he was telling me. "So, if other women in the past have been in on these scams, why would you disobey your orders by helping me? What makes you so sure that I'm innocent?"

"The look on your face this morning in the hotel. It was one of pure bewilderment, of panic. I have seen it many times before. I am tired of Claude's games, and I could not allow another woman to go through this."

"But I could just be a good actress, like the other women."

Julien shook his head. "No one can pretend *that* well. You were a mess. And I know a person like you would have nothing to do with a dirty scam artist like Claude."

The cab zoomed around a corner, causing me to slide right into Julien. I gripped his knee and lifted my face to his. "Thank you for believing me."

A hint of softness passed through his big brown eyes, but he quickly blinked it away.

The cab came to an abrupt stop in front of the train station, making me realize my hand was still on Julien's knee. I pulled it away and waited while Julien thrust a wad of bills at the cabdriver before letting us out.

As Julien bolted toward the station, I followed behind him, exhausted, sweaty, thirsty, and starving, but most of all, grateful that he was going to help me when it seemed that no one else in this godforsaken country would be on my side. I couldn't believe Julien had received orders to let me flounder with the French police...and even more so, that he'd ignored those orders.

We dashed into the bustling train station and zigzagged across the crowded main floor, where travelers strolled past us, pulling their mini suitcases behind them, munching on baguette sandwiches. Once we reached the ticket window, Julien rambled on in French to the attendant, and I remembered again that I didn't have any money to contribute. But Julien didn't say anything. Instead he handed over a credit card, then collected two tickets and gave one to me.

"Thanks," I said hesitantly, hoping that someday I could repay him.

"*Pas de problème*," he responded.

A massive escalator transported us to an open-air platform, where herds of people crowded around the large display screen, waiting to depart on one of the several trains pulling into the station.

"Are you hungry?" Julien asked.

I didn't want him to spend any more of his money on me, but I was starving. And, at this point, I would've considered going to a nude beach if it meant I could have a bottle of water.

I nodded. "And thirsty. Really, really thirsty."

"Come, I will get you something to eat and some water. I noticed you did not drink the wine on the bus."

"Call me crazy, but I didn't think more wine was going to help."

He grinned, making that dimple pop into his right cheek again. "No, I guess not."

As we walked toward a small group of cafés on the other side of the station, I bent down to adjust my painful heels. It took all my willpower not to toss them in the trash can to my left and just walk around barefoot.

"Ahem," Julien said loudly.

I peeked up to find him raising a brow, then realized I was still in this tiny red dress and was surely giving Julien and everyone else in the train station a show. I popped back up, smoothing the dress down over my butt.

"What?" I shot back as Julien's gaze remained fixated on me.

"Why don't you sit down, and I will get us something to eat. Okay?" he said, the mischievous smile on his face telling me that he'd just gotten an eyeful. Ugh.

I spied an open seat to my left and decided it wouldn't hurt to take him up on just one more offer. And the thought of walking around in these heels for another second made me want to cry. "Okay, thanks."

"Is a sandwich all right? Ham and cheese on a baguette?"

"Actually, I'm a vegetarian."

"You don't eat meat?"

"That's right. No meat."

"Wow, no wine. No meat. I cannot imagine. What *do* you eat, then?"

"A sandwich with cheese and some vegetables would be great."

Julien turned on his heel and headed toward the café. A weird feeling passed through my stomach as I watched him walk away from me, his broad shoulders firm and unmoving as his muscular arms swung back and forth—his stance not threatening, but strong all the same.

I sank back into my seat and shook it off. I probably just needed to eat.

Massaging my throbbing temples, I glanced up at the giant clock hanging from the center of the station. It was one o'clock. My plane would be taking off any minute now from Charles de Gaulle airport, and in eight hours Paul would be waiting for me back in DC, wondering where I was.

I had to find a way to contact him so he didn't go and wait for me. Paul would be worried sick, because there was no way I would ever miss a flight. He would think something horrible had happened to me. And then he would call my dad and my sisters and get everyone all riled up. Maybe I could use someone's phone on the train and pay them for the international call. But I didn't have any money. And I couldn't keep taking Julien's money. I didn't even know the man. And, supposing I could use a phone to call Paul, what would I say?

I would have to lie. I could tell him that I had another work meeting tomorrow and that I had to stay or else I would lose my job.

Or I could just tell him the truth.

But since the truth involved me allowing another man to come into my hotel room and the fact that I didn't remember most of the night after that point, there was no way I could tell him. Especially considering that in six days, we were supposed to walk down the aisle together and promise to love each other forever, for better or for worse.

This was definitely for worse.

In that moment, though, sitting alone in a Parisian train station so far away from home, I wished I could call Paul and tell him the entire truth. I wished I could trust that he would help me find a way out of this mess, and that he would be there for me when it was all over.

But I knew Paul. I knew how rational he was, how practical.

I knew if I admitted to him that I was running from the police, about to board a high-speed train with a man I barely knew to collect my passport so I could make it home in time for the wedding, he would be speechless. He wouldn't even be able to fathom that I, Chloe Turner—the woman who always had the situation under control, the woman whose family had nicknamed her "Just in Case Chloe" because she carried an entire medicine cabinet of drugs and first-aid supplies in her purse "just in case" her sisters or her fiancé or her dad or the random passerby in the street needed something—could ever find herself in this mess.

But here I was anyway. In a situation I felt I had absolutely no control over.

And I wished I could just call Paul and ask him to fix this for me, but I couldn't. I had to fix it myself.

Julien plopped down into the seat next to me, interrupting my thoughts.

He handed me a long baguette and two bottles of water. "*Voilà*," he said with a smile. "This should help."

"Thank you so much," I said in all sincerity. I'd never been more excited to drink water in all my life.

I guzzled the first bottle straight down without taking a break, then took a bite of my sandwich.

"It is good? Your sandwich?"

"Yes. Perfect. Cheese and veggies, just what I asked for. Thank you again."

He smiled. "Good. I am glad. You were getting a little…euh… what is the word in English? Grouchy?"

I frowned.

"Yes, you seemed grouchy. Food and water will help."

I didn't respond. I just kept eating and drinking, slowly wiping out the remainder of my ghastly hangover. Just as I was finishing up my sandwich, our train pulled into the station.

"*On y va.*" Julien stood and motioned for me to follow him.

"What does that mean?" I asked as I wiped the corners of my mouth, feeling infinitely better than I had all morning.

"It means 'let's go.'"

I smoothed down the tiny dress, which stuck to me like a dryer sheet, and brushed a few strands of my ever-frizzing hair off my shoulders, then followed Julien down the platform and onto the train.

Inside the roomy, comfortable train car—which happened to be *much* nicer than the cramped train I usually rode from DC to New York for business—Julien and I plopped into adjoining seats and let out a collective sigh. The minute my head hit the cushy headrest, I felt like I might pass out. I was exhausted.

I slipped my heels off and kicked them under my seat before curling my legs up underneath me. "How long is the train ride to Annecy?" I asked.

"Seven hours," he responded as he stretched his arms overhead and pushed his feet out into the aisle.

"Seven hours? Where exactly is Annecy?" My panic threatened to return in full force as I calculated the amount of time it would take to get there, find my passport, return to Paris, and book another flight.

"It is a small town in the French Alps. There are many small stops along the way, and since we have to go through the mountains, it takes longer."

"Once we get there, will you know where to find Claude? And my passport?"

"Yes. We will find him, get your passport, and you can be on the first train back to Paris in the morning. This will all work out, Chloe, I promise you."

For the first time in the last few hours, Julien didn't smirk or laugh. His brown eyes shot intently into mine—making me feel, against all odds, like I could trust him.

"Thank you," I said softly.

He gave me a goofy smile before running a hand through his messy hair and stretching farther back in his seat.

Another odd feeling tugged at my stomach as I leaned back into the comfy chair and closed my eyes.

It must've been from eating all of that food and drinking so much water after not having anything all day, I reasoned. And not to mention the rough night I'd just had.

As I began to drift in and out of consciousness, I thought of my dad and my sisters back home. What were they going to do when they found out I hadn't come home on that plane? The thought of worrying them was unbearable. After all we'd been through years ago losing Mom, I'd remained the strong one. Even through my father's debilitating bouts of anxiety, Sophie's foray into recreational drugs, Lily's incessant string of bad boyfriends, and Magali's constant need for a motherly figure, I'd been the one everyone in the family had always counted on to keep it together.

And I had kept it together. No one had ever needed to worry about me.

Until now.

I squeezed my eyes tighter, willing the tears away. What I wouldn't give to have my mom back. Even for just a day. To tell me what to do. To calm my sisters and my dad down, and for once, take the burden off my shoulders.

As my breathing deepened, taking me only seconds away from a comatose sleep, a memory of one of the last moments I'd spent alone with my mother passed through my mind. It was so fleeting, so quick, that I wondered if it had actually happened or if I was just dreaming it up.

She'd taken me to the C&O Towpath by the Potomac River for a walk, just the two of us. Her belly was so big with my baby sister Magali that she couldn't walk very fast, but she'd insisted on getting outdoors. She couldn't stand being cooped up in the house.

"Mom, how did you think of the name Magali for the new baby?" I'd asked as I gazed up at her beautiful green eyes and her flowing auburn hair, a mirror of my own.

She smiled warmly at me as she took my hand. "Before your dad and I were married, I took a trip to France by myself. And I became friends with a beautiful woman over there named Magali, so that's how I came up with the name."

"If you were marrying Dad, why did you go to France by yourself?"

"Sometimes a girl just needs to spread her wings," she said.

Then she tilted her head up to the sunlight and smiled as she wrapped her arms around my bony shoulders and led me along the sparkling river.

"You'll understand one day, Chloe," she said as she gazed down at me with a look that only a mother could give her daughter.

Back in Paris, the train jetted smoothly down the tracks while the memory of my mother's sweet voice lulled me into a deep sleep.

SIX

As the train rattled me awake, I noticed Julien shoving something in his pocket.

He cleared his throat, then shifted awkwardly in his seat.

"Did you have a nice nap?" he asked.

"Mm-hmm," I said. "How long has it been?"

"I think we have been on the train for about two hours now, but I do not wear a watch, so I am not sure."

My stomach tightened as I thought of Paul heading to the airport in just a couple of hours.

I rubbed my aching forehead, trying to think of a way I could get in touch with him. I had to call him before he left for the airport and at least ward him off for another day or two before I could get home.

"Do you know if we're stopping anywhere soon where I could buy a phone card and use a pay phone to call home? I have to call my fiancé as soon as possible. It can't wait any longer."

Just as Julien opened his mouth to speak, a loud beep sounded from his jeans.

"What was that?" I lowered my eyes to find a small lump in his pocket.

"I think there might be a stop in one or two hours. So you could try to call then. But there won't be much time," he said, ignoring my question.

Another beep emanated from his jeans pocket. Julien's eyes darted around the train car, avoiding mine. It was the first time I'd seen him look nervous all day.

"You have a phone in there, don't you?"

"I do not know what you're talking about."

"You specifically told me you didn't have a cell phone earlier, remember?"

"Precisely."

"So then what is beeping in your pocket?"

"There is nothing—"

It beeped again.

Without thinking, I reached across his lap and shoved my hand into his jeans pocket.

"Hey, what are you—"

I pulled out a black phone and glared at him.

"Why would you lie about something as simple as having a cell phone?"

Julien grabbed the phone out of my hands and shoved it back into his pocket. "This phone is for official government use only. I cannot allow you to make personal calls on it."

"Fine, but why didn't you just say that before? Why did you lie about it?"

"I can tell you are one of those women who, when there is something you want, you will not stop until you get it. I am right, no?"

When I didn't respond, he pulled his phone out of his pocket and handed it to me. "I am sorry I didn't tell you I had a phone. Call whoever you like."

I turned the phone over in my palm, realizing that talking to Paul was actually the *last* thing I felt like doing right now. "Will my call to Paul be traced or anything?"

"No, it will not be traced," Julien said, the discomfort in his face evident. "But make it fast. And be careful what you tell your fiancé. He is a lawyer, no?"

"How did you—"

"Chloe, it's my job to know these things."

Shaking my head, I flipped the phone open and dialed Paul's number before I could change my mind. I shifted toward the window so I could have at least a little bit of privacy.

"Paul Smythe," he answered after the second ring.

I pictured my fiancé standing there in a light-yellow polo shirt paired with khaki pants, his dark hair combed to the side, his lips tightened into a thin line, and his eyebrows knitting together, the way they did anytime he answered a call from an unknown number.

"Honey, it's me, Chloe."

"Chloe? Where are you calling from? Shouldn't you be on the plane already?"

"There's been a problem, actually, and I wasn't able to take my original flight."

"What kind of problem?"

"There's been a crisis with the conference, and they need me to stay a bit longer to run damage control. I spoke to Angela, and apparently my job is on the line if I don't stay and get things worked out." My insides squirmed with each lie I told. This was horrible.

"That's outrageous. The wedding is this weekend. Sophie flies in tomorrow, and both of our families will be in later this week. I need you here. How could Angela expect you to do this?"

"I have to stay until the kinks are fixed. I don't have a choice."

"How long is that going to be?"

"A day or two at the most…hopefully. I'll be in touch though to let you know. And I promise, when I get home, I'll handle my dad and my sisters. I know things can be a bit stressful when they're all in town."

"A *bit* stressful?"

"Okay, really stressful." Paul was an only child, and whenever my sisters descended upon our house, he usually found a reason to stay late at the firm so he didn't have to come home and deal with them. He'd always said it was too much estrogen in one room.

"I need you to deal with Sophie for a day or two, and I should be home before the rest of them fly in. So no need to worry, okay?"

Paul sighed loudly into the phone. "I was hoping we could do dinner tonight." He stopped to clear his throat. "I have some exciting news."

"Really?" My tense shoulders disengaged as Paul took the spotlight off my lies.

"If you're going to be home in a day or two anyway, we can just talk about it then."I wondered if I really would be home in a day or two. "Can you just tell me now?"

"I wanted to tell you over a nice dinner, but I've been offered a position at that small firm I was telling you about, Robins and Miller." I could hear him smiling over the phone.

I racked my brain to remember which firm that was. Paul had been unhappy with the slow growth at his big DC law firm, and he'd been hoping to find a smaller firm, where he could be a bigger fish, so to speak. "That's great, honey. Remind me again, though, which one was that?"

"It's the one in Pennsylvania."

My stomach dropped. "Pennsylvania? The one in that really small town?"

"I know what you're going to say, Chloe. But this could be a great opportunity for us. I mean, just think, with the money I'd be making, I could buy you a beautiful house with space and a yard. No more living in a crowded town house in the city."

"But I love our town house in DC. And we talked about this. There aren't any jobs for event planners in small towns like that."

"I know, but sweetie, wait until you see the offer they made me. I'd be making so much money, plus the cost of living there is so low, you'd never have to work again."

"But I love my job. I want to work. You know that."

"I know you do. And I don't want to take that away from you. But you'll be thirty soon, and I've been looking at real estate there, and I found some amazing homes that I know you would love...and they're in a great school district."

School district?

Just as I was about to respond, Julien's leg pushed against mine. I'd almost forgotten where I was for a second. My secret-agent travel buddy lounged back in his seat with his eyes closed, hands propped behind his head, legs relaxed out to the sides, invading my space. At least he appeared to be sleeping. Which hopefully meant he was not listening to this conversation.

Paul continued, "I'm thirty-two now, and neither of us is getting any younger. We should really start thinking about having a family. This could be it for us, Chloe. This could be our chance."

"We've talked about this before." I lowered my voice and turned my face back toward the window. "I have an MBA, and I did all that work so that I could have my own career. And I know I've said that I want to have kids someday, but I don't know if I'm ready for all of that yet. I don't know if I'm ready to leave the city for good."

"I know, darling. It's just that this is a huge opportunity for me, and if you could be happy for me and give it a shot, I think it would be good for us in the long term."

"But we don't know anyone there, and you'll be at work all the time. What am I supposed to do?"

"Chloe, sweetie, I'm sure you'll make friends. There will be lots of other women and mothers in a small town like that. You can read all those books you've been dying to read or take walks in the neighborhood, or take up cooking."

And then it hit me. Paul was talking about his mother. This is exactly what had happened with his parents. They'd left the city back when his father was offered a position he couldn't refuse at a firm in a small town in Maryland. And that's when Paul's mom became pregnant with Paul.

He wanted me to be just like his mother. But I wasn't like her. I had goals and dreams, and I loved my job. I didn't want to move away from the city and take care of a house and have kids. Not yet, anyway.

"Can we talk about this when I get home?" My forehead resumed its throbbing.

"Sure, sweetie, but, well..." Paul trailed off, and I could see him then, pacing in circles around the house, the way he always did when he disagreed with me.

"Yes?"

"It's just that...well, promise me you'll think about it, okay? This could be good for us, and I—" Paul's voice was suddenly cut off.

"Paul, are you there?" I pulled the phone away from my ear and realized the train was now racing through a tunnel.

I'd lost the call completely. And as I stared down at the phone, I had no urge to call him back.

I carefully laid the phone on the seat next to Julien so as not to wake him. I needed some time to process all of this.

But just as I was leaning my head up against the window, gazing out at the green, rolling hills that reappeared as we emerged from the tunnel, Julien shifted in his seat next to me.

"You're a terrible liar," he said.

So he hadn't been sleeping after all.

I scowled in his direction. "It's rude to eavesdrop on other people's conversations, you know."

He pressed a few buttons on the phone, then tucked it back into his pocket. "Trouble in paradise?"

I shook my head at him and laid my temple back up against the cool window. "Thanks for your concern."

"It sounds to me like you are with a man who is not so much of a man, if you know what I mean."

"Are you seriously trying to say that my fiancé, the man I love, isn't a *man*?"

"Yes. And you, *chérie*, are *not* a woman in love."

"How can you even say that? You have no right to make judgments about my life. You know nothing about me, and nothing about Paul. If he were here right now, he would—"

"He would run away like a scared little boy."

The sound of Julien's French accent suddenly had the same effect as the Catholic nuns I'd had in grade school scratching their long fingernails down the chalkboard.

"No, if he were here, none of this would've ever happened," I clipped.

"And if you really loved him, none of this would've ever happened either."

"What do you know about love? Have you ever actually been in love?"

Julien's lips tightened into a thin line, giving me no response.

"So that's all I'm going to get? You listen to my entire *private* conversation with my fiancé, you make judgmental remarks about my relationship, but you're not willing to share any details about *your* life with me?"

Julien's deep-brown eyes focused on mine. "I can just tell, by the way you talk with him, you are not truly in love."

"So if you're such an expert on love, where is she? The woman *you're* in love with?"

"I am not in love with anyone. I know what I know because many women have been in love with *me* before. I can spot them a mile away, *chérie*. But you are right. Your life is none of my business. I just think that a man and woman who are about to be married should make decisions together, no?"

I swallowed the lump in my throat and turned my face away from Julien.

I didn't want to move to Pennsylvania. I'd been more than clear about that the first time Paul had mentioned it. But I knew my fiancé, and when he got an idea in his head, it was close to impossible to shake him of it.

I would shake him of this one, though. I had to.

At least he hadn't accepted the position yet. And as soon as I got home, we would talk it out and Paul would see my point of view.

But then I remembered that when I did arrive home, we'd have even bigger issues to discuss—such as my stolen engagement ring, a fraudulent bank account, and the night I'd spent with a stranger... just to name a few. Ugh.

"I messed up my one chance at love." Julien's deep voice cut through my thoughts. "And I don't like to see others mess up their lives too, that is all." With that, he stood abruptly and headed down the aisle of the train, leaving me alone and speechless.

As the train rumbled down the tracks, I took a deep breath in an attempt to forget about my conversation with Paul, and even more so, about Julien's projections onto my life. He didn't know what he was talking about. He was clearly pinning his own fears and insecurities from his screwed-up love life onto me.

And in less than a day, I would never have to see Julien again.

While this thought should've comforted me, I noticed that the giant knot that had formed in my stomach over the course of the day wasn't loosening up in the slightest. And as I stared out at the looming, gray clouds now hovering over the white stone cottages off in the distance, I realized that this was the first time since those early years after my mother had died that I'd felt so helpless and so utterly out of control. I yearned to hide in one of those cottages and wish away everything that had taken place in the past twenty-four hours.

But I couldn't. I was on a train with a man I barely knew who was telling me I didn't love my fiancé.

That was ridiculous. Of course I loved Paul. Of course I did.

SEVEN

A light summer breeze kissed my cheeks as Julien and I stepped off the train in Annecy.

The sun had just set, but streetlamps lit the way while I struggled to keep up with him, my heels digging into the backs of my feet, giving me no mercy whatsoever.

After jetting across a busy intersection, we wound through a sea of dimly lit cobblestoned streets, combing past the crowds of jolly, wine-drinking tourists who were lounging and smoking cigarettes at the endless array of outdoor cafés.

I spotted a couple feeding each other large, steaming bites of chocolatey dessert crêpes, the woman's expression one of pure ecstasy as she licked a drop of gooey Nutella off the man's spoon. For a split second, I found myself wishing I could trade places with her. What I wouldn't give to be on vacation in some fairy-tale town, eating chocolate off my lover's spoon without a care in the world.

Julien's stern glance snapped me back to reality.

"Hurry, we are almost there," he said, all the while never breaking his brisk stride.

I ignored the throbbing in my feet and powered forward. I hadn't said a word to Julien after our conversation on the train, and I didn't see any reason to. I would follow him to retrieve my passport, and then I'd get right back on the train to Paris—*by myself* this time. With no judgment from the mysterious French agent, who didn't know me at all.

After crossing over a small river that flowed through the town, we squeezed past the meandering tourists and sped down a pedestrian-only cobblestoned walkway. The delicious aromas of melted cheese and chocolate wafted out onto the street, making me feel faint.

Julien took my hand and led me to a miniature table at a café on the corner. "Have a seat, drink a glass of wine, and I will be back in fifteen minutes." He pulled out his wallet and handed me ten euros.

Have a glass of wine? Seriously?

"Where are you going?" I asked, not following his direction to sit down.

"Do not go anywhere or talk to anyone," Julien instructed before turning and leaving me at the café by myself.

"But why can't—"

Julien swiveled back around and marched up to me, leaning in so close that his lips just barely grazed my ear. "The place I am going to may not be safe." He pulled the chair out and laid his hand on my shoulder. "Please, sit down and do not worry. I will be right back."

I noticed a weariness in Julien's eyes that I hadn't seen all day. He gave me one last serious nod before heading back down the crowded cobblestoned street and leaving me alone at what would've been the most charming café I'd ever been to, had it not been for the fact that I was sitting there alone in a tight red dress baring my skin to every sleazy French guy who happened to saunter past. Not to mention the fact that we were hunting down an evil con man to find my passport.

My eyes remained glued to Julien's back as he strode down the pathway, and just when he was barely visible, I shot up from the table.

I didn't care what he'd said. I needed to know what in the hell was going on, and I wanted my passport back.

Much less gracefully than Julien had, I stumbled my way over the rocky cobblestones in my heels. I spotted the back of Julien's head and his gray T-shirt not too far ahead of me as he took a sharp left underneath a stone archway. I slowed down so he wouldn't notice me then peeked around the archway to find him messing with a bloodred door across a quiet alley.

After a few seconds of jimmying the handle, he managed to open the door and slip inside. As the door clicked shut, I realized that sneaking in behind Julien was probably my only chance of making it into that apartment building, and I'd just missed it.

I brushed a strand of hair out of my eyes and let out a frustrated sigh. I probably should've just listened to him and stayed back at the restaurant. But this part of town didn't seem unsafe. So why hadn't he let me come with him? He didn't have a problem taking me into the country cottage in Giverny earlier and beating up that man right in front of me.

As I was trying to decide if I should wait it out in the alley or head back to the café, a flash of wavy auburn hair—almost the exact color and length of my own—caught my eye. I focused in on the woman, who stood a couple of blocks down the street, wondering why I felt so drawn to her. Just as she was about to round a corner, she stopped and pivoted to the side, her profile now clearly visible to me.

I blinked my eyes and did a double take. There was no way that what I was seeing was real. But as I took a few steps toward her, there was no mistaking it.

That woman looked *exactly* like my mother.

She disappeared around the corner, and without thinking, I found myself trekking across the street, rounding the corner, and following this woman with red hair and a face I longed to see again.

She stayed several steps ahead of me, winding through the dark, empty cobblestoned streets so quickly I could barely keep up. I had no clue where I was going, but nothing could've stopped me. I had to see her face one more time.

I struggled to catch up as her slim figure whipped around another corner, but just as I traced her path around the bend, she was gone.

Poof. Just like that. As if she'd disappeared into thin air.

I frantically combed the street where I was certain, *certain*, this spitting image of my mother had just turned, but she was nowhere to be found.

My hands trembled, and a couple of stray beads of sweat slid down the back of my neck as I stopped to catch my breath. Was I losing it? Thinking I'd seen my mother walking through an alley in Annecy? What in the hell was wrong with me?

But when I pictured the woman's profile again, I couldn't deny it. She had looked *exactly* like my mom.

I leaned back against one of the buildings and peered around the street, trying to regain my bearings, when a tiny woman, not more than five feet tall with a head of long, golden-blonde hair emerged from a small garage. She turned and lowered the clanking metal door to the ground, being careful not to let it slam. Then she locked it with a massive key, stuffed the key into her pocket, and cautiously checked to either side before booking it down the street. She visibly startled when she caught my eye, but quickly flicked her eyes back to the path ahead and kept walking.

I shook my head, wondering if she was an illusion too. What was up with me? I must've been severely dehydrated.

And now I had no clue where I was or how to get back to Julien. I should've just stayed put, like he'd told me to. Ugh.

I decided to follow the tiny woman, hoping she'd be heading back to the main part of town, which would hopefully bring me past the door Julien had broken into just minutes before. But as I turned the corner, she too was gone.

Okay, I really needed some water.

I walked alone for several minutes, weaving in and out of the winding streets, when suddenly a crisp breeze cut through the dark alley.

To my relief, the deep-red door loomed at the end of the tiny *rue*, and a massive man—well over six feet tall—was unlocking it with his muscled, tattoo-bearing arms.

I don't what came over me then—maybe it was a gut instinct, or curiosity at what was lurking behind this red door that I wasn't allowed to see, or fear of standing alone in that alley for another second and seeing another phantom woman—but I suddenly found myself running to catch the red door before it clicked shut.

And I made it, just by a hair.

I held the door in place for about thirty seconds as I listened to Tattoo Guy's black boots scuffing down what sounded like a long hallway. When I didn't hear his footsteps anymore, I cracked the door open just the tiniest bit and peeked inside to find complete darkness. My heart pounded through my chest as I listened once more to be certain he was gone, then slid through the doorway, trying not to make a sound.

After closing the door as quietly as I could, I reached for the wall and tiptoed down the clammy, pitch-dark hallway until my eyes began to adjust. A flicker of light emanating from a doorway down the hall caught my eye.

I peeled my heels off my aching feet, then crept up to the door and pressed my ear against the rough wooden panel. I immediately recognized Julien's deep voice, but there was another voice too—a woman's.

I couldn't quite make out what she was saying, but I knew one thing for sure. She wasn't speaking French. She was speaking English. With a posh-sounding Australian accent.

As I leaned closer in an attempt to understand their conversation, the door inched open. I leaped to the side, plastered my back against the wall, and held my breath, praying they hadn't seen me.

My pulse raced, telling me to run, but I clenched my fists and stayed put. After about thirty seconds, with no changes from the other side of the door, I inched closer once again.

My heart caught in my chest at the sight that was now clearly visible inside the apartment.

Lying across a plush, white couch was a striking woman with legs that went on for miles. Jet-black hair spilled over her shoulders and ran the length of her torso. Her curvy figure was barely covered in a black, slinky dress that accentuated her snow-white skin.

Her oval-shaped green eyes gazed upward as she unraveled the red, silky scarf that hung loosely from her neck.

And there, standing over her, was Julien. Firm and unmoving, his head cocked down toward her. I could only imagine the expression that passed across his face as Seductress stood up, wrapped her scarf around his shoulders, and pulled his chest into hers.

The place I am going to may not be safe, he'd told me.

Humph. *She* was dangerous, all right.

"I don't know anything about a painting," she hummed in his ear. "And as for Claude, well, I hadn't seen him in almost two years before he showed up earlier today. And now you, Julien. *My* Julien."

I tore my eyes away from them as a wave of nausea passed through my stomach. What painting? What was Julien not telling me? And was *this* the woman he'd spoken about on the train? The one chance at love he'd messed up?

Just as I was about to bolt and never look back, a glimmer from the other side of the door caught my eye.

And that's when I saw it. My engagement ring, lying carelessly on a dirty coffee table, next to a slew of passports.

Suddenly I couldn't have cared less about Julien or that woman or whatever he was about to do with her. I lifted my hand up to the door, but just as I was about to barge in, a bulge of muscles wrapped around my neck, cutting off my air supply.

I gasped for breath, but when none came, I panicked. I tried my best to squirm, but before I could move a muscle, the grip on my neck released and the bulging arms shoved my body through the door.

"What the hell is going on in here?" the man behind me boomed in an accent identical to the woman's. "And who the hell is this bitch spying through your door?"

Julien whipped around, his brown eyes the biggest I'd seen them all day as I stumbled to the ground, heaving to catch my breath.

Seductress tossed her scarf to the floor and charged toward me, her eyes now narrow little slits. But Julien reached me before she did. In one swift movement, he pulled me up from the floor and blocked me with his body.

"She is not a threat. She is just a friend I am traveling with, and neither of you will lay a hand on her." Julien's voice echoed through the small, cluttered apartment as he shielded me from their menacing glares.

I sucked in a deep breath as I wondered why I hadn't just listened to Julien. Did I really think I could handle everything on my own?

The man who'd pushed me into the apartment approached Julien, and I noticed then that he was the same man, covered in tattoos, who I'd just seen enter the building. He must've been hiding in the shadows, waiting for me. A chill ran down my spine just thinking about it.

A look of disgust fixed onto his face as he eyed Julien. "You and Claude make me fucking sick. You sleep with my sister, you use her to run your stupid cons, and then you leave her. Every time."

"You are right about Claude. But I am a different man. I have no interest in harming your sister," Julien responded without so much as a hint of fear in his voice.

"Then what the hell are you doing here?"

"I needed to ask her a few questions, that's all. And she was more than happy to answer them." Julien's snarky tone challenged the angry Australian.

The corners of Seductress's lips curved into a devilish grin as she slithered toward Julien and shoved her looming brother out of the way. She stood inches away from Julien's face, so close I could smell the alcohol and cigarettes on her breath.

"Julien Dubois," she breathed into his ear. "*You* were the one I always wanted."

She brushed her full lips up against his cheek before running her long forefinger down the middle of his chest.

"I didn't come here for that, and you know it, Marie." Julien pushed her hand off his chest, took mine instead, and led me to the door.

But just as we were about to leave this dodgy apartment, I remembered my ring.

I would not leave without it.

When I turned back toward the coffee table in search of the sparkly diamond that had been lying there moments before, it was nowhere to be found.

Aware that both Tattoo Guy's and Seductress's eyes were glued to my back as Julien pulled me through the doorway, I leaned close to him and whispered in his ear, "But my ri—"

He didn't let me finish my sentence as he whipped me out into the dim hallway and slammed the door behind us.

"But my ring!" I hissed again as I slipped my dreaded heels back onto my sore feet.

"Don't talk until we get outside." Julien gripped my hand as he led me out into the cool night air.

Once outside, I yanked my hand from his grasp and crossed my arms over my chest. "My engagement ring was lying on that coffee table. We have to go back in there and get it!"

Julien grunted as he stalked farther down the alley without me.

"I'm serious! I have to go back in there. This is not an option."

Julien flipped around, his eyes flashing, his hand stuffed into his jeans pocket. Then he reached out for me.

"No, I am not holding your hand again. Who knows where that hand was before I arrived. And another thing," I spouted. But I didn't get a chance to finish when I noticed what Julien had placed in the palm of my hand.

My engagement ring.

I stared down at the large diamond shimmering underneath the faint glow of the streetlamp, my head spinning in circles.

"But how did you…?"

"I told you I would help you, did I not?" Julien flipped around and headed back underneath the stone archway.

I hobbled to catch up with him. "And my passport? Did you find it?"

He shook his head before pulling a cigarette out of his jeans pocket and lighting up. "No passport."

"But there were all those passports on the coffee table. What about those?"

"Yours was not there. I checked." His tone grew impatient as he blew a puff of smoke into the night air.

"But how can I trust that you actually looked? I saw you in there with that...*woman*. You didn't seem too focused on getting my passport back."

Julien's gaze fixed on the ground ahead of him and his jaw clenched before he spoke. "It was not what it looked like. And you had no right to follow me. I asked you to stay at the restaurant. I knew what I was doing, and you, thinking you know how to do everything, had to run in and ruin the whole operation."

"I'm sorry for ruining the operation, but there are clearly things you're not telling me. What does any of this have to do with a *painting*?" I asked.

Julien flicked the cigarette onto the curb and took a sharp right up the river. "That is confidential information. You shouldn't have been there to hear it in the first place, so forget you ever did."

"Fine. So what now?" I said, realizing that after all of this madness, we still hadn't found Claude or my passport.

"We will get a hotel for the night, and we can take the first train out of the city tomorrow."

A sinking feeling gripped the pit of my stomach. What was I going to do? How was I going to get home? What if I went back to Paris and the police were still after me? And if those transfers really were tied to illegal activity, Paul would certainly be hearing about it soon. And how would I ever begin to explain the past twenty-four hours to him? How could I let him and my family down like this?

I peered down at the engagement ring I held in my hand. That diamond had once symbolized the security of the life I was to have with Paul.

But in one day, the safety net I'd worked so hard to build for myself had been swept out from under me. And all because I'd allowed some sweet-talking French man to feed me a few glasses of wine.

I followed Julien through the winding streets of Annecy in silence as I held the ring in my palm, physically unable to slip it back onto my ring finger. I wondered then, as I thought of Paul, if he too felt that we weren't just one, but many oceans apart right now.

EIGHT

I'd never been so happy to see a regular, paved sidewalk. After following the cobblestoned street along the river for a few minutes, we finally arrived at a main intersection with normal sidewalks and streetlights. It was a miracle I hadn't sprained my ankle with the amount of times I'd slipped in my heels on those damn uneven stones.

The river that flowed through town fed into a huge lake, its silky waters shimmering under the moonlight. Instead of continuing toward the lake, Julien took a left down the paved sidewalk and nodded for me to follow him.

That's all I was going to get now? A nod? Like I was his dog or something?

"Where are we going?" I asked, suddenly feeling so exhausted I could've curled up on a bench and gone to sleep in two seconds flat.

"There is a hotel up ahead. It is called Splendid Hôtel. We will get a room there for the night."

"Splendid," I replied dryly.

A tiny smirk emerged from Julien's lips.

"Should I even ask why you would be smiling at a time like this?" I asked.

"I am just thinking that my…what I mean to say is that *Claude* must have seen a very different side of you last night when he followed you up to your hotel room. I don't imagine this is the side I will be seeing tonight?"

"French men, American men, you're all the same." I sighed, removing my gaze from the mischievous look brewing in Julien's eyes. "One minute you're furious, the next minute you're thinking about sex."

"You are the one who is engaged, and who is about to spend *another* night in a foreign hotel with a *different* French man, *chérie*."

"Thanks for pointing that out. Where is the hotel again?"

"You ask, and I deliver." Julien gestured to his left.

The Splendid Hôtel awning hovered overhead.

I followed him into a quiet lobby, thinking about what he'd just said. He was right. *I* was the one who was engaged, and who, for the second time in a row, was about to spend the night in a foreign hotel with a guy I'd just met. I was so deeply ensconced in this mess, though, I didn't know how else to emerge on the other side without trusting Julien one more time.

Julien pulled out a credit card and paid for our room, leaving me to ponder the fact that I'd known him for less than twenty-four hours, and yet there wasn't even a tiny part of me that felt frightened at the thought of spending the night in a hotel room alone with him.

Scanning back through the events of the day, with the exception of the vicious punches he'd thrown at the police officer in the hotel bathroom and at the balding man in Giverny, nothing about Julien had scared me. In fact, it was just the opposite. He had this fiercely protective nature about him, as if no matter what disaster came our way, he would handle it...and he would protect me in the process.

I'd never met anyone like him.

Then again, I'd never met anyone like Claude, and my sleaze-bag, con-man alarm signal clearly had not gone off the night before, when he'd smooth-talked me. Maybe my gut instincts weren't to be trusted after all.

At least this time I had nothing left for anyone to steal. And at this point, I would've actually paid Julien to steal my heels and this slutty red dress so I wouldn't have to wear them for another second.

After Julien collected our room key, we waited for the elevator together.

"You know, once all of this is figured out, I'll pay you back for everything," I told him.

"That is not necessary," Julien said, pushing the button once more.

The bell dinged, and when Julien opened the door, he revealed the tiniest elevator I'd ever seen.

"After you," he said.

The two of us crammed against each other in the tight space, our chests and knees knocking together.

I tucked a strand of my ever-thickening hair behind my ear, suddenly feeling awkward and nervous. I diverted my eyes toward the wall.

"Seriously, though," I said. "I'll pay you back as soon as I get home."

Julien lifted his forefinger up to my lips.

"Shhh." He grinned at me, a mischievous gleam in his eye. "When you are around me, you can relax. I won't tell anyone."

Julien dropped his hand, his fingertips brushing over mine. A wave of heat pooled below my abdomen as tingles shot up my spine, making me feel light-headed. I swallowed hard as I broke his gaze.

Before I could say anything else to cut the weird tension that had filled up the stale elevator air, we arrived on the fourth floor. I took a deep breath as I followed him down the slim, dark hallway.

Julien unlocked our door, revealing a minuscule room containing a less than generous double bed, a tiny wooden desk and chair, and absolutely no floor space.

We stood in the doorway together and stared at the bed for a moment before Julien spoke.

"I am sorry. There were no rooms with two beds left. And all hotel rooms in France are small. Well, except for the Plaza Athénée."

I was so tired, I didn't know what to say. I mean, the man had shuttled me around France all day trying to find my passport, he'd retrieved my engagement ring, and he'd paid for my food, my train ticket, and now this hotel room. What was I going to do? Tell him to sleep in the wooden chair?

I plopped onto the bed and kicked my heels off my feet, which were red, swollen, and covered in blisters.

"Ouch," Julien said as he crossed to the other side of the bed and peeked inside the bathroom. "Your feet do not look happy. I will give you some privacy in case you want to take a shower. I'll be back in thirty minutes. Okay?"

"Thanks," I said.

Julien smiled kindly in my direction before letting himself out of the room.

Before I knew it, my back had plummeted into the mattress, my head like a dead weight that was too heavy to hold up for another second. I stretched my arms out to the sides and lifted my tired legs onto the bed while I stared up at the ceiling.

If I had focused long enough on the way the paint swirled in endless circles above me, I could've forgotten what was actually going on. Or at the very least, fallen asleep. But the throbbing in my feet was too painful for me to ignore, and more than that, whenever I closed my eyes, my insides heated up again, just as they had in the elevator with Julien only moments before.

As I forced myself up to a sitting position and shook off the heat that stung my cheeks, I spied the hotel phone on the desk across from me. Sophie would be flying into DC the next day, and she had no idea I wouldn't be there when she arrived. The thought of my sister staying alone with Paul for even a day made me queasy. They didn't just dislike each other, they *loathed* each other. Paul couldn't stand Sophie's constant chatter, question asking, and general lack of practicality, and as Sophie had so eloquently put it in her e-mail to me before I'd left, she wasn't a huge fan of the giant stick up Paul's ass.

I'd stopped trying to make them like each other long ago.

I picked up the receiver and dialed Sophie's cell, deciding I would tell her the exact same story I'd told Paul. I had no other choice. If I gave her even an inkling of the truth, the whole family would know something was wrong within two minutes of me hanging up.

"Hello?" she answered.

"Soph, it's me, Chloe."

"Dude, you need to tell your future husband to take a chill pill."

"What are you talking about? When did you talk to Paul?"

"I called the house about an hour ago to see if you were home yet, and he was freaking out."

"So, I guess he told you I have to stay in Paris for another day or two."

"Yeah, he didn't sound too happy about that, and he was flipping because he just tried to call you at the hotel and they said you're not a guest there anymore?"

I rested my forehead in my hands, preparing myself to lie for the third time that day.

"Oh yeah, um…I forgot to mention to him that Angela had me switch to a more reasonably priced hotel so we don't rack up the company credit card since the extra days here weren't planned."

"Well, you better call him and let him know. He said he really needs to talk to you, like *now*. Something about your checking account being on hold. I guess he tried to use your debit card and it wouldn't work. He was rattling on about it forever on the phone. He sounds really stressed, Chloe…not that it's any different from how he usually acts, but still. I think with the wedding coming up this weekend and everything, you should really get home."

I had nothing to say, except that my life was turning to complete shit.

"Chloe, are you there?"

"Mm-hmm," I mumbled as I squeezed my eyes shut and tried to breathe.

"So is this the hotel number where you're staying? Do you want me to give it to Paul so he can call you there?"

"No! I…um, I mean, no. I'll call him in a little bit. Don't trouble yourself."

"Oh, it's no trouble. I mean, I *am* your maid of honor, and you've barely let me take care of anything for the wedding. Which, by the way, can you believe you're getting *married* in less than a week?"

"No, Soph. I can't. I really can't."

"So tell me about Paris. What are the French men like? Are they sexy? Or are they super skinny?"

"*Sophie.*"

"What? I mean, I know you're about to get married, but that doesn't mean you're dead. It's not like you can't look at another man besides Paul for the rest of your life."

"Fine. I guess you could say they're…*interesting.* Not that I've really had much contact with them. I mean, you know I'm here for work." I cringed as I glanced around the hotel room. If she only knew.

"Work, work, work. You could at least have a little fun if you're going to be there for another day or two. You know how stressful it's going to be when you come back with all of us in town for the wedding. I talked to Lily and Magali and Dad this morning. They were stressing me out just listening to them. You've got to get home."

"I know, Soph. I know."

"Well, keep us posted on when you'll be back. Until then, it'll be me and Paul holding down the fort."

Oh, God.

"I will, Soph. Can't wait to see you."

"Me too. Love you."

"Love you too. Bye."

I hung up with Sophie and briefly contemplated calling Paul, but decided to take a shower first. I was sweaty and exhausted, and my feet hurt. Plus, I needed time to figure out what I was even going to say to him. The only two options were to keep lying to him or to tell him the truth. And if I kept lying, the lies were going to spiral out of control. I would have to tell him that I'm staying in a new hotel. Which, by the way, I wouldn't even be in tomorrow. And Paul wasn't an idiot. He would notice that none of this was adding up.

And now the checking-account disaster. I had no clue how I would even begin to explain that.

The other option—telling Paul the truth—still didn't feel like a viable option to me if I still wanted to get married this weekend.

So, lying it was.

I stared at the phone, and as the queasiness piled up in my stomach, I turned away and headed to the shower.

After twenty minutes of standing underneath a blazing-hot stream of water in a comatose state, not willing to think about my mess of a life for another second, I wrapped myself up in a towel, only to realize that I was going to have to put that dreaded red dress back on to go to bed. Ugh.

Just as I was about to slip the minuscule sliver of a dress over my head, there was a knock on the bathroom door.

"Yeah?"

"I bought some pajamas for you," Julien called.

"Oh, thanks," I replied, surprised at his thoughtfulness, and grateful to toss the red dress into a heap on the bathroom floor.

"Do you want them?"

"Oh yes, thanks." Cracking the door open a slit, I reached for the pajamas.

Julien had bought me a small purple T-shirt with *Annecy* written on the front in bubbly white letters and a pair of light-blue linen pants. To my surprise, he'd also chosen the perfect sizes.

Clean and tired, I emerged from the bathroom. Julien sat at the desk, eating a sandwich.

"Thank you for the clothes," I said as I plopped down on the bed and attempted to comb out my long, wet hair with my fingers.

"I got you a sandwich too," he said, sliding a plastic bag across the bed toward me. "Just cheese and vegetables. No meat. And there's a bottle of water in there too. No wine."

"Very funny."

Inside the bag, in addition to the sandwich and the water, there were also two toothbrushes—a pink one and a blue one—and a small tube of *dentifrice*.

I peeked up at Julien munching on a gargantuan bite of his sandwich, and despite the things he'd said to me on the train and the questionable events that had just taken place with the freaky Australian duo, I felt immensely grateful that he was taking care of me. And somehow I knew in my gut that I'd been right to trust him. He'd been right about the fact that I should've stayed put when he went to find my passport, and he'd even managed to steal my ring back.

I could explain a stolen passport to Paul. But how would I ever have explained my missing engagement ring?

I realized then that I still hadn't put my ring back on. The lonely diamond shimmered underneath the light of the desk lamp, next to Julien, who was looking straight at me as he chomped on his sandwich.

"You are thinking very hard over there," he said in between bites. "What are you thinking about?"

"Oh, I…I don't know. I'm just really confused, I guess, about everything. I spoke with my sister while you were out. She talked to my fiancé, and he was upset because the bank has placed a hold on our checking account."

Julien threw back a gulp of water, then cleared his throat. "Claude works quickly. He knows what he's doing."

"So what should I do? I mean, at this point, it seems inevitable that Paul is going to find out the truth."

"If we can find Claude tomorrow, there is a strong chance of getting your passport back, and you can be on the first plane back home."

"But if the police are looking for me, and if the transfers Claude made out of my account are now apparently tied to illegal activity, how will I even get through customs at the airport?"

Julien swallowed his last bite and crumbled up the wrapping into a ball before tossing it in the wastebasket. "You do not need to worry about that. I work for the government, remember? I will see to it that you get through customs with no problems."

"But you told me that even the people you work with won't believe that I'm innocent. That many of the women before me were actually working *with* Claude. So how will you ensure that I'll be able to leave?"

"You have to trust me, Chloe. I know what I'm doing."

"Who do you work for? Is it like the French equivalent of the CIA?"

"That is confidential. You already know too much as it is."

I narrowed my eyes at him. "Fine. If you can't tell me who you work for, then I want to know who that Australian woman was back at the apartment, and what the deal is with the painting."

Julien sighed. "I guess I am not going to be able to avoid your questions any longer, am I?"

"Not unless you want me to keep asking them."

"I for sure do not want that."

"Okay, then start talking," I demanded.

"Marie is a woman Claude uses to run cons with…and he sleeps with her too."

"And judging by what her brother said, you do as well…*sleep* with her, that is."

"No, that is not—"

I held my hand up to quiet him. "Never mind, I don't want to know. That's none of my business, anyway. If you're undercover, I suppose you have to do certain *things* to be 'one of them,' as you said."

Julien raised an eyebrow at me, his dimple popping into his right cheek as he smirked. "Why do you care if I sleep with Marie or not? You are engaged, no?"

My cheeks boiled as I tore my gaze from Julien's. "I don't care. I'm just trying to get the whole picture of what in the hell is going on here."

"Trust me, this is a complicated mess, and the less you know, the better."

"You never answered about the painting."

"There is no painting," he replied matter-of-factly.

"So why was that woman saying she knew nothing about a painting and then you told me after we left that it was *confidential*?"

"I used that to distract her so I could get other information without her realizing it. Marie, as you could see, is not exactly the smartest woman."

"So there is no painting?"

"No painting. But I found out where Claude is headed next, and Marie said he still had a batch of passports with him to sell, so it is very possible that he still has yours."

"Where is he going next?" I asked.

"Lyon. It is a city two hours from here by train. We can leave in the morning."

"I still don't fully understand why you would go to all this trouble to help me. Especially if your orders were to leave me with the police and find Claude. I mean, you're putting your job at risk for me and we haven't even found Claude yet. Why would you do that?"

"You really don't stop with the questions, do you?"

When I didn't gratify him with a snarky response, Julien sighed. "Fine. There was this…this woman I used to know…" He trailed off, fixing his gaze on a coffee stain on the carpet.

"Your one chance at love?"

He lifted his eyes to mine but didn't answer, so I took that as a yes.

"She was a victim of one of Claude's cons. Like you are now. And I do not want to see one more woman go through what she went through."

"What happened to her?"

Julien stood and headed toward the bathroom. "I think I have answered enough questions for one night." With that, he closed the bathroom door and left me alone on the bed, wondering what could've possibly happened to that woman that was worse than what had already happened to me.

I finished my sandwich while Julien took a shower, and as I stood to throw the wrapping in the trash, something on the desk caught my eye.

Julien's cell phone.

I glanced over to the bathroom door, and still hearing the shower running, I picked up his phone. I didn't know what exactly I was looking for, but I needed to know more. More about who he worked for, the painting that he claimed was only a "distraction," and why on earth he'd risk his job for a woman he'd just met.

Scrolling through his phone, I quickly located his text messages, then clicked on the most recent one. It had come in the night before from a contact named G. D.

My breath caught in my throat as a picture, not a message, loaded onto his tiny cell phone screen.

It was a picture of me.

The same one the cops had shown to the hotel manager earlier that morning at the Hôtel Plaza Athénée.

Underneath the photo was a message that read:

La femme s'appelle Chloe Turner. Si tu veux trouver le tableau, empêche cette femme de parler aux flics. C'est urgent.

I had to write this down. I couldn't remember enough French to understand the entire message. I yanked the desk drawer open in search of a pen and paper, but didn't find anything. Just then, the shower stream switched off from inside the bathroom. Julien would be opening that door any second now.

Lunging across the bed to reach the nightstand, I opened the drawer and found a pen next to a pad of paper. Underneath the Splendid Hôtel heading, I scribbled the text message down, tore the piece of paper off the pad, folded it up, and pushed it into my bra. I hurried back across the room, fiddled with Julien's phone to bring it back to the main screen, then returned it to its exact spot on the desk.

Just as I made it onto the bed, Julien emerged with a towel wrapped around his waist. His dark-brown hair was all wet and messy, and his lips curved upward into that disarming grin I'd already seen a few times that day, revealing the dimple in his right cheek.

"That was a nice shower, was it not?" he said as he used another towel to dry off his ears.

"Mm-hmm," I mumbled, trying *not* to look below his face at his rock-hard abs or his tan, muscular shoulders. I rubbed my hand over my chest and felt the folded piece of paper hiding in there, then smiled back at Julien. "It was the best shower I've had in a long time."

NINE

The sound of the door clicking shut jolted me awake. I opened my eyes to find Julien dressed in his clothes from the day before, a preoccupied look passing over his features.

"Sleep well?" he asked.

"Mm-hmm," I mumbled. "Like a rock."

"Is this what you are like when you share a bed with a man?"

"Excuse me?"

"When your fiancé takes you to bed, do you go to sleep immediately?" Julien whipped open the drapes, letting in a stream of bright light.

I pushed myself up to a sitting position and squinted as my eyes adjusted. "What are you implying? That I'm frigid?"

He shrugged his shoulders. "Just wondering."

I stood up in a huff.

"Do you live together?" Julien asked. "You and your fiancé?"

"Yes, of course we do. Why are you grilling me? I just woke up."

"Is he able to please you?"

My jaw dropped. "Did you seriously just ask me that?"

"What is the problem?"

"I just met you yesterday—that's the problem. If you think I'm going to discuss my sex life with you, you're crazy."

Julien shrugged and stifled a smirk. "Don't get so upset. I am just curious. I know that when people move in together, sometimes the romance goes away."

"Have you ever lived with anyone?" I asked him.

"No."

"Well, if you must know, things can get less exciting once you've lived with someone for a while. Not that I'm saying that's the case with me and my fiancé, but for many couples, yes, that can happen. Of course you can still come up with ways to spice things up."

He lifted a brow. "Such as?"

I ducked into the bathroom and splashed some water on my face. "Use your imagination."

Julien popped his head around the corner and caught my eye in the mirror. "I have a very vivid imagination."

"Yes, you proved that to me during your little nude beach stunt on the Newlywed Tour Bus from Hell yesterday. So charming," I muttered as I looked at my flushed cheeks in the mirror and closed the door on Julien's laughter. "What time is it?" I called through the door.

"It is nine thirty. I have just returned from the train station."

"Why did you let me sleep so late? Can we get a train out of here soon?"

"Actually, there is a problem."

I whipped the bathroom door back open again. "What kind of problem?"

Julien ran his hand through his hair. "There is a *grève*."

"What's a *grève*?"

"What is the word in English?" Julien sat down on the edge of the bed, tapping his chin with his forefinger. "A strike?"

"A strike?"

"Yes. That is the word. All of the transportation workers are having a strike today. There are no trains."

"What do you mean, there are no trains? How can this be possible?"

"It is quite normal in France. There are *grèves* all the time."

"We have to leave, though. We can't waste any more time. What about renting a car?"

"Not possible. They are on strike too. All the businesses relating to transportation are on strike. We are stuck."

I stared at Julien in disbelief. This couldn't be happening. "Why are you acting so calm?"

"You think I am happy about this? What can I do, though? It is not as if I am in control of the transportation situation in France," he snapped.

"But there has to be something we can do! Is there *any* way we can get to Lyon today?" I stood up and paced back and forth next to the window.

"I have left a message for someone who may be able to pick us up and take us to Lyon. We will wait for a call back. If that does not work, the strike will only last for one day. We can take the train to Lyon first thing tomorrow morning. Claude has a girlfriend he stays with, so he will be there for at least a couple days."

"Are you sure?"

"Yes, I am sure."

"Just like you were *sure* we would catch him in Giverny, and then in Annecy? I'm starting to think you're not the best undercover agent after all. I mean, why can't one of your fellow agents come and get us? How is it possible that we're stuck here?"

"I told you, I have left a message for the one person who is able to take us to Lyon, but the details of my job, of my connections, are to be kept confidential. And if you want to insult my job abilities, that is fine. But I'd like to know, do you have a better plan?"

"No, but still. This is insane. What are we supposed to do in the meantime?"

The tense look in Julien's eyes faded as they combed their way down my body. "I could come up with a few ideas."

I crossed my arms over my chest and stalked over to the window. "Oh, my God. This cannot be happening to me."

Julien stood from the bed and grabbed his phone off the desk. "You American women—so uptight. Come, I take you to breakfast, and we can discuss ways to lighten you up." Julien eyed the red dress lying over the back of the chair. "First, we need to get you some new clothes."

"In case you're forgetting, I don't have any money on me," I told him, my insides cringing at the thought of wearing those scuffed-up black heels and that awful red dress for another second.

"I will take you shopping. It will be fun."

I scrunched up my forehead. "Shopping? Fun? No man thinks shopping is fun."

"You mean no *American* man thinks shopping is fun. You forget, I am French. We are a very different breed. There are great shops in Annecy. Get dressed. It's time for a real French breakfast."

"If you think I'm going to run around eating and shopping in some obscure town in the French Alps with a man I barely know, acting like everything is okay when my wedding is in five days, you're insane! I'm going to find a way out of this city, with or without you."

Julien arched an eyebrow. "Oh yes? How?"

I stared at him blankly. Clearly I had no plan. And my stomach was growling something fierce.

"Fine. I'll come with you. But only because I'm starving and I don't see any point in sitting in this hotel room by myself."

After a quick shower, I tucked the piece of paper with the text message written on it back inside my bra, making a mental note to be sure to translate it as soon as possible.

My two choices in apparel were either the skimpy red dress or the pajamas, and with either option, I would be sporting my three-inch black heels. As much as that damned dress made me think of Claude and what I may or may not have done with him two nights prior, I decided to wear it. I simply could not bring myself to walk around outside in pajama pants and high heels. After I finished in the bathroom, I found Julien lounging on the bed, flipping channels on the TV.

He lifted his eyes from the screen, his chocolate-brown gaze landing on my chest.

"What are you staring at?" I snapped, hoping he didn't notice the flush spreading up my neck.

Julien's gaze flicked up to my face. "I am just thinking that for all of his flaws, Claude has good taste in women's clothing. No?"

Men.

"I need to call my fiancé before we leave," I said, taking a seat next to Julien on the bed and slipping on my heels.

"Did you not just speak with him yesterday? He thinks you are working, no?"

I peered down at my watch. Julien had a point. Paul *would* think I was working right now, and it was only three thirty in the morning there. Waking him up in the middle of the night had never been a good idea, so maybe I should wait until he was up for the day.

The tightness in my stomach dissipated the slightest bit. I could talk to him later. No need to make the situation worse than it already was.

"Okay, I'll wait. Let's go."

Julien smiled at me, revealing his big dimple. "*On y va.*"

Julien ushered me through the front door of the hotel, and as I stepped out onto the sidewalk and took in the view of the crystal-blue lake surrounded by tree-covered mountains, I forgot about my feet hurting, about the minuscule red dress I was wearing, about Paul, about our checking account, about how much Julien was grating on my nerves, about everything.

I'd never seen anything like this place. It was breathtaking.

"I told you it was beautiful here," Julien said as he placed his hand on my arm. "I will show you all around after breakfast. Come."

I followed Julien but couldn't keep my eyes off the scene that unfolded with each step through this enchanting town. White boats speckled the enormous, sparkling lake. They floated aimlessly, with no cares, nowhere to go, no race to run. Small, laughing children frolicked in the grass, their parents lined up on benches under lush trees, the view of the mountaintops just beyond the leaves that swished in the breeze. The air was cool and refreshing and smelled of pine. As we turned our backs to the lake and walked into town, the mouthwatering scent of chocolate mixed with coffee drifted out into the cobblestoned streets, making my empty stomach growl.

The lake funneled into a bubbling stream that flowed peacefully through the town. Vibrant bundles of pink, purple, and white flowers spilled over the small pedestrian bridges that stretched across the stream. Meandering tourists strolled up and down the path, shooting pictures of buildings the color of sunset, their shutters open to let in the fresh mountain air.

I remembered walking past this area the night before, but in the daylight, it was a completely different story. *Charming* didn't even begin to touch what this town was. It was a real-life fairy tale.

Julien led us to one of the cafés that lined the stream and pulled out a chair for me at a table that had a perfect view of the majestic lake, the towering mountains, the sweet-smelling flowers, the chirping birds, the rustling trees—all of it.

He sat down across from me and grinned. "See, spending the day in Annecy is not so bad. You do not have places like this in America, am I right?"

I thought back to our town house in DC, near Dupont Circle. It felt light-years away. "No. There is nothing like this in the States. Nothing at all."

A tall, dark-haired server with a breezy smile on his face appeared at our table. "*Bonjour, Mademoiselle, Monsieur. Vous voulez quelque chose à boire?*"

"*Un café pour moi, et...*" Julien turned to me. "Do you want a coffee?"

"*Un café pour moi aussi,*" I said to the waiter, hoping my accent was comprehensible. "*Et je...*um...*je suis une question?*"

The server's eyebrows knitted together. "*Oui, Mademoiselle?*"

I thought I'd just told him I had a question. Or had I said I *am* a question? Shit. Whatever, he got the point.

"*Il a y...*I mean, *il y a une grève?*" I managed to spit out.

"*Oui, Mademoiselle, il y a une grève aujourd'hui.* And, I speak English, if you would like."

Why hadn't he told me that right away? Wasn't I just screaming *stupid American tourist*?

"So all of the transportation systems are on strike today? Trains, buses, rental cars, everything?"

"Yes, everything."

"Do you know of any way I can leave this city and get to Paris or Lyon, for example?"

"No, Mademoiselle. I am sorry. Unless you have your own car, there is no transportation in or out of Annecy today. Surely another day in Annecy could not hurt. No?" He gestured to the picturesque scenery surrounding us.

"Of course not. *Merci.*"

Before the server moseyed off to another table, Julien added, "*Monsieur, deux pains au chocolat aussi, s'il vous plaît.*"

Julien raised an eyebrow at me. "Did you think I was lying?"

I shrugged. "I'm just watching out for myself."

"Why would I lie about the strike?"

I thought of my picture on Julien's cell phone and the strange text message with my name in it. "Who knows?"

Julien smiled. "Did you think I wanted to spend the day with you?"

"No, that's not what I was thinking. I just—"

"I did not know you spoke French," Julien cut in as he pulled his pack of cigarettes out of his pocket and laid them on the table.

"I don't really *speak* French. I took a little bit in college, but that was a long time ago."

"Your accent is good, though. You know, most Americans who come here have horrible accents. I want to tell them, go back to your country and speak English. But you, you have a nice..." Julien trailed off as his eyes traveled over my body.

"I have a nice what?"

He grinned. "Accent. You have a nice accent. You would do well here if you learned more of the language."

The server set two mini cups of coffee down in front of us along with two fluffy croissants, dark chocolate bursting from the middle.

"*Merci*," I said before devouring the first few bites of my buttery pastry, savoring the warm, gooey chocolate that melted on my tongue. I was so hungry I could've eaten five of them.

I tried to pace myself, but within seconds, only a sliver of the chocolate croissant remained.

Julien chuckled. "Along with bad accents, Americans have bad food."

"We do not," I said through a mouthful of pastry, which I washed down with a sip of strong espresso. "Have you ever been to the States?"

"Yes, as a matter of fact, I have, and your food is nothing to brag about."

"Not all Americans eat at McDonald's, if that's what you're thinking."

"It is clear that *you* do not eat at McDonald's because you are thin and healthy. But most Americans are not so thin, am I right?"

"Do you have something against Americans?" I asked, wishing Julien would shut his mouth so I could enjoy my pastry in peace.

"No, not at all. I am simply making observations. This is how I make my living, you know. I observe. Take you, for example. You are sitting here in one of the most beautiful places in the world, eating a delicious pastry, and yet, you are tense. You cannot allow yourself to relax even for one second to enjoy such a beautiful day, even though there is nothing you can do at the current moment about your predicament."

"And this is the first time I've seen you outside without a cigarette in your mouth," I shot back. "Eating too much McDonald's might be a cause of obesity in America, but aren't you aware that smoking causes cancer?"

Julien sipped his coffee and shook his head at me. "American women, French women, you are all the same."

"What's that supposed to mean?"

"Always trying to tell the man what to do. What is good for us. What is bad for us." Julien's lips curved upward into a devilish grin. "Why not just live a little and stop worrying so much?"

"I don't tell Paul what to do. And I don't worry all the time."

Julien raised his eyebrow at me again.

"Stop doing that."

"What?"

"That thing you're doing with your eyebrow."

He let out a low laugh before taking a large bite of his croissant and stretching back in his chair. "It is fun to make you mad, you know that?"

"And it would be even more fun if you would be quiet and *allow* me to enjoy the view."

Julien snickered under his breath, took a cigarette out of the pack, and lit up while I finished my chocolate croissant and breathed in the crisp mountain air blowing off the lake. And just as I felt a few of my worries being swept away at the sound of the stream rushing by, Julien tossed a couple of coins onto the table, grabbed my hand, and pulled me up from my seat.

His jaw was tense, his eyes narrow. "Follow me."

"But I didn't even finish my coffee," I insisted.

"*Now,*" he said, yanking me down the sidewalk and around the corner, his eyes darting over his shoulder the whole way.

So much for enjoying the moment.

TEN

"What the hell was that?" I snapped after Julien let go of my hand and resumed his usual nonchalant stride.

"It was time to go." He took another puff of his cigarette.

"Did you see someone? Those scary Australians from last night? Or the police?"

Julien kept walking, his gaze straight ahead, his lips sealed.

I shook my head, not sure what to think. One minute I felt like Julien was being honest and trying to help me, then the next minute something crazy would happen and I was back to square one, realizing I had no clue what was really going on.

"Come, I know a nice shoe store a block down the street." Julien glanced over his shoulder once more.

"You really expect me to go shopping with you and pretend like that didn't just happen?"

"Nothing happened," he stated very matter-of-factly.

"Fine. *Nothing* happened. We'll pretend that you didn't just see someone who we are now running from."

"At the moment, we are running from no one." He glanced down at my feet, the skin raw and pink. "I am buying you a new pair of shoes." Julien stopped and opened the door to his right, then gestured for me to go inside.

I left Julien's side, trying to forget about the stunt he'd just pulled at the café and hoping Tattoo Guy and Seductress weren't after us. I picked up a pair of gray-and-white sneakers and turned them over in my hands, my temples throbbing as I thought of how much time we were wasting by staying here for another day. Paul would be waking up soon. What would I even say when I called him later on?

"Hey, honey. Just taking a little detour to a fairy-tale town in the Alps with this undercover French agent I met yesterday. Oh, and by the way, he kissed me in the lobby of the Plaza Athénée, I slept in the same bed with him last night, and he took me shopping. Can't wait to get home for the wedding, though!"

God, what a freaking disaster.

"Those look nice. Want to try them on?" Julien stood next to me, a little too close.

I gazed down at my red dress. "I don't think they'll really go with my outfit."

"No problem. We will get you something more comfortable to wear. I don't imagine you want to walk around Annecy all day in this seductive dress. Am I right?"

"I'm not going to let you buy me new clothes too. This is ridiculous. Shouldn't we be spending our time trying to get the hell out of here?"

"I already explained to you, I made a call to the one person who is close enough to come to Annecy and pick us up, but I haven't heard back. With the nature of my work, there are unfortunately no other options without ruining my cover. I will call again in a minute, *after* I buy you some new shoes." His eyes darted out the store window, then back to me. "Unless we want to sit in the hotel all day, we may find ourselves running some more, and with you hobbling around in those high heels, you are slowing us down."

Gripping a shopping bag full of socks and my new pair of snazzy sneakers, I followed Julien out of the store, trying to stay calm. Trying to "go with the flow" and "enjoy the moment," since it appeared that I had no other choice.

A few feet down the sidewalk, he stopped abruptly, grabbed my hand, and spun me around in the other direction.

"What is going on?" I hissed as I attempted, unsuccessfully, to disentangle our hands.

"*Rien*," he said with a roll of his eyes. "Nothing. I am taking you to another store I know. It is called Camaïeu. I think you will like it."

"Okay, then why are you holding onto my hand with a death grip and making me walk a hundred miles an hour?"

He flashed his obnoxious smirk. "I told you that you would need the sneakers."

"Just tell me what the hell is going on," I snapped. "*Who* are we running from?"

Julien opened the next door we came to and shoved me inside ahead of him. "You shop. I will be in the corner making a phone call."

"What? Who are you calling?" I asked, wishing I could bug his phone so I could find out what was really going on.

"*Vas-y*," he said. "I will only be a minute." Julien spun around and disappeared behind the racks of stylish clothing, leaving me dumbfounded in the middle of the store.

A sleek saleswoman appeared by my side. "*Je peux vous aider, Mademoiselle?*"

"Um…no, *je*…um…"

"You speak English?" She smiled at me with kind, hazel eyes.

I nodded, my mouth still dangling open.

"Come with me. I help you shop." She placed her hand on my shoulder and guided me through the store, picking out an assortment of jeans and tops along the way while I smiled distractedly and scanned the racks for Julien.

Just as she was setting up a dressing room, and I was beginning to wonder if Julien had left me here for good, he popped around the corner, holding a plum-colored T-shirt. He held it out for me. "Here, I think this will look good with your hair."

"What were you doing?" I asked as I took the shirt from him and tossed it into the dressing room.

"Making a call, like I said."

"So, can we get out of here soon? Is this person going to come get us? And who is it, by the way?"

"Her name is Camille. And no, she hasn't answered her phone yet. I left her another message."

Was Camille one of Julien's girlfriends? A guy like him was certain to have at least a few women scattered around France.

While he certainly had a protective, sweet side to him, he also didn't strike me as the commitment type. His *one chance at love* he'd referred to on the train was probably a goldfish he'd forgotten to feed.

"It didn't take you that long just to leave a voice mail," I remarked. "Who else did you call?"

Julien's eyes flickered as he placed his hands on my shoulders and pushed me into the dressing room. "Just try on the clothes. I make you a promise that I will get us out of Annecy as soon as I can, and I will. There is nothing more for you to question." He dropped his hands from my shoulders and shut the door in my face.

"I will wait here," he called through the door. "Show me when you're done so I can see."

"Humph," I snorted. Like I was actually going to play dress-up with him and show him each outfit. I didn't even want to be here. I mean, yes, I couldn't say I wasn't looking forward to trashing my heels and this ridiculous dress and changing into some normal, clean clothes, but that was beside the point.

The point was that this situation was completely out of control, and judging by the way Julien had had one eye glued over his shoulder since we'd left the café, we weren't safe here. We needed to get out of Annecy and find Claude as soon as possible.

I threw on a pair of dark, boot-cut jeans and the plum T-shirt and decided it would do. Just as I was about to strip off the shirt, Julien cracked the door open. "Let me see."

"Hey!" I said, pulling the shirt back down over my stomach. "Ever hear of knocking?"

His eyes scanned the length of my body, resting a little too long on my chest. "I was right. This shirt does look nice with your hair. Do you not think so?"

I pushed him out of the dressing room and shut the door back in his face.

Maybe Julien was gay, I thought as I glanced at myself in the mirror, catching a glimpse of the strawberries that had appeared on my cheeks.

Then I remembered his shameless glimpse of my chest and the way his mischievous eyes had scanned my body earlier that morning in the hotel room *and* at the café. No, he definitely wasn't gay.

I recalled the last time Paul had gone shopping with me and the exasperated look he'd plastered across his face each time I walked out of the dressing room. Julien was right about one thing—French men *were* a different breed. A weird breed. A breed *I* definitely wasn't used to, and as soon as I could get home to Paul, a breed I wouldn't have to worry about or come into contact with ever again.

At the register, as Julien pulled out his credit card, he insisted that I get a navy-blue top I was about to put back as well as a chunky, beige cardigan sweater to go over everything.

"It might get cold tonight," he said, tucking his card back into his wallet.

"That's the least of my worries."

On my way back to the dressing room to put on the new clothes, I noticed a few other men in the store with their girlfriends, pleasant looks on their faces, no mumbling or complaining going on. Something must've been in the water here...or in the wine. This was not normal.

I emerged from the dressing room in my new sneakers, jeans, and the plum-colored T-shirt.

Julien smiled at me. "Now at least your clothes are relaxed."

I chose not to respond and instead brushed past him. It was time to get out of here and figure out a plan. Julien reached for the door, but surprised me as he rested his other hand on the small of my back. He kept his hand there until I'd passed through the doorway and walked out onto the sidewalk.

Heat crept up my spine all the way to the tips of my ears as his hand slowly slipped off my back.

"Thank you for the clothes," I said, focusing straight ahead on the sidewalk, wondering why Julien's touch made me feel so off balance. It's not as if I'd never had physical contact with a man other than Paul.

Well, okay, I hadn't had *much* physical contact with other men… okay, fine, I couldn't remember the last time a man other than Paul had placed a hand on me. And to tell the truth, I couldn't remember the last time Paul had placed his hand on my back the way Julien just had. Not that there was anything wrong with that—Paul just wasn't a cuddly, touchy-feely kind of guy.

"Like I said before, it is no problem," Julien said.

I continued to focus on the road ahead. I would be home soon and would never again have to worry about other men making me blush. "So, what now? Should we call that girl again? Camille?"

"She will call me back soon."

"Are you sure?"

"Yes, positive."

Julien's reassurance didn't mean much to me anymore. He'd been sure about a lot of things up to this point. Sure that we would find Claude *and* my passport in Giverny, and then in Annecy. Would Camille coming to save us from the transportation strike be another thing he was "sure" about but that didn't come to pass?

Just as I was beginning to ponder what we would do if Camille didn't pull through, Julien stopped and peeked into a store called Darjeeling. This time, though, instead of jeans and T-shirts clothing the mannequins, their smooth white bodies were strung in racy lingerie.

He lifted both eyebrows this time and shot me a sly grin. "You probably would like some clean underwear too. No?"

"Are you kidding?"

"No, I am serious. You are probably wearing the same pair for a couple days now."

"What about you? You don't have a change of clothes with you either."

"I was only planning on being away from home for a day at the most. Do you need the underwear or not?"

As I mulled it over, I realized I would love a few pairs of clean, comfy underwear to replace the pair I'd been donning the past day and a half. And I *would* pay him back. So it's not like I'd be indebted to Julien forever.

Oh, what the hell. "Come on," I told him as I opened the shop door. "You will *not* be watching me try anything on this time, and I'm not getting anything…you know, crazy."

Julien's eyes crinkled as he laughed. "Suit yourself."

I strolled through the store in search of black, or white, cotton bikini briefs—the kind of underwear I normally wore. I wasn't a thong girl, and even if I had been, I wasn't about to buy a bunch of lacy, provocative thongs while Julien was trailing along at my side.

I'd never been in a French lingerie store before, though, and the problem was, there didn't seem to be anything that *wasn't* provocative. Rows of lacy, transparent bras in purples, grays, light greens, and blacks paired with matching transparent boy shorts and panties lined the walls. I had to admit, I'd never seen lingerie more beautiful, but who was I kidding? This was awkward. And I was engaged. Just thinking of Paul made me uneasy as I strolled through the aisles of gorgeous, sexy French lingerie with Julien, who was acting as if we were shopping for something as benign as apples.

After making a round through the entire store without picking up a single thing, I turned to Julien. "I don't think there's anything for me here. We can just go."

"What? You do not wear lingerie like this at home? Even with your fiancé?"

"That's none of your business."

Julien crossed the store and picked up a white bra with gray straps and a little gray bow in the middle that came with a matching pair of white, non-transparent boy shorts. "What about this? Would you not even wear something this prude in front of him?"

"That's not prude! That's…well, it's sexy. And yes, of course I would wear that in front of him. We've been together for eight years. It's not like I'm afraid to show myself to him."

"The question is not if you are afraid. The question is, do you even wear lingerie with him? Ever? Because the way you are walking through this store, with your hands in your pockets, not touching a thing, I imagine the answer is no."

I yanked the bra and underwear set out of his hands and pushed past him toward the dressing room. Julien chuckled behind me, making me want to turn around and smack him. Who did he think he was, constantly questioning my relationship with Paul? Our level of intimacy was just fine, and it wasn't like I was actually going to divulge the details of our sex life to him.

Besides, he was totally wrong about me and Paul. Sure, I wasn't wearing sexy lingerie every night of the week and giving him stripper lap dances like Julien's girlfriends probably did for him, but we'd been together for eight years, and it was normal for the passion to die down by that point. Paul was stable. And he'd known me since I was twenty-one years old. What did Julien know about that kind of stability? Obviously, nothing.

Inside the dressing room, I continued to stew over Julien's rude comments as I pulled the text-message note out of my bra, reminding myself to translate it as soon as possible. I tucked the note into my jeans pocket, slipped on the new bra and underwear set, and regarded my reflection on the mirror. I hadn't checked the sizes before I'd ripped them away from Julien, and I quickly realized the cup on the bra was a size too small. Other than that, though, it *was* a gorgeous set.

Julien's voice sounded on the other side of the door. "I found another one you might like."

A raspberry-colored bra with fuchsia straps and a matching pair of lacy raspberry panties with little pink bows on either side appeared under the door. I took them from him without responding and decided that while I was stuck here, two pairs of clean underwear would be better than one.

After slipping on the second set, I flipped around to check myself out in the mirror. Wow. This one was…well, it was hot. It was the sexiest, most beautiful bra I'd ever worn, without a doubt. Not that I thought *I* was that hot in it, but I had to admit, it made my chest look pretty nice. I always had a hard time bra shopping in the States because everything had so much padding, which made me look top-heavy.

But there hadn't been any padding in either of these bras, so it was just me, *au naturel*. And I liked it. I liked it a lot, actually.

Just as I realized I was beginning to enjoy myself, I remembered where I was and what I was doing. I was lingerie shopping with a mysterious French agent who had a picture of me on his cell phone and wasn't telling me everything. It was time to get the hell out of here and get that text message translated.

As I was about to slip off the bra, Julien burst through the door of the dressing room, his eyes as wide as quarters.

"What are you—" I began, but wasn't able to finish or cover myself up because Julien had wrapped his arms around my all-too-bare waist. He lifted me up onto the dressing room bench then stepped onto it himself, smashing his warm body into mine.

"Shhh," he whispered, lifting his finger to my lips.

A booming male voice echoed through the store. My mind flashed back to the night before—to the bulging muscles around my neck.

It was Tattoo Guy.

I lifted my eyes to Julien's and gave him a knowing glance. Staying still, I leaned my back against the wall, my body completely exposed except for the racy lingerie strung onto me, my short legs resting against Julien's jeans. His hands stayed firmly planted on my shoulders, his cheek touching mine, his hot breath on my neck, as we listened to Tattoo Guy shop for lingerie with a woman who I was assuming was his girlfriend.

"This would be right sexy on you," he growled in his Australian accent.

"Wouldn't you like to see," she purred.

Footsteps entered the dressing area, then padded into the room next to us.

"Show me," he said.

"Oh, baby," she responded.

The girlfriend giggled while Tattoo Guy made a grunting noise. The wall between us shook as the two of them slammed up against it, and the heavy breathing commenced.

"Oh yeah, right there," she heaved in a low voice.

I arched my eyebrows at Julien. Seriously? They were going to go at it on the other side of the wall, in a public place, no less, and we had to just stand here and listen?

The corners of Julien's mouth slid upward just the tiniest bit.

Oh, my God. He is actually enjoying this. The man who we were hiding from was about to have sex with some woman in the room next to us, and Julien was pressed up against my almost naked body, thinking this was funny.

I glared at him, careful not to make a sound, even though I wanted to shove him off me and bop him in the head.

He wiped the near grin off his face and resumed a serious look, his eyes not breaking my gaze. And as Tattoo Guy and his girlfriend began pounding into the wall, Julien slid his hands down to my waist, stepped off the bench and guided me down with him.

Moving swiftly and silently, he stuffed the white lingerie set inside of the cardigan sweater he'd just bought me, then crammed them both into the shopping bag. I opened my mouth to ask him what the hell he was doing, but a low groan from the other side of the wall reminded me to shut it.

Julien motioned for me to put my clothes back on.

He wanted me to walk out of this store wearing the raspberry lingerie underneath my clothes? He wanted *me* to steal?

I mouthed a big fat *no* to him, but as he pointed to the pounding wall, then ran his eyes up the length of my body, his pupils lingering on my chest, I remembered that this bra was practically transparent. I grabbed my clothes off the floor and threw them back on.

Once I was clothed, Julien led the way out of the dressing room, opening and closing the door in complete silence as Tattoo Guy carried on his public display of affection in the next room over.

Julien leaned into my ear. "You go first. I'll be out in a second."

My heart thudded in my chest, my face burned, and I was sure, absolutely sure, that the saleswoman was going to start screaming and call the police, and that a loud, scary alarm would go off, and that I would be in prison for the rest of my life for stealing this stupid, transparent, gorgeous, raspberry-colored lingerie set.

Instead, I smiled at her and jetted out onto the sidewalk. No alarms, no police. Nothing. It didn't matter, though. I knew the truth: I was officially a criminal. I was a slimy shoplifter. And as if that wasn't all, I'd just allowed another man to see me in the sexiest lingerie I'd ever worn.

But then again, Claude had obviously seen me in my underwear too, just the other night. Ugh.

I scuttled down the sidewalk and around the corner to wait for Julien. As I thought about the way he'd been pressed up against me, his hands on my bare skin, his cheek touching mine...my entire body felt weak all of a sudden. My stomach flopped. My ears were hot. I felt dizzy and shameful and excited all at the same time.

Julien appeared at my side, donning his devious grin. "I am impressed."

"About what?" I demanded, trying to ignore the butterflies dancing around my stomach.

Julien did his characteristic eyebrow raise.

"What? You're impressed that I stole? That you made me a thief?" I snapped, wishing he would go away. Wishing I didn't feel so weird all of a sudden.

"No. It is not *that* I am impressed about, although that was quite a surprise."

"I don't want to know, then," I said as we wound through the streets, my pulse still racing. I had a pretty good idea what he was talking about, but I was going to pretend I didn't. And as Paul's face flashed through my guilty conscience, I realized that just for today, it would be easier that way.

ELEVEN

Julien and I wound back through the town toward the hotel, passing by a *crêperie*, a *pâtisserie*, a *boulangerie*, and a *fromagerie* along the way. The smell of Nutella, fresh pastries, fluffy breads, and tangy cheeses emanating from their open doors made me feel light-headed from hunger. Tourists and locals strolled along the sidewalks, baguette sandwiches in their hands, munching and chatting, not in a hurry to be anywhere.

As I noticed a young French couple strolling along ahead of us, their clasped hands swinging back and forth, I felt that familiar pang I'd felt when we'd first arrived the night before—wishing I could step into their shoes and be someone else for the day. Someone who was visiting this gorgeous little town for fun. Someone who wasn't worried about the fact that she'd just shown her body to a French guy she barely knew when she was engaged to be married in a few days...and who couldn't get the electricity she'd felt from his hands on her bare skin to leave her memory.

I glanced over at Julien, taking in his large brown eyes, his messy chestnut hair, his strong cheekbones, and as my stomach churned, I knew what I needed to do.

I needed to call Paul.

"You are okay?" Julien asked as we neared the hotel.

I nodded, keeping my gaze on the sidewalk. "Just hungry, that's all."

"You know, it was not my intention to make you uncomfortable in there."

"Then why did you do that? You knew I was barely dressed. And I know I don't need to say it again, but I'm engaged."

"It would not have been good if that man had seen us. Like you saw last night, he does not care for me or for Claude, and now you are on his list too. We have enough problems. We do not need one more."

"Who is he, anyway? Some kind of gangster? I mean, it's not like he owns the town of Annecy."

"The story is too long and complicated to get into. Trust me. We don't want to see him or Marie again. It will only lead to more trouble."

"I have a feeling that all of your stories are too long and complicated to get into, aren't they?"

Julien didn't respond as he held the hotel door open for me, then rode the elevator in silence.

Back inside our hotel room, I dialed Paul's number, ignoring Julien's presence behind me.

"Hello?" Paul answered, with more than a hint of panic seeping through his voice.

"Paul, it's me."

"Chloe, I've been trying to get a hold of you. With your cell phone gone, the only number I have for you is the Plaza Athénée, but they said you're not a guest there anymore?"

"Sorry, I forgot to tell you. Angela had me switch to a hotel that's a little less expensive so we don't rack up the company credit card. Seeing as how the extra days weren't planned."

"Jeez, Chloe. It's not like you to forget to tell me where you're at."

"I know. Things have been a little hectic over here."

"This job is getting too stressful. I don't like what it's doing to you. You should be home, preparing for the wedding. And when the wedding is over, it would be nice if you could take a break from all of this event-planning business."

It didn't sound like Paul was going to forget his offer of stay-at-home mommyhood in suburban Pennsylvania anytime soon.

As my resentment festered silently at that thought, Paul kept talking. "Also, I tried to use our debit card yesterday, and it wouldn't go through. I called the bank and they said they've put an indefinite hold on our account due to potential fraudulent activity. I explained to them that you're in Paris for business, but they said it was more than that. They're doing an investigation, Chloe, and they refuse to take the hold off the account until they're finished."

"That's weird," I said, rubbing my throbbing temples.

"You still have possession of your debit card, right? That wasn't stolen too, was it?"

Shit. What am I supposed to say?

"No. I have it right here." *God, what am I doing?*

"Fine. I'll call them again today. We still have a few final bills to settle before the wedding. Not to mention our normal bills, which come out of that account. Just hold off on using your card for now until I get this figured out. You can use the company card while you're there, right?"

I stole a glance at Julien and noticed him pretending to mess with his phone. "Hmm? Yeah, the company card is fine."

"Are you all right, Chloe? You sound a little distracted."

"I'm fine. Just really busy with the conference, you know. Still working out the kinks."

"So when will you be home?"

"Hopefully by Wednesday."

"Wednesday? I thought you said a day or two at the most." Paul's voice rose in agitation.

"I know. I don't have a choice, though. I'm the only planner here handling the messes that have come up, so I have to stay."

"Have you thought any more about Pennsylvania?"

I let out a quiet breath as Julien went into the bathroom and closed the door behind him. "Let's talk about it when I get home, okay? I have a lot going on here right now, and that's something we need to talk about in person."

"Promise me you'll think about it and really consider it, okay?"

"Okay, Paul. I will. I'll think about it. I hate to run, but I have to get back to work here."

"Can I have the hotel number where you're staying?"

"You know, I don't have it on me at the moment. I'm calling from a colleague's cell phone. I'll call you later on before I go to bed. And don't forget to pick up Sophie at the airport tonight. Her flight comes in at seven."

Paul sighed loudly into the phone. "I really wish you were here right now. I can't believe this. Just make sure you get home by Wednesday. Your dad and sisters are arriving then, right?"

Ugh. "Yes. I'll be back by then. I promise. And I'll try for earlier, but no guarantees."

"And don't use the debit, okay?"

"Got it."

After hanging up the phone, I rested my head in my hands and closed my eyes. *God, what a mess.* But what was I supposed to do? Should I have told Paul that my entire wallet was stolen, so at least the debit-card fiasco would make a little more sense? I hadn't thought any of this out, and I hadn't realized it would go this far—that I would be seven hours from Paris, letting the lies roll off my tongue each time I talked to the man I was marrying in just five days.

I gazed down at my engagement ring—which I had slipped back on that morning before leaving the hotel—and silently thanked God that Julien had gotten it back. I couldn't even imagine what Paul would've said about that. I had no idea how I would explain the rest, but at least I had the ring.

Julien appeared at my side. "You are okay?"

"Yes. No. I don't know."

"You talked to your fiancé?"

"Yes." I narrowed my eyes at him. "I just talked to my 'not a man' fiancé."

"I am sorry I said that yesterday. I do not know him, but…never mind. I should not have said that."

I shot up from the chair and paced the room. "What am I going to tell him when I do finally get home? How is the illegal activity on my bank account going to be cleared? How is he not going to find out what really happened? And if he does find out, is he even going to want to marry me this weekend?"

Julien reached for my shoulders and pushed me down onto the bed before sitting next to me. "Like I told you, I have seen Claude do this many times before. I can't promise that things will go well once you go home, but I can at least help you get there."

"Why do you have my picture on your phone?" I demanded, not willing to just go along for the ride anymore.

Julien's voice caught in his throat as he opened his mouth. "What?"

"I looked at your phone last night when you were in the shower. You had the same picture that the police had of me, with some strange message underneath that had my name in it. What's going on?"

"You already know everything that is going on, Chloe. I told you I work for the government, and I have been assigned to find and arrest Claude. There is nothing more to tell."

"That's funny, because when I asked you how you knew it was me in the hotel lobby yesterday morning, you said it was the signature red dress and the bewildered look on my face. You failed to mention the fact that someone had sent you my name and my picture. Who sent it, and what does the message say?"

Julien stood abruptly and walked to the window, where he avoided my gaze…and my questions.

That was it. I'd had enough. I walked over to him, grabbed his face, and pulled him toward me so he couldn't avoid me for another second.

"Don't ignore me! I've gone along with everything you've told me, I've followed you around this damn country, and all the while, I've been lying to my fiancé, who I'm marrying this week! The *least* you can do is explain to me what the hell is going on and why you have my picture on your phone."

Julien didn't break my gaze this time. "The connections I have in my job…they are powerful, Chloe. And like I already explained to you, I am under strict orders *not* to help you, but instead to let the police deal with you. After all, my agency does not know for sure that you are innocent, so they would rather let the police interrogate you while we focus on finding Claude. But there is one friend of mine—the government agent who assigned me to this case and who is very high up—who made a promise to me a couple years ago after something very bad happened to one of the women that Claude scammed. He promised that if Claude started up again, he would assign me to the case so that I could personally take him down. And so I could make sure nothing like that ever happened again to another woman. He sent me the picture that the undercover cop took of you at the hotel that night and told me that if I stopped you from going to the police and helped get your passport back from Claude, he would make sure you are able to leave the country without any trouble."

"Okay. Assuming that's all true, I still want to know what happened to that woman that you would go to such lengths to make sure it never happened again. And in the text message, I read the word *tableau*. It means 'painting,' am I right?"

"Yes, it does. There is more to this story than you need to know, Chloe. Or than I can tell you. It is a long story, and it is nothing you need to worry about."

"There you go again with your long stories."

"I am trying to help you, Chloe. I am being honest, and I need you to believe me. Because what happened to her..." Julien turned his face from me as his eyes glazed over. "It was a nightmare. And I won't let it happen again. Not to you or to anyone else."

"What *exactly* happened to her? Why won't you tell—"

"She's dead," he said flatly.

A chill ran down my spine as I stared at him, only silence filling the gap between us. Suddenly a sharp ring sounded, making me jump backward a foot.

Julien pulled his phone from his pocket and checked the caller ID.

"It's Camille."

TWELVE

The call lasted no more than two minutes before Julien shoved his phone back in his pocket and smiled at me, all traces of his grim memories wiped away.

"Camille is coming to get us."

"Right now?"

"In a couple hours. But she will take us to Lyon tonight, so we won't have to wait until tomorrow morning to find Claude. In the meantime, we will wait here in the hotel."

Julien plopped down on the bed, grabbed the remote, and flicked on the TV, his long body stretching out over the burgundy comforter.

I sat on the corner of the bed, feeling something pull at my stomach.

"Is Camille another agent…or is she one of your girlfriends?" I asked.

Julien laughed. "*One* of my girlfriends? How many do you think I have?"

I ran my eyes down the length of his body. "Well, from the way you've talked, I just assumed that—"

"I told you I wasn't in love with anyone."

"Yeah, but that doesn't mean you don't have women that you…"

"That I what? Sleep with?"

I nodded.

Julien scrunched up his forehead. "What is the word you use in English for this sort of person? A slut?"

I chuckled. "Yeah, that's one way of putting it."

"So you think I am a man slut?"

"I didn't say that…I was just wondering about Camille, that's all."

"Camille is my sister," he said, pinning his intense eyes on me.

"Oh. I didn't know you had a sister. Why didn't you just say that before?"

Julien shrugged. "For the record, I do not have several girlfriends. At the moment, I don't even have one."

My stomach flip-flopped again and I thought back to what had just happened at the lingerie store and how weird I'd felt afterward. I needed to get some fresh air. By myself.

"I'm going to take a walk across the street to the lake," I announced. What did I care about Julien's love life, anyway? It was none of my business.

Julien turned the volume down on the TV. "It is best to stay here for now and wait for Camille."

"But you said she wouldn't even be here for another couple hours, so I don't see the point of just sitting here. Plus, it's gorgeous out there. What happened to relaxing and enjoying the moment?"

Julien shot me a stern look, his eyes filled with impatience. "Just stay in the hotel for a couple hours with me. It is not that big of a deal."

I crossed the room and opened the door. "I need some fresh air. I'll be across the street."

Just as I was about to close the door behind me, Julien caught it with his hand, grabbed my arm, and pulled me back into the hotel room.

"You are not walking around Annecy alone. I will come with you." He picked up my shopping bag of clothes and nodded toward the door. "*On y va?*"

"You don't have to come—" I began, but Julien had already ushered me into the hallway and closed the door behind us.

So much for getting some alone time.

"Women," he muttered under his breath as he trailed behind me down the hallway. "*This* is why I do not have a girlfriend, you see?"

"I'm capable of taking care of myself, you know. I did just fine before I met you yesterday."

"Correction—before you met Claude. After that, it seems everything is out of your control, no?"

As the elevator doors opened up, I bolted past Julien and out into the fresh mountain air. I didn't wait for him as I crossed the street to the tree-filled park that jutted out into the sparkling lake. I wished he would just leave me alone for five seconds. His incessant jabs were driving me nuts. Plus, every second I spent alone with him made me feel like I was betraying Paul—because I was. I was lying to him. And to my entire family.

Just as I was about to sit down on one of the park benches facing the water, hoping to clear my head, Julien grabbed my hand. "I have an idea. To pass the time, we will take a boat ride. Come."

He led me across the lawn a little too quickly until we reached a large group of chatty, laughing tourists who were waiting to board a massive white boat that looked like a small cruise ship.

Julien snapped his head to the side, his eyes searching the pathway leading back into town. He slid his arm around my waist and pushed me toward the boat.

"Do you see that guy again? Why are you acting like this?" I asked.

Before Julien could answer me, I discovered the reason why he'd rushed me across the park—it was Officer Laroche and Officer Fournier, charging down the sidewalk, their eyes combing the lawn we'd just run across.

Julien pivoted so his back was facing them, his body pressed up against mine, his arm still cinched around my waist. "Don't look over there," he mumbled. "Just get on the boat."

As we climbed the stairs up to the deck of the boat and pushed our way through the crowd to get to the other side, I noticed that all of the other passengers were dressed nicely—the men in collared shirts and ties, the women in dresses—and they all seemed to know each other already.

"Do you think they saw us?" My pulse raced as Julien let go of my waist, causing me to trip and bump into a large display of calla lilies. What were calla lilies doing on a tour boat?

"No," Julien said. "But I knew it was only a matter of time before the police tracked us here."

"Us? You mean *me*?"

A beat passed before Julien responded. "Yes, of course."

Before I had a chance to consider his hesitation, a man dressed in a black-and-white tuxedo appeared at our side. "*Champagne?*" he asked in a French accent as he thrust a tray of bubbly glasses at us.

Why were they serving champagne on a tour boat? I scanned the faces surrounding us and gasped as I caught sight of a woman in a sparkly white gown. A wispy veil glided down her back as she leaned over to kiss a tall, lanky man in a black suit.

Oh, my God. We were crashing a wedding. If I was the event planner at this wedding, I would have thrown us out immediately.

Julien plucked a glass of champagne off the tray. "*Merci,*" he said, not fazed in the slightest by the situation.

"Put that back!" I whispered.

"*Et vous, Mademoiselle?*" the waiter asked me.

"No, *merci,*" I responded.

"What is the problem?" Julien asked, the innocence in his voice making me want to grab the glass of champagne out of his hands and throw it in his face.

"If you haven't noticed, we're crashing someone else's wedding! We have to get off this boat."

Julien peeked over my shoulder and nodded toward the park. "Of the two options, I would rather be here."

As the wedding cruise pulled away from the dock, I turned and spotted the two police officers walking right past where we'd just been standing.

"This is why I did not want to leave the hotel room," Julien said in an irritating, singsong voice.

"Oh, so now this is my fault."

Julien arched an eyebrow, then downed a sip of champagne.

"Stop it. Stop doing that. It's making me crazy."

He laughed, then took another gulp, bigger this time. "Mmm. *C'est bon.* You should try some."

"This isn't funny." I grabbed Julien's arm and dragged him to the edge of the boat, hoping none of the guests would notice we didn't belong here. "Do you know how much money a wedding like this costs? We have no right to be here, let alone take part in the celebration." I nodded toward his now-empty glass of champagne.

"What do you propose, then? Jumping off the boat?" His smirk widened.

"You think everything is one big joke, don't you? I mean, do you actually think no one is going to notice? Look at how we're dressed. You're in the same jeans and T-shirt you've been wearing for the past two days." I lowered my voice and smiled as a couple of chatty guests walked past.

Julien waited until they were gone. "If you keep shouting at me, yes, people will begin to notice. But if you calm down and act like you're *happy* to be here with me, *your date,* everything will be fine."

"I'm not acting like you're my date. And don't even think about pulling a stunt like you did yesterday on that awful newlywed tour bus."

The lines around Julien's eyes crinkled as he laughed at the memory. "That was quite funny, was it not?"

"It was not."

"Oh, thank God," came a high-pitched Southern drawl behind us. "Did I hear you two speaking English?"

I flipped around to find a short, middle-aged woman with bleached-blonde bangs curled about an inch off her forehead, puffy cheeks smothered in pink blush, and pearly white teeth glinting in the sunshine.

"Um, yes," I answered hesitantly. I did not want to have a conversation with anyone on this boat.

"I thought I heard my native tongue over here." Her smile dimmed as she eyed the two of us—me in my jeans and sneakers, Julien in his beat-up black boots. "I don't remember seeing y'all at the ceremony."

"Our flight into Paris was delayed, and we had to rush to Annecy. No time to change, you see." Julien slid his arm around my waist. "We are so happy we made it."

"Oh, you poor dears! You must be exhausted! At least you made it in time for the cocktail cruise. You'll have time to change before the reception tonight."

"Mmm." I nodded. Thank God this wasn't the reception. It would last only an hour or two at the most.

"Are you friends of Luc's or Charlotte's?" she asked.

"Charlotte," I blurted, hoping we could get this woman to leave us alone.

"I can't believe we've never met! I'm Charlotte's aunt Liza from Florida. Well, from Texas, originally. But anyhoo, I just can't believe our Charlotte is all grown up and marrying a French man!"

"It is true. Time goes too fast," Julien said, his eyes flickering in amusement. "Chloe and I are hoping to have a wedding as beautiful as this when we get married." He grabbed another glass of champagne from the waiter's tray. "It is just a matter of time. Right, *chérie*?"

Aunt Liza clasped her hands over her heart. "Now aren't you two just the sweetest things." Her strong, floral-scented perfume assaulted my nose as she leaned forward and whispered in my ear. "And from what I hear, French men are dynamite in the bedroom."

"Mmm," I said, wishing I could shrivel up and disappear. This was horrible. Just horrible.

"Chloe and I are waiting until marriage." Julien turned and nuzzled his nose into my cheek. "Isn't that right, *chérie*?"

I wrapped my arm around his waist and pinched the skin under his T-shirt as hard as I could while keeping a smile plastered across my face.

"Y'all are going to have quite a wedding night. Well, it was great meeting you two lovebirds. I'm off to grab another cocktail. Can't let them go to waste!"

I breathed a sigh of relief as Aunt Liza sauntered off, her thigh-length fuchsia dress sloshing a little too high with each step in her three-inch leopard-print heels.

"You are the worst liar I have ever seen," Julien said in between champagne sips.

I placed my hands on the edge of the boat and took in the view of the white cottages that speckled the mountainside off in the distance. "You're not that great yourself. *Waiting until marriage?*"

"I thought you would appreciate that. It seems like something you would do."

"I am not waiting until marriage, for your information."

"Oh, really?"

"Really."

"Have you ever experienced a man other than your fiancé?"

"What? You have no business asking me that."

"What does it matter? After tomorrow, you may never see me again anyway. Just answer the question."

"Fine. I've been with Paul since college, so he was my first, and he's my last."

Julien's face contorted, a look of near horror passing through his eyes. "But how do you know he is the right one for you when you have never experienced someone else?"

"I don't need to sleep around to know that I'm marrying the right person. And besides, it's not like sex is the whole relationship. It's just one part—a small part, really."

"A *small* part?"

"Well, for you I'm sure it's the *only* part of a relationship. But for me, other things matter too. Like compatibility and stability."

Julien let out a dramatic yawn. "Boring, boring. What about the passion?"

"I have passion. We have passion."

Julien nodded to the newlyweds at the front of the boat who were locked in an almost inappropriate embrace—her hands ruffling through his short, brown hair, his lips trailing from her mouth down to her neck. "Do you have that kind of passion, with your fiancé?"

I swallowed the lump in my throat. "Of course. Of course we do."

He raised his right eyebrow at me, then resumed watching the newlyweds swap tongues. "I don't believe you."

"You're unbelievable, you know that?"

"No, I am French. And the French man is quite different from the American man." He gestured to the breathtaking scenery as the boat carried us farther into the clear blue lake. "Look at what the world has to offer you. You should not limit yourself so young."

Julien turned to me then, the wind blowing his hair back, his big brown eyes lighting up under the intense sun. "You are how old?"

"I'm twenty-nine. You?"

"I'm thirty-four. And I have had thirty-four years of a passionate life. Can you say the same?"

"No, I can't. I'm only twenty-nine, remember?"

"Anyway, all I am saying is—"

I placed my forefinger on his lips to shut him up. "Shhh. For all your talk about enjoying life, you sure don't know when to be quiet and enjoy the moment."

Julien took my hand off his lips and held it for a few seconds before placing it back on the railing of the boat. Butterflies raced through my stomach at the feel of his touch and patches of heat stung my neck.

"You are right," Julien said softly. "There is no need to ruin the moment with words."

I pulled my eyes away from his and focused ahead on the mountains, willing the redness that danced on my cheeks to go away. And as I tried to concentrate on the scenery—the gorgeous mountains all around us, the bright-blue sky and the puffy white clouds overhead, a majestic white castle on an island in the middle of the lake—all I could think about was the patch of Julien's skin brushing up against my shoulder ever so slightly, sending tingles up my spine and making me feel light-headed and dizzy.

I closed my eyes and let out a long, quiet breath. I'd never spent this much time alone with a man other than Paul. And I was just emotional, worried, and tired after everything that had happened. That's all it was. And I loved Paul. No, we weren't the most passionate couple, but we'd been together for eight years. Passion—I mean real, sensual passion—wasn't supposed to last past the first year, was it?

When I opened my eyes, Julien's gaze remained fixated on me.

"What were you thinking about?" he asked, his expression and his voice even softer than before.

"I…I don't know. Just that…"

My mind went blank as Julien's face squared directly in front of mine, his brown eyes burning right through me, making all of my practical beliefs, my rationalizations, my need to constantly be in control of the situation, fly right out the window.

"Yes?" he prodded.

I tore my face from his and breathed in the warm summer breeze blowing off the trees. "Nothing. I wasn't thinking about anything."

THIRTEEN

At my insistence, Julien and I trailed along the edge of the boat, careful to steer clear of the bride and groom and all of the chatty guests. When we came upon a table piled high with fluffy squares of bread, chocolate-covered strawberries, and pots of steamy fondue, I realized I was ravenous. I hadn't eaten anything since the chocolate croissant that morning.

Julien shamelessly loaded up a plate of food, not the least bit concerned that we were uninvited guests at this party.

"It is totally inappropriate to take their food," I told him as I eyed the melted cheese, wishing it didn't smell so damn good.

Julien answered by taking a seat at an empty table, sticking a fork in a block of bread and plunging it into the fondue. "This business you have of always following the rules," he said through a mouthful of bread, "it is no fun." He gestured to the waiter, who brought us two glasses of red wine.

Julien lifted one of the glasses to his nose, swirled it around, and took a whiff. "The wine in Annecy is exquisite. I am going to take a glass. You?"

I raised my eyebrows at him without responding.

"I take that as a no. You will regret it, though. You may never come back to Annecy again, and it would be a shame to miss out on the wine."

"I'm sure Claude probably said something like that to me the other night to get me to drink."

"He did more than that," Julien mumbled before stuffing another massive bite of fondue-covered bread into his mouth.

While Julien munched on his feast, I thought about what he'd just said. I still couldn't remember much at all about the night I'd met Claude in the hotel bar. I could only conjure up those same images I'd had the next morning when I woke up hungover. Claude's voice, convincing me to have a glass of wine. Claude tipping the glass past my lips and feeding me an olive. Then a couple of fleeting images—me leading him up to my room, bumping my shoulder into the wall, and Claude putting me to bed. That was it. I didn't remember the conversation we'd had. How many glasses I'd drunk. If he'd kissed me. If I'd talked about Paul. Or how I'd ended up *mostly* unclothed.

After Julien finished chewing, I locked eyes with him. "What did you mean when you said that Claude probably did more than that? I thought you said he doesn't sleep with the women."

"I am not talking about sex."

"What else do you think happened, then?"

"Do you remember how many glasses of wine he gave you?" Julien said.

"Not really. I mean, I guess I only remember one."

"You are probably accurate, then. You probably only had one, maybe two at the most."

"I know I don't drink much anymore, but there's no way one or two glasses of wine could've gotten me drunk enough to invite him to my room, let alone erase my entire memory of that night. It had to have been more."

Julien shook his head. "You think a skilled con man is only going to use a few glasses of wine to get what he wants?"

"Are you saying…?"

Julien nodded, tapping his fingers along the smooth white tablecloth. "It is likely that Claude put something in your drink."

"I was drugged?"

"I'm not saying for sure. But it is very possible, yes."

I shook my head as I stared straight ahead at Julien, speechless. How could I have been so naïve? It's not that the thought hadn't crossed my mind—I wasn't an idiot. It was just that everything had happened so fast, I hadn't had enough time to really consider what might've happened to me that night. Instead I was in survival mode, running damage control on the mess I'd created for myself back home.

"Why didn't you mention the fact that Claude drugged me? Why is this just coming up now?"

Julien set his wineglass down on the table. "First of all, it is *probable* that he drugged you, but it is not a fact. Second of all, would it have made a difference if you had known earlier?"

"Of course it would've made a difference! If I had known there was a strong possibility I'd been drugged, and that was the reason I'd invited Claude up to my room, I could've told Paul what really happened. I could've gone to the police immediately, and they could've run a drug test to see that I was telling the truth. That I have nothing to do with whatever crazy scams Claude is pulling!"

"I hate to ruin your nice idea of how this all would've worked out if you had known, but it would not have gone so smoothly. I promise you," Julien said, his usual blasé tone disappearing.

"Whatever. I think the best thing for *me* to do at this point, whenever we get off this damn wedding boat, is to go back to the police, tell them I was drugged, and then tell Paul the truth. Because if I was drugged, how can anyone possibly think any of this is my fault?"

"You are forgetting that the police are not only after Claude, but after you as well. They think you could be working with him."

"This is infuriating! I am as straitlaced as they come! Once they run an investigation on me, they'll see that there's no way I could have anything to do with a despicable human being like Claude."

"You may be right, but by the time they finish the investigation, you will miss your wedding. This is why I am helping you, Chloe."

"Well, I'm sorry, but your help doesn't seem to be getting me home any faster. And what about that woman? The one who died? Was *she* working with him?"

Julien's eyes glazed over again, like he was remembering something he didn't want to think about. "No, she was like you. She had no idea."

"What about your super-high-up government agent friend, the one who texted you my picture? What if he tells the police that I'm innocent? Wouldn't they have to let me go home?"

"Chloe, even my friend does not know for sure if you are innocent. Do you see? He is just keeping his promise to me because of what happened to Valérie."

So *Valérie* was her name. Finally, a tiny detail. "I see."

I looked past Julien out to the clear, glistening lake and wished I could jump in, swim to some remote little village in the mountains, lock myself up in a cottage, and stay there forever. Because I didn't see how any of this was ever going to work out.

I didn't even notice that Julien had walked back over to the food spread and filled up another plate. "You look pale," he said, setting the plate down in front of me. "You need to eat."

He stuck his fork into a square of bread, dipped it into the steaming fondue, and lifted it to his lips. "Mmmm," he mumbled as he chewed. "*Délicieux.*"

I brought my focus back to the boat, to the cheerful wedding guests mingling around the deck, the sound of the French language bubbling through the air. And something about them—their unhindered joy, their contagious excitement—made me think of my mother. She had been like that. Always excited. Always rushing to embark on the next adventure. I had been like that too when I was younger...before she died.

I knew then, with absolute certainty, that if she were here, no matter what mess was going on in her life, no matter the fact that she was not a guest at this wedding, she wouldn't have dreamed of letting this food go to waste.

I picked up my fork, pierced a square of bread, dipped it into the melted cheese, and plunged it into my mouth.

Closing my eyes, I felt some of the stress leave my body. Nothing had ever tasted so good.

Then, for once in my life, without obsessing about breaking the rules, I reached for my glass of red wine before Julien had a chance to steal it, and took a sip. And before setting the glass down, I took another.

Julien grinned at me, and as if reading my mind, he said, "Life is short, no?"

As I let the fruity liquid wash down my throat, I eyed the messy-haired French man beside me, his darkened five o'clock shadow, his distinct cheekbones. And despite this unimaginable mess I'd entangled myself in, I laughed. *Nothing* was going as I had hoped, but at least Julien had been right about one thing—the wine here *was* exquisite.

A few minutes later, the picturesque town of Annecy came into view, and the wedding cruise glided in toward the dock. Julien checked his phone as we stayed planted at our hidden little table at the back of the boat. "Camille is almost here," he announced.

I finished my plate of food in lightning speed and felt an inkling of relief. At least we were about to get off the boat, out of Annecy, and away from those police officers. And hopefully then we'd be one huge step closer to finding my passport.

I tossed my plate into the trash and stood. "I'm going to go use the restroom. I'll be right back." I jetted across the back deck of the boat, hoping I could make it in and out without having to talk to anyone. Inside the bathroom, there were two stalls. One was already taken, so I took the other one and moved as swiftly as I could. I made it out before the other person, and just as I was washing my hands, a soft, sweet voice sounded behind me.

"Excuse me, I think you dropped this."

To my horror, there stood the bride. Her smile disappeared as she searched my face, no doubt wondering who I was. She held out a piece of paper for me, which I realized was the text message note. It must've fallen out of my pocket.

"Thank you," I mumbled, dread rising from the pit of my stomach.

"Are you...have we met?" she asked, the sweetness in her voice still present despite the confused look in her eyes.

I held out my hand. "I'm Chloe. And I...I...oh, God. It's no use. I'm so sorry. I got on the wrong boat. It was a total accident."

"You got on the wrong boat?"

"I meant to get on a tour boat, you know, to go see the mountains, and we were rushing from...well, it's a long story, but basically we meant to get on another boat and accidentally got on your wedding cruise instead. I know how awful this must seem to you. I'm an event planner, and I'm getting married this weekend! If anyone did this to me, I would be furious. Outraged. I'm so sorry."

The bride's big brown doe eyes focused in on me, and just when I thought she was going to whack me in the face with her beautiful bouquet of white calla lilies, she started laughing. "Don't worry about it! I hope you had a good time while you were here."

"Really? You're not angry?"

"It was an accident, right?"

"Yes, trust me. I would *never* purposely crash someone else's wedding. It makes me sick just thinking about it."

She smiled. "I wish I would've known you when I was planning this thing. It sounds like you take your job really seriously."

"I suppose I do."

She reached for the door handle. "Good luck next weekend with your wedding. I bet you're so excited."

A smile plastered across my face. "So excited," I echoed, even though, at that moment, I couldn't conjure up a single ounce of excitement for my own wedding day. And considering the possibility that I might actually get my passport back in a few short hours, I wasn't sure why.

"It was nice meeting you, Chloe. I hope the rest of your trip goes well. And do me a favor. Relax a little, will ya?"

I stood, dumbfounded, as she left me alone in the bathroom. I stared down at the note in my hand, and without thinking, I burst through the door. "Hey, Charlotte!" I called out.

She flipped around, her long, sparkly dress swishing at her heels. "Yes?"

"You don't speak French by any chance, do you?"

"Sure, I used to be a French teacher."

"I know I've already intruded enough, but would you be willing to take a quick look at this note and translate it for me?"

She walked over and took the piece of paper in her French-manicured hands. "Hmm, all together, it means, 'If you want the painting, stop this woman from speaking to the police. It's urgent.'" She handed the note back to me. "Is this from a book you're reading? Sounds like a good one."

"Yeah, a book. Thank you, Charlotte. You were really helpful." The words spilled numbly from my mouth as I watched her walk away from me, my head spinning in circles.

Julien *really was* after a painting? Had he been lying to me all along? Did he even work for the government?

Why had I followed him?

What had I done?

I stormed past all the jolly, drunk wedding guests to where Julien was standing alone.

"I'm not coming with you," I told him as the boat docked.

"What did you just say?"

"I *said*, I'm not coming with you. You've been lying to me all along, and I'm done."

"What are you talking about?"

I left Julien's side and joined the line of guests filing off the boat. He caught up with me and grabbed my arm. "What are you talking about?" he hissed into my ear.

I shoved the text message note into his stomach. "The bride used to be a French teacher. She translated this for me. Looks like you haven't been telling me everything I need to know after all."

Julien's eyes combed the note, but I was already off the boat and pacing down the sidewalk toward the town. As soon as I found those two police officers, I would tell them everything they wanted to know.

Julien rushed to my side, grabbing hold of my arm again, trying to slow me down.

"Get off me!" I snapped, jerking my arm from his grasp.

Julien walked briskly to keep up with my stride. "Okay, you are right. I lied to you about the painting. But it has nothing to do with you. Everything else I've told you is true. And if we don't go to Camille's car now—"

"How can you say that when the message clearly says to stop me from going to the police so that *you* can get some painting you're looking for? You've obviously been lying to me about being an undercover agent, about everything! And I've been desperate and dumb enough to believe you. I'm done listening to you. I'm going to go talk to those police officers and tell them everything that's happened to me. And then I'm going to call my fiancé and tell him the truth. And if you don't get your precious painting back as a result, you know what? I couldn't care less! You have strung me along these past two days with nothing but lies, and it's time for me to go home." With that, I jogged across the busy intersection through the swarms of tourists, searching for any sign of men in police uniforms.

"Chloe, wait! Chloe!" Julien came up behind me on the street corner, grabbed my shoulders, and spun me around.

"I know I haven't been completely honest with you, but you have to trust me. If you don't leave Annecy with me right now, you will not make it home in time for your wedding."

"Is that a threat?"

"No, it is a reality. If you talk to the police now, before I have a chance to work everything out, it could ruin you, Chloe. It could ruin your life."

"Are we talking about Miss *Valérie* again? Did she even exist, by the way?"Julien's eyes hardened as his lips formed into a tight line. "I told you, she is dead. This is not a joke, Chloe. You are dealing with a situation and a group of people you know nothing about. I know what they are capable of." He dropped his hands from my shoulders and shook his head at me. "But if you don't believe me, fine. Go talk to the police. You will see, it will not work out as you are hoping."

I left Julien standing alone on the sidewalk as I raced past the rushing stream, my sneakers skimming over the cobblestones, doubt boiling up inside of me. What if I went to the police, told them I'd been drugged, and gave them any information they wanted about Julien or this painting, and they *still* thought I was in some way involved in Claude's dealings? What if they still insisted on keeping me in France for questioning and wouldn't let me leave in time for my wedding? What if that part of the story was true?

I flipped around to find Julien still standing in the same spot, watching me walk away. "You do see how crazy this all looks from my point of view, don't you?" I called out to him. "I mean, if you were me, would you believe you?"

He walked up to me. "No, you are right. I would not."

"Then just tell me the truth. Do you even work for the government?"

"Yes, I am working for the government…not quite in the capacity that I originally told you. But I do work for them. That is the truth."

"I'll pretend for a minute that I believe you and that I have a clue what you're talking about, but first I want to know what is going on with this painting? Why do you need it so badly? And why would me talking to the police stop you from getting it back?"

A large group of high school–age French kids barreled past us, joking and flirting with each other. Julien waited until they'd passed, then cornered me. "If I tell you the story of the painting, you have to promise you will never mention it to anyone, especially to the police. You must swear."

"Okay, I swear," I said, unsure now if I really wanted to be let in on whatever deep, dark secret he was about to reveal.

Julien took my hand and led me down one of the cobblestoned alleys until we came to a quieter area of town. The tourists had evaporated, and the only sounds came from a few pigeons cooing about, looking for scraps.

He scanned the street before stopping on a deserted corner. "It is not a mistake that I am on Claude's case. Besides wanting to stop him from committing another fraudulent crime and hurting another innocent woman, I also have a personal reason to find him."

"The painting?" I asked.

Julien nodded. "The painting is a Manet. It has been in my family for over one hundred years."

"A Monet? Like Claude Monet in Giverny?" I asked.

"No, a *Manet*. Édouard Manet. Like Claude Monet, though, Édouard Manet was a nineteenth-century French impressionist painter."

"I see. So where is the painting now?"

"That is the problem. Claude has stolen it."

"So that's why you're *really* trying to find Claude? To get this painting back for your family? Is it just because it's worth a lot of money?"

"Yes and no. Like I said, the painting has been in my family for over one hundred years. My grandfather's father passed it down to him, then down to my father, and so on. It has special meaning in our family, and we would have never thought of selling it."

"So Claude just comes to your house one day and steals it?"

Julien glanced at me nervously then blew out a loud breath. "Chloe, there is one more thing I haven't told you. I thought you would've figured it out last night at Marie's house when she said my name, but you didn't seem to notice."

I thought back to the night before, my mind now a fuzzy haze full of clues, lies, and secrets. I couldn't remember what she'd said. I'd been too focused on getting my ring back and getting the hell out of there.

"I don't remember. What did she say?"

"She called me Julien Dubois."

"Dubois? But isn't that Claude's…"

Julien placed a hand on my arm. "Yes, Dubois is Claude's last name...and it is mine as well. Claude is my brother."

I pulled away from Julien's grasp, not able to believe what he had just told me. "Claude is your *brother*? How could you not have told me this? What in the hell is going on?"

"Shhh," Julien said as an old couple sauntered past us.

"Don't shush me. Just tell me the truth. All of it," I demanded.

"Just two weeks ago, my father passed away. No one in the family has seen Claude for two years. He found out about my father, though, and came home for the funeral this week. My mother was devastated, but to have her youngest son back, you see, was a gift for her. She thought Claude would stay for a while, that maybe he'd changed. We all did. But instead, the morning after the funeral, Claude was gone. And so was the painting. My mother said to let it go. It was not worth chasing him around the country to find this painting. But when my mother and I met with the bank to discuss the business of my family's vineyard, which my father had been running for years, we found out that my father had not been wise with his money, and if we didn't come up with a large sum of cash immediately, we would lose everything. The vineyard, our home, our land."

I sucked in a breath. "So that's why you need the painting? To sell it and buy your family's vineyard back?"

Julien nodded. "You see? You and me both. We need something important from Claude. This is why we must work together."

My head throbbed trying to put all the pieces of this jagged puzzle together. "So that whole story you told me yesterday about Claude's operation infiltrating the police—the *mole*? It was all just a lie to convince me to follow you?"

A somber expression swept over Julien's face. "Yes, I am sorry. That part of the story was not true. I had to say that to—"

"And the part about you being an undercover agent? Also not true, I suspect? I mean, call me crazy, but I'm having a hard time believing that you're really a government agent who has been assigned to track down your own brother."

"No, Chloe. This part is not a lie. For the past two years, I have been working with the government on a contractual basis, so to speak, going undercover to help them find and arrest other con men like Claude. Technically, I have not been assigned to Claude's case. I am the most qualified person to find him, though, since he is my brother. And once he stole the painting, it was not an option. I had to go after him."

"So why didn't you just tell me all of this right from the start?"

Julien ran his hand through his messy brown hair. "I did not know if I could trust you."

"But you expected me to trust you? Even though you started off by telling me a huge lie to divert me from the cops?"

"I know it does not make sense to you. But I know Claude. I know what he does, how he works. And I can help you get your passport back and get home safely. You are an innocent woman mixed up in this stupid mess my brother has created, and in addition to getting the painting back, I *do* want to help you."

"Well, then explain to me *why* you won't get the painting back if I talk to the police. After all, that *is* why you lied to me in the first place about Claude having a mole on the inside, right? I'd really like to know that I haven't been running around this damn country with you for nothing!"

"There are two reasons you should not talk to the police. The first is what I have already told you about all of the women who've worked with Claude in the past, and the fact that the police will not believe you when you say you are innocent and Claude stole everything from you. You saw this for yourself that morning in the hotel, no? They will suspect you are working with him and will have to complete an entire investigation before your name can be cleared. That is not a lie, Chloe. I did not lead you away from the police for nothing."

"But even still," I cut in, "let's say we get my passport back, and you and your high-up government connection clear the way so I can get through customs and go home in time for my wedding. When I get home, I'll still have to deal with the fact that there has been fraudulent activity concerning my bank account. So my bank at home is still going to be running an investigation on me, right? I mean, how am I going to deal with that when I'm trying to get married?"

"I spoke to my government friend while you were in the bathroom on the boat, and he promised me that if we can get your passport back from Claude, he will not only help me to get you through customs, but he will clear your name from the investigation."

"Are you serious? Who is this guy?"

"I told you, he is a good friend. And he is very high up, so he can take care of these things."

"Okay. If that's even true, then why can't I just go to the police now with him backing me up?"

"This friend of mine is taking my word for it that you are not involved with Claude's scams. That does not mean that he can just tell the police that you are innocent. They must run a complete investigation first. Plus, he cannot tell them that he is in contact with me, tipping me off about where Claude is. He would lose his job if they knew, since I'm not supposed to be messing with Claude's case at the moment. But, once you are back in the United States, he can help clear your name, and then only your bank at home will be handling the situation. And once your name is cleared here, your US bank will have no reason to question you. You will tell them your card was stolen and they will refund you the money."

My head resumed its spinning as I tried to make sense out of all of this madness. "You said there were two reasons I shouldn't talk to the police. What's the second one?"

"The first one is not enough for you to believe me?" Julien asked, a smirk spreading across his face.

"Yes, I'd say the first one is enough. But I want to know everything. I don't want to be running around following you with no clue about what's really going on."

"Fine. If you talk to the police, besides making it difficult for you to get home in time, it will make it next to impossible for me to get the painting back. You will provide new evidence as to Claude's whereabouts, and once they clear you—which like I said, will take some time—they will have enough evidence to finally convict Claude. And if they find him and take him in *before* I get to him and find the painting, my family…they will lose everything. But if I can find Claude first, get your passport, and find out what he did with the painting, we can both get what we want. And then the police can have him."

Julien placed his hands on my shoulders and looked me in the eye. "Do you understand everything now? Do you believe me?"

Just as I was opening my mouth to respond, Julien grabbed my hand and started running.

"What—" I began, but as I whipped my head around, I spied the two police officers rounding the corner where we'd just been standing. They shouted something in French and took off after us.

My heart hammered in my chest as I picked up the pace, running as fast as I could alongside Julien.

We turned the corner, and without warning, Julien pulled me into a skinny alleyway. We ran single file between two tall stone buildings until Julien pulled me into a tiny, hidden alcove.

As we scrunched into the cramped space together, Julien pulled out his cell phone and tapped away on the keypad.

"What are you doing?" I whispered.

"I am telling Camille to come to this street to pick us up."

I realized then that it was official.

I, Chloe Turner, the girl who'd never done anything wrong, who'd never cheated or skipped a day in school, who'd never stolen so much as a cotton swab belonging to someone else, who'd never bagged out on her responsibilities to her family, her fiancé, or her job, was a wanted suspect running from the police.

FOURTEEN

Five minutes of tense silence later, Julien peeked out into the alley. "Stay here," he told me as he crept toward the street, checked both ways, then motioned for me to follow him.

When we emerged, a cherry-red Smart car screeched around the corner and came to an abrupt stop in front of us.

Julien opened the door, revealing a petite girl with tanned skin and shoulder-length chestnut hair—the exact color of Julien's—tucked behind her ears, a few light strands dangling over her high cheekbones.

"Camille," Julien said, his tone razor sharp. "Why did you bring this car? I told you I have Chloe with me."

Camille's eyes danced as she shrugged back at him. "*Maman* wouldn't let me bring her car. You know she hates driving the Smart."

Julien peered down the road. "There is no time to argue. We must go."

Julien climbed into the passenger's seat while I stood on the sidewalk, staring into the smallest car I'd ever seen, wondering if Julien really expected me to: (a) continue to follow him after all of the crazy information he'd just revealed to me, and (b) sit on his lap.

Maybe they thought I'd fit in the trunk? Did this thing even have a trunk?

Julien reached for me. "Come. I know you're not happy, but we have no choice. You'll have to sit on my lap."

I glanced up at the sky, hoping for an answer, for some guidance. Should I keep following this guy? Keep running from the police? Was he finally being honest with me now? Could I really trust Julien?

I squeezed my eyes closed.

"*Go.*"

My eyes popped open, searching for the woman who'd just whispered *go* in my ear, for that familiar voice that sounded so much like...my mom.

But all I found were Julien's and Camille's intense stares shooting me down from inside the minuscule car.

Julien squeezed my hand. "Everything I just told you is true, Chloe. I promise I will help you make it home. You have my word. Now, come. Get in the car."

Oh, God.

Camille bit her bottom lip as she watched me climb into the car, bump my head on the ceiling three different times, and finally settle onto Julien's lap.

"Sorry," she said to me with unapologetic eyes. Then she turned to Julien as she started the car. "I don't think the seat belt will stretch that far to hold you both in. You have to hold on to her, Julien. We're going for a ride."

Julien wrapped his arms around my waist, and as my neck curved at an unhealthy angle, I had no choice but to press my cheek into the top of his head and rest my entire body against his. And just as Camille took off down the road and ripped around a corner, I spotted the two police officers running down the street. Camille took another sharp left as Julien gripped my waist, making sure I didn't fly into his sister.

"Do you think they saw us?" I asked as a bead of sweat slid down my forehead.

"No, they were looking the other way. As long as we get out of this city now, I think we will be safe," Julien said.

Camille rolled down the window, letting the warm summer breeze whip through the car. She turned to Julien. "Nothing with you is ever safe." And with that, she stomped down hard on the gas, leaving the enchanting town of Annecy in her wake.

As Camille ran two red lights, whizzed around four tight corners, and made at least seven illegal passes all within the first fifteen minutes of our car ride, it became clear to me that erratic, dangerous driving ran in the family.

At least when I'd ridden with Julien, I'd had my own seat and a seat belt. This time I was smashed between Julien's rock-hard body and the all-too-low ceiling of a Smart car.

If Paul could see me now, he would die. He would just die.

"How long is the drive to Lyon?" I asked, praying that it was a short ride away.

"An hour and a half," Julien answered, his grip tightening around my stomach as Camille took another sharp turn. "But with her driving, it will be less."

I didn't know if my neck could survive another five minutes at this angle, let alone an hour and a half.

"Can I just…" I began as I attempted to shift my butt off Julien's thigh so that I could lower my head and straighten my neck out.

"Here, let me." Julien grabbed my hips and shifted me farther over onto his right thigh. "Did that help?"

"Not really. My neck is at a really bad angle."

Julien swiveled his face toward mine, making our noses touch. "You can relax your head and let it rest on me. I don't mind."

My face heated up as Julien held my gaze for a second before fixing his eyes on the road.

I hesitated, not wanting to give in, but as each bump produced a neck spasm, I decided to take him up on his offer. I was already smashed up against him with his arms wrapped around my waist. And it's not like Paul was in the car watching me. He couldn't have fit if he tried.

With my head now resting on Julien's shoulder, I eyed Camille. A light-gray T-shirt and a pair of dark jeans covered her thin, elegant figure, and a silver cross dangled from her neck. Lengthy eyelashes framed her deep-brown eyes, and a dab of lip gloss shimmered on her thin lips. She stretched her left arm out the window, clipping the wind as it flowed between her fingers.

"Do you think Claude knows we're looking for him?" I asked.

Camille shot Julien a sideways glance.

"She knows," Julien said.

Camille lifted a brow in Julien's direction. "What do you mean, *she knows*?"

"I told Chloe about the painting. About everything. So you don't have to hide anything in front of her."

Camille whipped her head toward Julien as a shrill voice escaped from her lips. "*Pourquoi t'as fait ça? T'es dingue? Tu ne la connais même pas! T'es vraiment stupide, Julien.*"

All I could catch from Camille's sudden rampage were the words for "why" and "stupid." I really needed to buy a dictionary for moments like these, but I could guess that she was asking Julien why he'd told me and then calling him stupid for doing so. Unless she'd been calling *me* stupid, which really wouldn't have been fair, seeing as how she'd known me a whole ten minutes.

Julien's voice boomed into my ear. "*Oui, je la connais. Et elle a ses propres problèmes! Elle se marie dans une semaine, donc elle a besoin de son passeport. Tu vois? Elle s'en fiche du tableau.*"

"*Alors, pourquoi tu lui as dit?*" Camille demanded.

"*Elle voulait savoir la vérité, et j'ai confiance en elle. Donc, pourquoi pas?*"

I tried my best to piece together what they'd just said. I thought Julien had responded by saying something about how I have my own problems—like getting my passport back and getting married. Then I heard him say something about the painting. Maybe something like why would Chloe care about the painting when she had her own problems? Yes, that must've been it. Then Camille asked him *why* again. She was probably wondering why Julien needed to tell me about the painting if I had my own reasons for needing to find Claude. Then he'd said the word *confiance*, which, if I remembered correctly, meant "trust." So maybe he'd said he trusted me.

Hmmm. I was remembering more French than I thought I would, which was making the car ride a lot more interesting. Of course, I could've been completely wrong about all of it. I tuned in again to see if I could pick up anything else, but now Camille was firing so rapidly at Julien that I couldn't decipher a single word. Julien shot in and yelled something back, and after this went on for another few minutes, a hammer pounding away at my temples, I decided I deserved to know what exactly they were discussing.

"Hey!" I yelled. They both stopped shouting and stared at me. "What the hell is going on?"

Camille's brown eyes flashed angrily as she turned back toward the road and continued yelling at Julien.

"She is upset that I told you about the painting," Julien said over Camille's high-pitched voice. Then he switched into French and snapped back at Camille. I wasn't able to pick up anything they were saying at this point. It was all going too fast.

"Speak English, Camille," Julien demanded. "It is rude to keep screaming in French when Chloe doesn't understand."

"I don't think she would want to hear what I have to say," Camille said with a huff as she ripped the car around the curvy mountain road, her pale cheeks now the shade of a cherry tomato.

As a wave of nausea passed through my cramping stomach, I closed my eyes and tuned out their bickering. Camille clearly didn't trust me with her family's secrets, but I had no reason to trust her either. She was acting like a complete maniac, jerking the car around these skinny roads, making me feel sick and out of control. Nothing about this situation felt safe anymore. Finally, the yelling stopped and silence washed over the infinitesimal space we shared in the car. The sick feeling in my stomach passed, and as I opened my eyes, I caught the blazing-orange sun disappearing behind the mountaintops. And for the first time since I'd woken up penniless in the Plaza Athénée, I acknowledged the real possibility that I might not make it home in time for my wedding. That, in the end, this wild chase through France might be for nothing.

Feeling a tear sting the back of my eyelid, I blinked it away, then squeezed my eyes shut once more and hoped with every last fiber in my body that somehow this would work out. That I would make it home in time for my wedding in one piece. But with crazy Camille at the wheel, I wasn't so sure.

The feeling of Julien's arms squeezing tighter around my waist startled me awake. Camille must've been taking another one of her extra-sharp turns.

I blinked my eyes, adjusting to the darkness that had now settled upon us. I hadn't even realized I'd fallen asleep. The neon clock in the Smart car flashed nine p.m. Shouldn't we have been in Lyon by now?

I lifted my head off Julien's shoulder and shifted to the right so that I could see his face. The minute I caught a glimpse of his profile—his clenched jaw, his lips sealed tightly together, his eyes wearily focused on the winding road ahead—a sinking feeling seized my gut.

Something wasn't right.

"What's going on?" I asked, not even attempting to hide the panic in my voice. "We should be in Lyon by now."

Julien kept his eyes focused on the darkness outside. "There has been a change of plans."

"What do you mean?"

"While you were sleeping, we received a phone call. Our mother is not well. We are on our way home, to the vineyard."

I squeezed my fists in my lap and just as I was about to open my mouth to tell them that I *needed* to be on a train to Paris tomorrow with my passport, and that we *had* to go to Lyon, I stopped. They'd just lost their father, and if their mother was sick now too, they didn't have a choice. They had to be with her.

"Where's the vineyard?" I asked.

"It is forty minutes north of Lyon. We were almost to Lyon when we got the call, so we just rerouted up north."

"How long do you think we'll stay?"

"I am not sure."

That nauseated feeling—which I was unfortunately becoming accustomed to—took hold in my stomach once again.

Julien's anxious gaze met mine. "I am sorry. I have no choice."

I nodded. "I understand."

I didn't know what else to say at that point, and even though I felt like I would explode if I didn't get out of that car immediately and figure out what the hell I was going to do, I realized I was stuck. And since Julien and his sister needed to find Claude as badly as I did, so were they.

Five minutes of tense silence later, Camille swerved off the main road onto a long gravel driveway, her foot even heavier now against the pedal. Julien's body stiffened against mine, letting me know this must be the path leading to his house.

The darkness that blanketed the sky couldn't mask the massive brick home that stood at the end of the driveway with a candle in each window, lighting the way. *This* was his family's home? It was gorgeous.

What if Julien wasn't telling me the truth? What if Camille had convinced him to drop me off at some random home in the country so they could retrieve the painting without the annoying American along for the ride?

I didn't think Camille could make this little car move any faster down the bumpy driveway, but she could. And she did. She had barely put the car into park before she flew out the door and ran up the walkway toward the house. I slammed my forehead against the roof as I climbed out of the car as fast as I could, and once I was out, Julien followed Camille's lead.

I rubbed my head and trailed behind them, realizing that they couldn't have been less concerned with my whereabouts as they jetted through the front door. Which meant this *was* Julien's home, and his mother really was ill. I was having a hard time wrapping my head around it all—that Claude was Julien's brother, that Julien needed to find Claude for the painting, and that Julien was still working for the government to bust other con men. This had become even more complicated and insane than I ever could've imagined when I first woke up with nothing to wear but a questionable red dress the day before, and now, to top it all off, I was at Julien's home, about to meet his mother.

Hesitating at the door, I suddenly remembered the auburn-haired woman I'd seen in Annecy the day before—the spitting image of my mother. And then the voice whispering "Go" in my ear. And now, as I stood on Julien's porch, I knew it was crazy even as the thought crossed my mind, but I could feel her here. Prodding my feet forward. Telling me to keep going.

I only hoped I wasn't losing my mind.

Inside the house, I followed Julien and Camille through a brightly lit foyer and into the living room, where a little woman with short, wispy black hair, a sunflower-yellow apron tied around her waist, and pale, plump cheeks lay on a sky-blue sofa. A doctor knelt by her side, packing up his things.

Camille rushed to her mother's side while Julien walked up to the doctor and spoke in hushed tones, the corners of his mouth turned down into a frown. I backed into the doorway and swallowed the lump in my throat as I suddenly had another flashback of my mom. This time, she was lying in a hospital bed, cold and unmoving. The scene of her lying there in the aftermath of her struggle to give birth to my baby sister was a vivid and unwelcome memory I'd often had nightmares about but had never allowed myself to remember while awake. Seeing Julien's mother lying there so pale and weak brought me right back to that moment, though. The moment where I'd had to say good-bye to my mom.

Except she hadn't been alive to say good-bye back.

I shuddered at the gut-wrenching memory, then thought about how horrible it was that Julien and Camille had just lost their own father and were now faced with an ill mother. And regardless of the tense car ride we'd just shared, regardless of all the bickering I'd done with Julien, regardless of the fact that he hadn't been truthful with me until earlier today, I sincerely hoped their mom was going to be okay.

Julien's mother opened her brown eyes—eyes the same exact shade as her children's—and smiled weakly at Camille.

"*Maman*," Camille whispered as she leaned forward and embraced her mother.

Julien continued speaking with the doctor, and I hoped by the way the tension had lifted from his forehead and jaw that whatever was wrong with his mom wasn't serious. He shook the doctor's hand, walked him to the front door, then reappeared be my side.

"Is she going to be okay?" I asked.

He ran a hand through his hair and let out a deep breath, as if he'd been holding it in for hours. "Yes, the doctor is hopeful that she will be okay. She had some chest pains and some dizziness, but it could be from the stress of losing my father, and now the threat of losing our home."

As I gazed around the spacious living room at the myriad of family photographs lining the sunrise-yellow walls, I could feel the life that this house had held—still held—for Julien and his family. And his quest to get the painting back made even more sense to me.

"I am sorry, Chloe, but the doctor has asked that we stay with her at least for tonight in case anything else happens. I know I promised you we would go to Lyon tonight, but..." he trailed off as his gaze wandered over to his mother lying on the couch.

"It's okay," I said. "I understand. We can go tomorrow, once she's feeling better."

"Yes, we will definitely go tomorrow." Julien walked over to his mother and kissed her on the forehead. She turned her head to the side, and for the first time, her gaze met mine.

Julien gingerly laid a hand on his mother's shoulder. "*Maman*, I want you to meet Chloe, my girlfriend."

Sending a tense glare in Julien's direction, I opened my mouth to protest. But when a sweet smile spread across his mother's face, I softened my glare and smiled back. What else could I do at that point?

FIFTEEN

Thankfully, Julien's mother was too tired for small talk, so Camille walked her upstairs while Julien took me back out to the car to retrieve my shopping bag of clothing.

The night air was thick and humid, and the humming of cicadas buzzed in my ears as I followed Julien down the steps toward the Smart car. After handing me my bag, he closed the car door, leaned up against it, and sighed.

"What a day," he said with a shake of his head. "No, what a week." He lifted his chin, planting his tired gaze on me.

I crossed my arms over my chest and resumed my glare. "Why did you tell your mother I was your girlfriend?"

Underneath the moonlight, the corners of Julien's lips twitched upward into a grin. It was the first time I'd seen him smile since the boat ride earlier that day. "What? If you were not engaged, would you not consider being my girlfriend?"

I shifted my weight and tore my gaze from his, hoping he couldn't see my cheeks turning red under the starry sky. Never in all my life would I have thought I could find someone like Julien endearing or attractive. But after seeing how much he cared for his family, and how far he was willing to go to save his mother's home, he suddenly didn't seem so...unappealing.

And just the fact that I was thinking that made the flush spread to my ears and made my heartbeat quicken.

"Relax, I am kidding." Julien pushed off the car and took a step toward me. "I told her that because she is too stressed to know any more about Claude and what he is up to. If I tell her that you are a victim of one of his cons, she will be devastated. She believed he was done with all of that. Like I told you, Claude is the youngest, and after everything she has been through with losing my father, she can't bear to know that her youngest child is out breaking the law and hurting innocent women. So for now, it is the easiest thing to say."

I waved my left hand in front of Julien's face. "Don't you think she'll notice my ring, though?"

"Maybe." Julien scrunched up his lips as he gazed at the sparkling diamond. "Just for tomorrow, could you take it off?"

"Take it off? I am not taking my ring off." Just because I was beginning to see the kindness underneath Julien's rough exterior didn't mean I was going to publicly renounce my engagement for him.

"Why not? It is just a ring, no?"

"It's not just any ring—it's my *engagement* ring."

"If my mom notices your ring, she may think that *we* are to be married. Is that what you prefer?"

"This is insane." I turned away from Julien, allowing my gaze to sweep past the house, to the rolling hills bathed in silver moonlight, the rows of well-tended vines rustling quietly in the gentle breeze. I wanted to go lie down on one of those quiet hills, fall asleep, and pretend that none of this had ever happened. That my life was just as it had always been before.

"I know. I am sorry, Chloe. Nothing is going as I had planned."

I tore my eyes away from the serene night that unfolded around us and shook my head. I didn't want to hear anymore. I wanted to be alone. "Could you just show me to my room?"

Julien took a deep breath. "Does this mean we are in agreement?"

"No, it means I'm exhausted and I want to go to sleep. In a bed by myself this time."

"Well...that will be a bit of a problem."

"What?"

"If we are sleeping in different bedrooms when my mother wakes up, she will know I am lying."

"You're saying your mom actually *wants* you to sleep in the same bed as your girlfriend?"

"I am thirty-four," Julien explained. "I am a grown man. She will know I am lying if you do not sleep in the same room as me. Then she will ask a million questions. And trust me: you do not want to be on the other end of my mother's questions."

"This is unbelievable," I muttered as I envisioned sleeping in the same bed as Julien yet again, and realizing that a teeny, tiny part of me was okay with that.

But I was engaged. And despite the kindness I'd seen in Julien tonight, that didn't change the fact that he'd been lying to me all along about Claude being his brother.

I shouldn't be okay with sleeping next to him again. What was wrong with me?

"It is not such a big deal," Julien said with a shrug. "It is not as if we have not shared a bed before."

"That was because we were sharing a *hotel* room. It was necessary. But this house is huge. You must have seven bedrooms in there!"

"Eight," he corrected.

"Whatever." I threw up my hands. "I can't sleep in the same bed with you again."

"Why not?" His lips curved into an obnoxious smirk. "You had no problem falling asleep next to me last night and then *on* me in the car today."

My cheeks burned as I turned my face away from him. "That was different."

"If it is anything like last night, you will curl up on your side of the bed and fall asleep immediately anyway. There is no reason to feel guilty, if that is what you are worried about."

"You're right. I'm going to be sleeping in the same bed as you *again*, taking off my engagement ring, and telling your mother I'm your girlfriend, all the while lying to the man I'm supposed to be marrying in a few days. No reason to feel guilty here at all."

"The man you are *supposed* to be marrying?"

"You know what I meant. The man I *am* marrying in a few days."

Julien snickered. "What is done is done. Come, I am tired. Let's get some sleep."

As I followed Julien back into the house, I peered down at my engagement ring, the large diamond shimmering under the moonlight. And I realized that in the rush to get out of Annecy, I'd completely forgotten about my earlier intention to call Paul and tell him the truth.

But as Julien let me into his bedroom and I stared at the small double bed we were about to share, I wondered if telling Paul any part of the truth would actually help at this point.

Julien pulled a pair of black shorts and a white T-shirt out of a tall brown dresser and threw them onto the bed.

"Do you have Internet here?" I asked.

"Of course." Julien walked over to his desk, opened up a drawer, and pulled out a laptop. He plugged it in and booted it up, then gestured for me to have a seat. "*Voilà.*"

I stared at the icon for the Internet, but decided I wasn't quite ready to deal with the minefield of unread e-mails I would certainly have waiting for me, not until I organized my thoughts a little more, anyway. Instead I angled the computer so that Julien couldn't see what I was doing, then pulled up a Word document and began typing a list of all the issues I needed to deal with.

1. *Construct story to tell Paul so that he will still want to marry me this weekend, even though I have lied extensively and have spent large amounts of time with two random French men over the past few days.*
2. *Contact Angela and tell her that under no circumstances is she to respond to any of Paul's calls or e-mails, should he try to contact her.*
3. *Contact Sophie and tell her to keep Paul, Dad, and sisters under control as they arrive, and not to kill Paul or let Paul kill them in the process.*
4. *Get my freaking passport back and fly home.*

I stared at my list and pushed all of the dread out of my stomach. I could handle this. I would figure it all out. I could do it. I'd start by e-mailing Angela and Sophie.

I pulled up the Internet and signed into my e-mail. Seventy-three new messages. And at the top of my inbox, there was one from Angela. Oh, God.

From: Angela Kelly
To: Chloe Turner
Sent: Monday, August 29 at 12:04 p.m.
Subject: Where are you?

Chloe,

Just spoke with Paul. He wanted the hotel number where you're staying in Paris. Mentioned something about you still being there to work out the "kinks" in the conference and seemed slightly irate with me for making you do this. Obviously did not make you do this as had no idea there were "kinks." Have been e-mailing you since yesterday morning to find out how trip went, but no response. Cell phone seems to be disconnected. What's going on? Are you still in Paris? Did the conference plans flop and you're afraid to tell me? I know I can be a bit of a bitch, but you can be honest with me. And as you are the most efficient, reliable person who has ever worked for this company, I doubt there are kinks. Plus company budget is not approved for extra days in Paris. And your fiancé is flipping out. And you're getting married THIS WEEKEND. Where are you? Please tell your fiancé I am not a heinous, slave-driver boss, as he obviously thinks otherwise. Hope I'm still invited to the wedding and you haven't run off with some sexy French man.

Angela Kelly
Kelly and Rain Premier Event Planning
Washington, DC

I deleted number two on my to-do list and changed it to:

2. Consider moving to small town with Paul, staying home, wearing apron, and reproducing, since career as event planner is obviously over.

From: Chloe Turner
To: Angela Kelly
Sent: Monday, August 29 at 10:18 p.m.
Subject: Re: Where are you?

Angela,

Everything is fine with the conference—there are no "kinks." I am still in France, though, which was obviously unplanned, and there has been some miscommunication between me and Paul. I'm sorry to have pulled you into this. Please, if at all possible, do not respond to any further calls or e-mails from him. Trust me, it's in your best interest. Not to worry. I will be home within the next few days and will be marrying Paul on Saturday. Just got sidetracked a bit over here. Also, I'm not using the company credit card and will be paying for my own flight home. Actually, on that note, if you've seen any suspicious activity on the card and have time to cancel mine, that would be great.

I will be sure to tell Paul you are not a heinous, slave-driver boss, and yes, of course you are still invited to the wedding. If I still have a job with you after all of this, I will be forever indebted.

Chloe

I took a few calming breaths before clicking on the next e-mail bomb.

From: Paul Smythe
To: Chloe Turner
Sent: Monday, August 29 at 12:03 p.m.
Subject: Angela, Checking Account, Pennsylvania

Chloe,

I just spoke with Angela, and when I asked for your new hotel number, she didn't have a clue what I was talking about. What is going on? Why isn't she aware that you're still in Paris?

Also spoke with the bank this morning. Two large transfers were made out of our account, and we can't touch the rest of our money until the investigation is cleared. Do you have any idea what is going on here? Are you absolutely sure your card is in your possession? They want to speak with you as soon as possible, which is why I contacted Angela in the first place.

None of this is adding up, Chloe, and I know there's something you're not telling me. With the wedding this weekend and your entire family descending on our house, you need to get home, and we need to talk.

Also, the Pennsylvania job is waiting on my response, and I think this could be the best thing for us. Think about it, and please, tell me what the hell is going on. This isn't like you, Chloe.

—Paul

I went back to my list and deleted number one. In its place, I wrote:

1. No freaking clue what to tell Paul.

"I know it is none of my business," Julien cut in, "but what are you telling your fiancé?"

A shirtless Julien stared at me with his huge brown eyes. I quickly averted my gaze from his chest and focused back on the computer screen. Couldn't he put a damn shirt on?

"I have no idea," I admitted, trying to forget about the way Julien's abs cut tightly into his tan torso, forming a perfect six-pack.

"This is all such a mess," I went on. "What could I possibly say to calm him down at this point? He's starting to get suspicious that there's more to the story than what I'm telling him. The bank has told him they're investigating the fraud on our account, and I've told him that my card is still in my possession. So none of it is adding up, and it shouldn't, because it's all a lie." Exasperated, I slammed the computer shut and swiveled around to face the still-shirtless Julien.

He sat down on the edge of the bed, his knee just a few inches from mine. "It is my family who has caused this mess for you, and I feel responsible. I will help you figure out what to tell him. If you'll let me."

"Because you're such an amazing liar?"

Julien smiled, but I caught the briefest flicker of hurt—or was it regret?—in his eyes.

I sighed. "Fine. What do you think I should tell him?"

Julien stood and reached across me, his bare chest rubbing against my shoulder as he flipped the laptop open again. "Scoot," he said as he sat on the edge of my chair, his forearms brushing against mine as he began typing, making me feel all dizzy and light-headed again.

"What are you—?"

"Trust me," he said, his fingers tapping wildly on the keyboard.

Ten minutes later, Julien had helped me come up with a plausible e-mail, which we hoped would tide Paul over for the next day or two until I was able to get home. We told him that my card had, in fact, been stolen, along with my passport, and that I was working with the US embassy to get it all worked out so that I could fly home within the next few days. We chose to leave out the details about Claude, the chase around France, the police who were hot on my trail, and the fact that I'd spent every minute of the past two days with Julien, and was currently scrunched up in a chair with him as he sat, shirtless, typing this e-mail to Paul.

I read over the e-mail about a hundred times before Julien finally convinced me to just send the damn thing and get some sleep. I ignored the frantic messages from all three of my sisters, my dad, the florist, the DJ, and the photographer. Instead I showered, brushed my teeth, and changed into my Annecy pajamas in Julien's bathroom. I returned to the bedroom to find him propped up on his pillow, reading a book under the soft lamplight, a pair of black wire-rimmed glasses framing his eyes.

I also noticed that he still hadn't put on his T-shirt.

As I tentatively pulled back the covers and slid into bed beside him, I realized that *this* was what Julien was like on a normal night—when he wasn't racing around the country chasing his brother, crashing weddings, and running from the police. I'd been with Paul for so long, I'd never really thought about what it would be like to share those intimate, end-of-the-day moments with someone else.

And I wondered, as I watched Julien relax back into his pillow and flip a page, why I felt so nervous all of a sudden. Why there were butterflies dancing around in my stomach.

And why, at the same time, this also felt strangely natural.

"What are you reading?" I asked as I laid my head on the fluffy pillow, trying to envision climbing into bed next to Paul and remembering how each night he liked to read over his notes for the next day's case—which had never made for relaxing bedtime conversation.

"It is a book on wine making. Now that my father is gone, I will be running the vineyard in his place…if we are able to buy it back."

I rolled over onto my side to face Julien, determined to ignore the weird feeling creeping into my chest. "Don't you know how to make wine, if you grew up here?"

"Yes, but it is the business side I must learn better. Even if we do succeed in buying back the vineyard, I have to find a way to grow the business quickly so we can make a profit and keep it going."

"Do you ever hold events here?"

"What do you mean?"

"Wine tastings, parties, weddings. That sort of thing."

"We have had an occasional wine tasting, but that is all." Julien rested his book on his bare stomach. "This is your work, no?"

I nodded. "If you opened up the property for events, you could bring in a ton of extra money. And it would be great exposure for your wine. Your sales would definitely go up...well, if the wine is good, that is."

"Of course the wine is good," Julien said, taking his glasses off and biting the end. "Hmmm. This is a nice idea you have. My father was a very private person, so he never liked this sort of thing. But my mother is quite different. She is outgoing and social. She would love to host parties or weddings here, and it would give her something to focus on now that my father is gone."

"Exactly. I have a client right now, for example—a senator's daughter—who's looking for an overseas destination site for her wedding. She doesn't want to do the typical, overdone tropical island wedding, though. They want something different. And from what I could see so far of the vineyard, this property could be a perfect fit for what she's looking for. I'd need to take a proper look around in the daylight, of course, but..." I trailed off as I noticed Julien staring intently into my eyes, his brow furrowed, his lips hesitantly forming a smile.

"What?" I asked.

"I am surprised."

"At what?"

"That you are talking as if you would actually set me up with a client to help my family's business."

"Oh...why are you so surprised at that?"

"I assumed when you returned home to your fiancé and your life in DC, that you would want to forget that any of this had ever happened. That you had ever met me and my family."

Julien was right. I'd never considered I would actually be in contact with him after I made it home, let alone send clients his way. But as I lay in bed with him, watching the way he looked at me, his muscular chest lifting up and down with each breath, for some strange reason I suddenly couldn't imagine leaving and never talking to him again.

"If you decide to host events at your vineyard, and if the property turns out to be as gorgeous as it looked at night, I would have no problem setting you up with some of my clients."

A goofy grin spread across Julien's face, his dimple popping into his cheek. "Your fiancé is a lucky man, you know that?"

My entire body flushed with heat at Julien's compliment. I swallowed hard, flipped onto my back, and stared at the ceiling, willing myself to think about Paul. But as I tried to picture my fiancé, his face wouldn't come into focus.

"I'm going to go to sleep now," I said, closing my eyes.

Julien switched off the lamp and set his book on the nightstand. Then he rustled under the covers until his foot rested ever so slightly on mine.

"Good night." Julien's voice carried softly through the darkness.

"Good night," I whispered. And as I opened my eyes and stared up at the moonlight reflecting off the ceiling, I felt something shift inside of me. I wondered, then, when I returned home, would I be able to pick up where I'd left off as if none of this had ever happened?

SIXTEEN

I woke to the sound of a bird chirping through the open window, and I squinted as the early morning sunlight peeked through a set of wispy yellow drapes. I turned over to find that I was alone in Julien's bed, the bedside clock telling me it was only six a.m.

Climbing out of bed, I slipped on my new cardigan sweater and padded into the hallway to find Julien. As I made my way to the stairs, I noticed that the house was silent. No clamoring of cupboards, no talking…nothing. Maybe Camille and her mother were still sleeping. But where was Julien?

I rounded the corner at the bottom of the stairs and peeked into the living room, and when I didn't find anyone in there, I headed farther down the hall to the next doorway, which turned out to be the kitchen. I circled the long mahogany table, taking in the brass pots and pans hanging neatly on walls the color of the sunset. When I spotted a half-eaten baguette lying in a bread basket next to an almost-empty miniature cup of espresso, a familiar scent engulfed me.

I stood motionless in the kitchen, trying to place it.

It was the smell of cologne. But it wasn't Julien's scent. It was different.

Why was it so familiar?

As I turned and walked back toward the door, running my fingers along the dark, smooth wood of the table, my hand brushed up against a piece of paper. The paper fluttered to the floor, revealing the word *Maman* scribbled at the top.

I picked up the note and tried to read the long French paragraph, but the handwriting was so rough I could barely make out the letters, let alone translate the words.

Then, at the bottom of the note, I spotted a name I recognized all too well.

Claude.

Suddenly the floor creaked behind me. I whipped around, catching a glimpse of slick black hair, a tall frame, and broad shoulders passing by the doorway.

My heart stopped in my chest as that same masculine scent flooded my nostrils once more.

It was Claude.

I dropped the note and ran through the doorway to see the front door slamming shut. Racing to the door, I swung it open and flew down the stairs in my bare feet. Claude was up ahead, walking briskly toward a small gray car.

"Claude!" I called out in desperation. "Stop, please!"

To my surprise, he stopped and turned around to face me.

And there he was again. Those chiseled cheekbones, those piercing blue eyes, those dangerous lips. Flashes of memories from the night we met ran through my mind like an old black-and-white film missing half of its slides.

He didn't speak, but the look of recognition that passed over his face showed that he remembered me. Oh yes, he remembered me.

"Do you have my passport?" I demanded.

"No." He swiveled back around on his heel and continued on toward the car as if nothing monumental was going on. As if it was totally normal that the woman he'd stolen everything from just a few nights earlier in Paris was at his family's vineyard in the middle of France at six in the morning, demanding her passport back.

"Okay, fine. Forget about my passport," I called after him as a rage like nothing I'd ever felt before boiled to the surface. "And forget about my bank account too. And the fact that you have single-handedly ruined my chance at making it home in time for my wedding! What would you care about me? I was just another one of your stupid victims. But what about the painting?"

He froze. "What did you just say?"

"I asked if you have the painting. You know, the one you *stole* from your own family? I know you're a thief and you couldn't care less about your unsuspecting victims, but how could you have done this to your family? To your mom? How could you have taken away the only thing that will help your mother buy this vineyard back?" I gestured to the acres of rolling green hills surrounding us, the orange sunlight flickering off the endless rows of vines. "They're going to lose everything because of you! It wasn't enough that your father died. Now you have to take away your mother's home too! She's sick now, because of you…you slimy French bastard."

I took in Claude's flashing eyes, his hard-set jaw as he stormed toward me. "What are you talking about? Buy the vineyard back?"

"When your mother went to meet with the accountant after your father's death, they learned that he'd left them in a state of financial ruin, and if they don't get that painting back, your sick mother is going to lose her home, her land, this vineyard, everything."

"Unbelievable." Claude turned, marched back to the car, and wrenched open the door.

"Where are you going?" I demanded, running after him.

Claude slid behind the wheel, shaking his head. "I cannot believe you fell for that. You are even stupider than I thought."

"No, you're the one who's making the mistake here. I mean, what do you think I'm doing at your family's vineyard? Why do you think your brother would drag me around the whole freaking country looking for you? Just for my passport? I don't think so. He needs the painting back so he can help your mom save their home… and what I'm assuming used to be *your* home too." I reached for the door handle. I wasn't about to let this guy leave the property.

A flash of doubt passed through his cold eyes, but then they hardened again as he zoned in on me. "You think you can actually trust what Julien tells you? You think he is innocent in all of this?

Where do you think I learned how to do what I do? I learned it all from him—*the expert*."

I staggered back, my fingers falling from the handle as Claude jammed the car into gear and shot me one last look. "And besides," he said, his chiseled features void of emotion, "the painting is gone."

With that, he sped off into the early morning sun, leaving me alone in a cloud of his dust.

MT-541-RW. MT-541-RW. MT-541-RW.

Taking the steps two at a time up to Julien's room, I repeated the sequence over and over in my head. I scoured the desk for a piece of paper and a pen, then scribbled down Claude's license-plate number. I'd be damned if I was going to let him get away with what he'd done.

I sat on the edge of Julien's bed for a minute to catch my breath, and to calm the sick feeling that crept up from my gut when I thought about what had just happened.

If what Claude had said was true, I now knew that my passport was gone for good. And with this whole bank-account-police fiasco I was wrapped up in, I doubted there was any feasible way I could make it home in time for my wedding.

And even though the threat of missing my wedding to Paul should've been the *only* thing on my mind, the last thing Claude had said to me made me feel even worse than the fact that I now had no way to get home.

"*I learned it all from him*—the expert."

After the events of the past two days, I wasn't oblivious to the fact that Julien was well versed in the art of lying. But to have taught Claude *everything he knew* would have meant that Julien had stolen from other women, the way Claude had stolen from me.

Suddenly Julien's words from that terrifying morning in the Hôtel Plaza Athénée flooded through my spinning head.

"*You think it is a mistake that Claude chose you, the cautious American with a hefty bank account and a wedding next week? Your life will be in ruins faster than you can blink. I have seen it happen to many women before you.*"

It was all making sense now.

Julien had seen it happen to many women before me because *he* was the mastermind behind the scams, not Claude. Julien wasn't an undercover agent *pretending* to be a criminal.

He was a criminal himself.

That's why he'd been so insistent on me staying away from the police. It's how he'd known the scary Australian duo in Annecy. And how he'd known every last detail of the scam Claude had pulled on me—how he'd stolen my PIN, tapped into my bank account, wired the money to an offshore account, drugged me, then left me looking like a hooker in that slinky red dress.

Julien had played the exact same scam on other women before me.

How could I have been so blind?

I imagined Julien, shaven and in a suit, prowling some rich hotel. Preying on innocent women like me. I felt the bile rising up my throat as I thought about how, despite the fact that he'd lied about Claude being his brother, I'd actually begun to trust him, to believe that he really wanted to help me. I'd even thought about sending clients his way!

God, what a fool I'd been.

Suddenly the image of Julien kissing me in the lobby of the hotel appeared in my mind. I closed my eyes and tried to picture Paul's face, just as I had the night before, but I couldn't draw it up. All I could think about were Julien's soft, warm lips. Julien pressing up against me in the dressing room of the lingerie store. Julien in his wire-rimmed glasses, reading his wine-making book, his dimple popping into his unshaven cheek as he gave me that goofy grin.

I shook my head in an attempt to erase the rage, the disappointment, the confusion bubbling over inside of me. If Julien had taught

Claude everything he knew, then Julien could be capable of anything. And I couldn't place my trust in him any longer.

I had to get out of here.

I still hadn't seen or heard anyone else in the house, and with no clue where they'd gone, I checked all the bedrooms—all eight of them—and still found no one. Peering out the window, I searched the rows of vines for signs of life, but came up empty yet again.

Just as I was trying to figure out a plan for how to get the hell off this vineyard and to a US embassy, a red flash caught my eye.

It was the Smart car, all two inches of it, parked right where we'd left it.

I threw on my jeans and T-shirt, then flipped open Julien's computer and Googled the Dubois family vineyard to find out where in the hell I was. After clicking through a few links, I nearly fell off my chair when I found the name of the town I was trapped in.

It was called *Saint-Julien.*

Seriously?

I looked up directions from Saint-Julien to the US embassy in Paris and found that it was about a four-hour drive away. I jotted down the directions on a clean sheet of paper, then searched around Julien's room for money, a credit card, anything. I didn't want to run out of gas on the way up.

I ransacked every drawer, every crevice, but found nothing. I sighed in exasperation, considering just leaving so as not to waste any more time, and then stealing gas at a gas station if worse came to worst, but then I realized I hadn't checked the tiny drawer in Julien's nightstand.

Inside, Julien had placed the same black wallet he'd been carrying around since I'd met him. I flipped it open and pulled out the blue credit card I'd watched him use to pay for our hotel, our breakfast, my shoes, and my clothes. As I turned the card over in my hand, I gasped. The name printed on the front wasn't Julien's. It was Claude's.

This whole time, Julien had been using a stolen credit card. His own brother's! Clearly there was no family loyalty left between the two of them. Why was I even surprised?

Since the one person I had no qualms stealing from in this whole scenario was Claude, I stuffed the card in my jeans pocket and decided I would drive to Lyon instead, then take a train from there up to Paris.

After tucking the wallet back inside the drawer and looking up a new set of directions to Lyon, I grabbed the paper where I'd scribbled Claude's license-plate number and ran downstairs to the foyer. There, on a side table, were the keys to the Smart car, lying in the exact spot where Camille had thrown them the night before.

The shiny silver car keys taunted me as my blood ran marathons through my veins. Could I do this? Could I really steal their car?

I was just taking it to Lyon, which was only forty minutes away. I could figure out a way to let them know where I'd left it if I really wanted to, so I wasn't exactly *stealing.* And if I wanted to get out of here before they got home, I didn't have another second to waste.

I grabbed the keys, jogged out to the tiny car, and for the first time since this whole mess had begun, I climbed into the driver's seat, started the engine, and took off by myself.

Speeding down the hilly country road, my hands shaking at the wheel, the wind whipping my hair in circles around my head, I realized why Julien and his brother had a thing for stealing. There was a certain exhilaration that came along with doing something forbidden. It was a feeling I'd never experienced before the past two days with Julien, and at the current moment, it was a feeling I hoped I'd never have to experience again once I left France for good.

I focused my eyes on the winding road ahead and forced myself to stop thinking about the fact that I was stealing this car from

Julien's family. It would be okay. I would figure everything out when I got to Paris.

And just as the trembling in my hands began to calm and the feel of the smooth steering wheel on my palms became comfortable, a navy-blue car that had just sped past me going the other direction pulled a U-turn and raced up behind me.

I floored the gas and checked the rearview mirror to see if I could make out a face.

As soon as I saw the messy brown hair and the cigarette dangling out the window, I knew exactly who it was. *Damn.*

I flicked my gaze back to the road but gasped when a razor-sharp curve snuck up on me and Julien's horn wailed behind me. By the time my foot hit the brake, I was already barreling down a grassy hill. I closed my eyes as a willow tree trunk crashed into the front of the car and the airbag inflated in my face.

After a few moments of listening to the sound of my own breath grazing over the airbag, I realized I was still alive. I lifted my aching head to find steam billowing up from the hood of the tiny car. The tree trunk was now only two feet away from my head.

So much for my big, brave escape plan.

Footsteps pounded down the hill and before I could even turn my sore neck, Julien pulled the door open and lifted me out of the car. He set me down on the soft grass and sat across from me, his breath heavy and fast.

"Are you okay?" he asked.

I rubbed the back of my neck, my hands shaking, my chest pounding. "I think so."

"Good," he said. Then he stood, walked calmly over to the crumpled car and pounded the roof with his fist. "*Putain!*" he shouted, then fisted the car again.

He turned to me, his eyes full of rage. "*T'es dingue?* What were you thinking?"

I stood on wobbly legs as I narrowed my eyes at him. "Oh, sure. You can teach your slimy brother how to manipulate women and ruin their lives, but I can't even steal a stupid Smart car and get away with it!"

"What are you talking about? Teach my brother?"

I let out a snort. "Guess who made a surprise visit to the vineyard this morning while you and your family were out doing God knows what?"

Julien's brown eyes widened. "Claude was here?"

I nodded. "Yup, and you know what else? He doesn't have my passport."

Julien's hands flew into the air. "Your passport? Your passport! *Putain!* Is that all you can think about? Where is he?"

I crossed my arms over my chest. "He's gone."

"What? You let him leave?"

"What was I supposed to do? Hold him down? Or even better, slip a drug in his drink and seduce him like you've probably done to hundreds of women?"

Julien rushed toward me, his eyes flashing with anger. "Why was he here?"

"He left your mom a note on the kitchen table. Horrible handwriting—I couldn't make out a word."

"What did he say to you? Did he give you any idea as to where he was going?"

A dry laugh escaped from my lips. "Are you kidding me? Claude actually *tell* someone where he was going next?"

Julien made an angry grumbling sound with his throat, then pounded his fist on the car yet again. "*Le salaud!*"

I jumped backward, not used to seeing him so furious.

Julien turned to me, his expression crazy with rage. "How long ago did he leave?"

"I don't know. Maybe a half an hour."

He marched past me up the hill. "Come on!" he shouted over his shoulder. "We can't waste any more time. We have to go after him."

I planted my feet into the ground. "I wouldn't bother. He said the painting is gone."

Julien flipped around. “That means nothing coming from him. He is a liar and a thief.”

“Funny, he said the same thing about you,” I replied coolly.

“He would.” He turned and continued climbing up the hill.

I wasn’t going anywhere with him. “So it’s true, then!” I yelled. “What Claude said. You taught him what he knows? How to steal?”

Julien’s voice boomed over his shoulder. “We don’t have time for this.”

“Just answer the question!”

He snapped his head around, his eyes burning right through me. “Yes, it is true.”

I stared at Julien, wanting to run up to him and pummel his chest with my fists. “God, how could I have been so stupid? I’ve wasted the past two days listening to you, following you, talking to you about my relationship, when all along, you’re just like him. You’re just like the man who put me in this horrible situation in the first place. I suppose you’ve been lying the entire time about working for the government as well?”

Julien kicked a clump of dirt and stormed back down the hill toward me. “Two years ago, when one of our cons went bad, and something terrible happened to that woman I told you about, Valérie…I quit after that. I was finished. But my friend, the one who is high up in the government, cut me a deal. If I went undercover and helped them bust other con men, I could stay out of prison. I am not proud of my past, Chloe. But I am a different man now. I understand the hurt I have caused others, and I will spend the rest of my life trying to make up for it.”

“And what exactly did you think you’ve been doing by lying to me this whole time? *Helping* me? And to think I was actually beginning to…to feel bad for you. Well, you know what? I couldn’t care less what happens to you or to your vineyard. You deserve whatever you have coming to you.”

Julien flinched, and for a second, I caught a flicker of hurt in his eyes. “It is not just *my* vineyard. It belongs to my family, to my mother. And I will not let her lose it. I am leaving now. You can either come with me, and I can help you get home, or else you are on your own."

"I don't need your help getting home."

Julien stared over at the Smart car, steam still sizzling up from the hood, then returned his deadpan gaze to me. "Suit yourself."

He turned on his heel and headed back up the hill without looking back.

I closed my eyes as a spasm shot up my neck. *Shit, shit, shit.*

"Wait!" I called after him.

Julien didn't slow down. I rushed to catch up with him, and as I joined his side, he didn't look at me, didn't even acknowledge my presence.

We climbed into the car together, the silence so thick it was suffocating.

"When we get back to your house, I'll find my own way home. I don't want your help," I told him.

Julien shifted the car into gear, the veins in his forearms bulging, a bead of sweat dripping down his forehead. "Fine," he said.

"Fine," I spat.

But as he sped down the road, a gut-wrenching feeling of dread gripped my stomach. What in the hell was I going to do?

SEVENTEEN

"Where is Claude's note?" Julien demanded as he slammed the car into park and shot out of the car.

"On the kitchen table," I told him. "Oh, and you might need this." I climbed out of the car and tossed Claude's credit card across the hood.

"What—" he began, but when he reached for it, his eyes widened. "You stole this? From my wallet?"

"It's not like it was even yours to begin with."

He shook his head at me, his mouth twitching, his brown eyes frantic, then tucked the card into his pocket and ran up the stairs to the house.

I searched the rolling countryside that stretched for miles around me, the rows upon rows of vines, hoping a solution would pop out at me. Something I'd missed. Some magical way I could work out making it home in time for my wedding without telling Paul or the rest of my family what was going on. Without having to speak to the police. Without worrying about the fact that I officially had no passport.

But there was nothing. No lightbulb. No magical solution.

Suddenly every muscle in my body ached. Cramps gripped my calves, my head pounded, and my breathing quickened. I braced myself on the side of the car, feeling like I might pass out. Something Julien had said to me the day before rang loudly in my ears.

He'd said that this whole situation could ruin me. That it could ruin my life.

Blackness closed in around me as my chest struggled to take in air.

No. I couldn't let that happen. *I wouldn't.*

I opened my eyes and forced the air into my lungs. I didn't need Julien's help. I just needed to use a phone.

⸻

"*Parlez-vous anglais?*" I said into the phone, cupping my hand over my mouth to muffle my voice.

"*Un moment, s'il vous plaît,*" said the woman who'd answered the emergency police line.

While I waited on hold, I stretched the ancient corded desk phone across the downstairs office and peeked down the hallway to make sure the coast was clear. Julien had been up in his bedroom, yelling on his cell phone, when I came back into the house moments before.

I listened for a moment and jumped when I heard his voice still booming upstairs. Closing the office door, I sat down at the desk and spread Claude's license-plate number out before me.

The numbers blurred. This would either be my ticket back home, or my ticket to jail. But I had to take a chance. I couldn't leave things in Julien's hands anymore.

A gruff voice spoke into the phone. "I understand you requested an English speaker."

"Yes, Officer. I'd like to report a theft. A couple of them, actually—all by the same man. Claude Dubois. He just left, and I was able to get his license-plate number."

"You said Claude Dubois? Is this correct?"

"Yes, Officer. That's correct."

"Hold for one second, please."

I tapped my fingers on the cool wood, my mind running a mile a minute, hoping I was making the right choice.

The officer's voice came back over the line. "*Madame?*"

"Yes?"

"I am going to transfer you to Agent Bertrand Martin. He will be able to help you, and he speaks English."

"Thank you."

Within seconds, the line picked up.

"Hello, miss. This is Agent Martin." His voice was deep and throaty, and he spoke with a thick French accent. "I am a government official in Paris. I understand you have information pertaining to the whereabouts of Monsieur Dubois, and that you would like to report a theft."

"Yes, I do. And that's *thefts. Plural.*"

"Of course, miss. But first, tell me your name."

A bead of sweat rolled down my temple. I wondered if some kind of siren would go off at the sound of my name. What if this guy was just waiting for me to say "Chloe Turner" before siccing the entire French police force on me?

There was no other option, though. I swallowed hard and took a deep breath.

"My name is Chloe Turner."

"Thank you, Miss Turner. Have you just seen Monsieur Dubois?"

I breathed a sigh of relief. He didn't sound at all interested in me. "Yes, in Saint-Julien, at his family's vineyard near Lyon."

"Yes, I am familiar. And the license-plate number?"

"MT-541-RW."

"Color and make of the car?"

"It was a gray Renault Twingo."

"Thank you, miss. And quickly, please explain the thefts."

"He stole my passport, my wallet, and a valuable Manet painting from his family's home."

There was a pause on the other line. "A Manet?"

"Yes, Officer, that's correct."

"When did the thefts take place?"

"He took the painting maybe about a week ago, and he stole my passport and wallet on Sunday, at the Hôtel Plaza Athénée in Paris."

"I see." Another long pause followed, then he cleared his throat. "Thank you for calling, Miss Turner. I will need to speak with you again and with a member of his family regarding the painting. Is there a number where I can reach you?"

Before I had a chance to answer, the office door flew open behind me. Julien towered in the doorway, staring me down.

I slammed the phone back into the cradle.

"What were you doing?" he asked

"I...I was just trying to call home. No answer, though."

Julien eyed me suspiciously. "Tell me the truth."

When I didn't answer, Julien glanced past me to the desk.

And then I remembered, Claude's license-plate number was lying there. *Shit.*

I tried to scoot so he wouldn't see it, but it was too late. He reached over my shoulder and snatched it off the desk. "This is Claude's?"

I nodded.

"Did you give this number to the police?"

I couldn't lie any longer. Julien wouldn't believe me anyway. I stood up and faced him straight on. "Yes, I called the police and gave them his license-plate number. Isn't that what you would do if you were me?"

Julien paced back and forth around the small office. "No, that is not what I would do. You are not thinking clearly. The police are after you and me. We have been running from them. They will be coming here. We have to leave. Now."

"I'm not going anywhere. The way I see it, I haven't done anything wrong. Well, besides running from the police. This was all Claude, and I have no choice but to talk to them if I want to get home. Now that we know my passport is gone, do you see that I have any other choices here? Because I'd love for you to enlighten me with more of your con-artist wisdom if you do."

"*Merde*," he said with a shake of his head.

I remembered that one from French class. It meant "shit."

"*Merde* yourself," I said, pushing past him.

"If you want to talk to them, go ahead. Like I have said, it will not go well. I will not be here when they arrive. It is not an option for me at this point."

"Where are you going?"

Julien walked past me in the hallway, grabbed his car keys, and opened the front door.

"*Where* are you going?" I called after him.

"It will be easier if I don't tell you. That way you cannot tell the police." He climbed into the car and skidded out of the driveway, just as his brother had done earlier this morning.

I couldn't believe he'd just left me here. Alone, again, at his family's vineyard. Where the hell were his mother and Camille? Before I had a chance to think about it another second, a different car pulled into the driveway.

This one was black and white and had a siren on the top.

Julien was right. It hadn't taken them long at all.

"Let's try this again. When did you first meet Claude Dubois?"

It was Officer Laroche, the tall, lanky, black-haired police officer who'd been chasing me around the country. I'd been sitting alone in a dull white room in a police station in Lyon for the past hour until he came in and seated himself across from me, his expression stern and unmoving.

"Like I told you, I met him on Saturday night at the Hôtel Plaza Athénée in Paris," I responded, trying not to fidget.

"You are saying that you had never seen or spoken with him before that night?" he asked in his strong French accent, his beady black eyes boring into mine.

"Yes, that's correct."

"As we discussed a couple days ago, I understand your wedding is coming up this weekend. Lying about the circumstances under which you met Monsieur Dubois will not help you make it home in time."

I gripped my knees with shaky palms underneath the table. I couldn't let him see how nervous I was. Otherwise he really wouldn't believe me.

"I met Claude on Saturday night. I've never even been to France before this trip."

"And what was the nature of your trip to France, exactly?"

"I was here on business. I'm an event planner, and my firm was running a language teacher's conference in Paris last weekend."

"I see." He jotted a few notes onto his pad before lifting his severe eyes back up to mine.

Each time he looked at me I wanted to shrivel up under the table and hide forever. This was terrifying. But I had to look him in the eye and keep my cool. After all, I *wasn't* lying, so I had nothing to be worried about.

"And why did your boss send *you* at the last minute?"

How did he know that? Had they talked to Angela? Or, even worse, to *Paul*?

"She got really ill and couldn't make the trip. I've been handling most of the details for this conference anyway, so I didn't have a choice."

"Even with your wedding coming up this weekend? Surely your boss would understand that you need to be home, preparing for your wedding day?"

Now he was starting to sound like Paul.

"Yes, but it was only supposed to be for the weekend. I was supposed to fly back to DC on Sunday, leaving me plenty of time to finalize the wedding details. Like I told you, Claude stole my passport, my wallet, my suitcase, everything. My boss obviously didn't know that something like this would happen to me the week before my wedding."

Officer Laroche lifted his bushy black eyebrows, his expression still cold, then scratched something down on his notepad.

"Tell me, Mademoiselle Turner, if you did not know Claude before your business trip, why is it that you are staying at his family's vineyard with his brother, Julien, and running from the police in the process?"

I opened my mouth to respond, but no words came out. Instead my pulse sped up and heat blazed across my cheeks.

But as a look of satisfaction spread across his already smug face, I sat straight up in my chair and decided I wouldn't let him talk me into a corner. I would explain everything, starting with the moment Claude slipped a drug into my wine.

Two hours later, after I'd told the entire story from beginning to end to both officers, I sat alone in the grim room, the uncomfortable chair digging into my back, hoping and praying that they would come in and tell me I could leave. That they believed me and that I hadn't done anything wrong, and that they were sorry I'd gotten wrapped up in this mess in their country. *And* that they would give me a new passport and pay for my plane ticket home.

Okay, maybe that last bit was taking it too far. But I really wanted to get the hell out of there. I mean, I was in a police station in Lyon. A *police station*. And they were questioning me. Me! I wanted to yell at them and tell them that I was valedictorian of my high school class, that I'd graduated summa cum laude from Princeton, that I was a smart, hardworking goody-two-shoes from DC who would never, *never* dream of stealing anything from anyone, let alone get wrapped up in a mess with someone like Claude Dubois.

The reason none of that mattered, though, was because I *was* wrapped up in a mess with someone *like* Claude—his brother, Julien. The police knew about the stolen lingerie in Annecy, and from the looks on their faces whenever Julien's name was mentioned, they knew *all* about his past.

But what could I do about any of that now? I told them everything I knew, and I was probably stupid to do any of this without a lawyer by my side, but what other choice did I have? I had to at least try to clear my name in the hope that I could get a flight out of France and make it home by Saturday.

I tapped my fingers on the metal table, suddenly envisioning myself locked up in some scary French jail, with no phone calls to make, no one at home knowing where I'd disappeared to, freaky cell mates trying to talk to me.

I shuddered and squeezed my eyes closed. *No.* I had to think positive. This would all work out. I shouldn't have run from the police, I shouldn't have stolen the lingerie, I shouldn't have done anything I'd done over the past three days, but I hoped I'd explained the whole story well enough to the police for them to believe my reasons for following Julien and to let me go home.

But no matter how hard I tried to envision those two officers walking back into the room, smiles on their faces, telling me it was all just a big misunderstanding and that I could go now, the image just wouldn't come. Who was I kidding? They weren't going to do that. I'd found myself knee-deep in a family of con artists who the police were just itching to convict. What reason would they have to not throw me into the mix when it clearly looked like I was in on it too?

As I sank further into my negativity, my stomach turning sour and sweat rolling down my neck, the door swung open.

I expected Officer Laroche and Officer Fournier to be standing there with handcuffs, ordering me into a dark, damp jail cell.

But instead, it was a younger man dressed in a black suit and a dark-red tie, his light-brown hair, hazel eyes, and chiseled cheekbones taking a striking resemblance to another man I'd been spending a lot of time with recently…no, that was ridiculous.

Oh, God. It was probably the French version of the FBI, coming to question me more. Or take me to federal prison. Or—

"Miss Turner," he said as he approached the table.

"Yes?"

He pulled a badge out of his coat pocket—a badge that looked all too similar to the fake one Julien had shown me in the hotel lobby the day before—and as he flashed it at me, my heart plummeted through my chest. This was it. I was officially done for.

"I am a special agent with the French government. I have reviewed the charges and—"

Oh, God. No. "Please, you have to listen to me. I haven't done anything wrong. I mean, yes, I ran from the police when I should've just talked to them. But I have nothing to do with Claude Dubois. I wouldn't even know how to shoplift a pack of gum, let alone pull the kind of fraud Claude has pulled on me. Please don't take me to jail. I'm getting married Saturday! You have to believe—"

"Mademoiselle Turner," the agent interrupted. "Please, calm yourself. I am not here to arrest you, or to question you further."

I lifted my eyes to meet his, and it was then that I noticed the warm look on his face...and again, I couldn't help but think that he looked *familiar*. "You're not?"

He smiled. "No, I'm not. I'm here to tell you that you can go now. The investigation on you has been dropped."

I stared at him incredulously. "Really?"

"Yes. Really."

I stood from the table, not sure what to do or think. I did know one thing for sure—I wanted to fling my arms around this guy's neck and plant a big, fat kiss on his cheek.

I restrained myself, though. "Thank you," I said. "Thank you so much."

My American politeness must've been a bit too much for him because he shifted uncomfortably and glanced toward the door.

"So I can leave now?"

"Yes, there will be no further questioning. Your bank at home will refund the money that is yours, and you are cleared to leave the country."

I stopped before opening the door. "Agent, you never told me your name."

He raised a brow at me. "I was wondering if you would notice. My name is Guillaume Dubois. I understand you have met *both* of my older brothers this week, *n'est-ce pas*?"

I nodded, unable to believe that my hunch had been correct. "So you're the so-called *friend* Julien told me about, the one who cut him a deal to keep him out of prison? You're the person he's been in touch with this whole time? It was you who sent him the text message with my photo and told him to stop me from going to the police. You've been tipping him off about where Claude is running to next, and you've kept him safe because you needed him to find the painting too...for your family."

Guillaume nodded. "Yes, that is all true. I am sorry you were brought into this mess, Miss Turner. It is the last thing Julien or I ever wanted."

I couldn't help but let out a snort. "Maybe that's true for you, but I have a hard time believing that Julien gives a damn about what happens to me—or any other woman, for that matter."

Guillaume took a step forward, his resemblance to Julien so strong, it took my breath away. "That is where you are wrong, Miss Turner. Did Julien ever tell you why he began running cons in the first place?"

"Does it even matter? What matters is that he stole from innocent women, ruined their lives, and taught Claude to do the same. I wouldn't be in this mess if it weren't for him."

"This much is true, yes. Unfortunately, Claude is much worse, and unlike Julien, *he* will never change. As for Julien, though, he began running cons as a teenager, to make up for my gambler of a father. He gave the money to our mother to help sustain the land and the vineyard, to help her keep her home, and to help support me, my brother, and my sister when we were very young."

"Did she know how Julien was earning this money?"

"Not until two years ago, when he was caught, no."

"So coming from this family of gamblers and con men, you logically became a government agent?"

Guillaume shrugged. "I found my own ways to cope with my father's shortcomings. And I also believed, mistakenly, that I could watch out for my brothers in this way. Help them from the inside, and make sure they never got in too much trouble. But, as you can see, my plan did not work so well…otherwise, you wouldn't be here. And after this point, as much as I care for my family, I am finished with all of it. I must take care of my own family, you see."

Guillaume took another step toward me, laying his hand on my arm. It was then that I noticed a silver wedding band on his left ring finger. "I am sorry for all of the harm my family has caused you, Chloe. And I know you don't want to believe me about Julien, but he is truly a different man now."

"It doesn't matter what kind of man he is, because I'm going home to my fiancé," I said coldly. "Thank you for your help, Guillaume. Clearly the Dubois family did at least one thing right in you."

I walked out of the stuffy little room and through the bustling police station, not even stopping to check if my two favorite officers were around. I didn't want to give them a chance to change their minds.

As I pushed through the double doors of the station, I knew I should've felt as if a weight the size of China had been lifted from my shoulders. I was cleared to leave the country. I was going to get my money back. No more running from the police. No more lying. No more hiding. I was done. I could leave.

But the weight wasn't gone. It was still there, in all its heavy glory. Guillaume's words swirled through my dizzied head, making me wonder why I cared so much about Julien and his motives.

I never had to see Julien or another member of the freaking Dubois family ever again. I should've been elated.

Out on the bustling sidewalk, I lifted my eyes to the clear blue sky and told myself to get a grip. It was time to figure out how to get home. It was time to go home to Paul. To get married.

To forget about Julien.

But when I brought my eyes back down to the busy street and glanced past all the tiny cars zooming by, I spotted a man with messy chestnut hair, a dark five o'clock shadow, and jutting cheekbones leaning against a familiar navy blue car. He had on a pair of worn jeans, a dark-red T-shirt, and black boots, and as he turned to the side and smashed his cigarette on the ground, his eyes locked with mine.

It was Julien.

EIGHTEEN

"So, you are a free woman." Julien's brown eyes were unreadable, his usual smirk gone.

"Why are you here?" I asked.

"I see that you have not learned a thing." He sighed as he thrust an envelope into my hands and turned around to open up the car door.

Inside the envelope, I found two folded sheets of paper. The first one had a train itinerary on it—a one-way ticket from Lyon to Paris. "What—" I began, but when I flipped to the second sheet, my voice caught in my throat.

Air France. One-way flight departing from Paris Charles de Gaulle. Arriving in Washington Dulles International. *Tomorrow.*

Julien was already seated at the wheel. "You leave tomorrow morning. In the meantime, you will stay at the vineyard. Come, get in the car." Julien's expression remained blank, his voice dry.

As I climbed into the passenger's seat, I noticed that his eyes were red rimmed with large gray circles underneath. The color had drained from his face, the scruff on his chin and cheeks was messy, and his dimple was nowhere to be found.

"You did all of this?" I asked. "The train ticket, the plane ticket, getting your brother to clear my name?"

Julien started the car, his tan forearms effortlessly shifting gears, his eyes focused straight ahead on the road. "There will be a man waiting for you at the train station in Paris tomorrow morning. He will hand you an envelope containing your passport."

"A real-deal passport?"

"It is not stolen, if that is what you mean."

"How did you get this so quickly? I just saw you a few hours ago, and somehow in that time, you've managed to have your brother clear my name from the investigation, you got me a new passport, a plane ticket, and a train ticket? I mean, really, *who* are you?"

Finally the tiniest of grins popped up on his face. "For spending over two days with an ex-con, you are not picking up very quickly." Julien pressed harder on the gas as we turned onto a country road, the city of Lyon disappearing in the distance.

I shook my head, trying to fit all of the pieces together. "So they've fully, one hundred percent, dropped the investigation on me?"

"Yes. They are not concerned with you any longer. After all, with the exception of running from the police and stealing a bra, you are innocent. It is Claude they want."

"Well, good. That's who they should've been after all along."

Julien's knuckles turned white on the steering wheel, his expression deadpanning.

Of course. *The painting.* If the police found Claude first, the painting could be long gone, and along with it, the vineyard.

"Can Guillaume help you find Claude before the police do?"

"That is what he has been trying to do. But now, it is out of his hands."

"How is it out of his hands? He seems to be pretty high up if he can just walk into a police station and tell them to let me leave."

"Guillaume can only do so much for me before he puts his job in danger. He has a wife and a new baby, and I cannot ask any more of him. This was my last favor."

I paused, not sure if I'd heard him correctly. "You mean *me*? *I* was your last favor?"

Julien's silence confirmed my fear.

I couldn't believe he'd done all of this for me when he'd only known me for a couple of days. *Why?* Why would Julien have even cared enough to help me after I'd wrecked his car, spoken to the police, and reported his brother, all against his will?

I thought of the gorgeous vineyard, the beautiful family home that Julien had grown up in, and how he'd just lost his father. I thought of his mother, the cute little woman lying there sick on the couch. Guilt washed over me. I didn't want them to lose their last chance at keeping their home because of me.

"There has to be something we can do. Do you have any clue where Claude might've taken the painting?"

"I cannot think of the painting for today," Julien clipped. "There are other problems I must attend to at home. You can stay at my house for the day, and I will drive you back to the train station in Lyon tomorrow morning."

"Thank you, Julien," I said softly. "You didn't have to do all of this for me."

Julien nodded, but didn't once turn to meet my gaze.

Resting my head, I allowed my mind to scan over the events of the past three days. Everything Julien had told me about what would happen when I went to the police had turned out to be true. They hadn't believed a word I'd said. They thought I was just another sleazy woman working the system with Claude, trying to pull one over on them.

And still, even after I'd gone to the police, Julien had figured out a way for me to get home, just like he'd said he would.

I stole another glance at Julien and realized I could not imagine him doing what Claude had done to me. I couldn't picture him looking all slick, walking into a hotel bar and stealing from an innocent woman. Not now. Not after he'd used his last favor from Guillaume on *me*.

The man sitting next to me, the man I'd spent every minute with for the past three days, didn't seem to have the heart to pull it off.

But the fact was, even though he'd supposedly done it to help his family, he still *had* stolen from other women just like me. And he'd taught Claude how to do it too. It was true that Julien had worked out a way for me to get home, but in a way he was still part of the reason I was here to begin with.

For that reason, I knew I should've been happy to leave Julien, to never talk to him again. Happy to return home to my normal life in DC, with my responsible, stable fiancé who wouldn't know how to steal something if it was handed to him on a silver platter.

But as the car bumbled along the winding country road, I wondered why I felt a sinking feeling in the pit of my stomach, and why, when I tried to picture Paul's smiling face waiting for me at the airport when I flew home the next day, I couldn't.

It just wouldn't come into focus.

"There is just one last thing I must ask of you before you leave tomorrow," Julien said as he put the car into park in his driveway.

"Okay…what is it?"

"When my mother comes home, we must still act, for the day, as if you are my girlfriend. And we must not tell her or Camille about you talking to the police or meeting with Guillaume. They will know what that could mean for our family. I will figure out a backup plan, but while I am thinking, I cannot deal with emotional women."

"Okay," I said, gazing down at my engagement ring. "I'll do it. Where *are* your mom and Camille, by the way? And where were all of you this morning?"

"My mother is in the hospital. We had to take her in the middle of the night last night."

"Oh." An immense pang of guilt washed over me. I'd been so focused on my own problems, I hadn't even thought of that possibility. "I'm so sorry."

"I have to go now to see how she is doing."

"Of course."

"The door to the house is open. I don't know how long I'll be, so you are free to eat or use the phone. I am sure you need to make a few calls."

"Thanks." I opened up the car door but stopped as I was about to climb out. "I really hope your mom is going to be okay."

"Thank you." Julien's eyes met mine for a quick second before they darted away.

"I'll see you later, then?" I asked.

"Yes, see you later."

Julien backed down the driveway and zoomed away, past the rows of vines, and out of sight.

I turned to face the massive house, its periwinkle shutters framing the windows, pink and white geraniums spilling over the flower boxes, vines wrapping around the dark-red brick. And as I padded up the walkway toward the front door, racking my brain to think of a way I could help Julien save his family's home, a warm breeze lifted under my nose, and brought with it a scent I hadn't smelled in years. A mixture of lavender and rosemary.

My mother.

I closed my eyes, breathing in that comforting smell. It was so strong and so real—as if she was standing right next to me. I could almost feel her soft hands brush over my cheek, hear her soothing voice telling me she loved me.

The scent engulfed me, made me remember her in a way I hadn't been able to in the seventeen years since her death. And in that moment, I knew that she was right here with me. And that maybe, in some strange way, she'd played a part in helping this work out for me.

I blinked my eyes open, then gazed up at the house and at the soft rolling hills that surrounded me. I felt as if I was seeing this place for the first time. Through my mother's eyes.

It was absolutely gorgeous. She would've loved it here.

But then as the wind picked up, it carried with it the comforting scent of my mother and left me alone, wishing I could see her again. Wishing I could ask her to help me find a way for Julien to save the vineyard.

And even more, wishing I could ask her to help me with what I was about to do.

"Paul, it's me. Chloe."

"Chloe, what the hell is going on? Where are you?"

"I'm still in Paris, but Paul, I have good—"

"I know you're not in Paris, Chloe. Two detectives came to the house last night and grilled me for hours. They had photos of you in some skimpy red dress, and they told me you've been running from the police? With some pair of famous French con-artist brothers. And they think we're wrapped up in some kind of scam with them? What the hell is this? I can't get caught up in all this shit. I could lose my career!" Paul's voice screeched at a pitch I'd never heard before.

"Paul, just calm down. I can ex—"

"Do not tell me to calm down. Just tell me what the hell is going on. And no more lies."

I flinched as I imagined Paul storming around our DC town house, yelling into the phone, no doubt waking Sophie up. Then I realized Sophie would've been at the house the night before, when the detectives showed up. Which meant she knew about all of this. Which also meant that now my whole family knew.

I took a deep breath as I tried to gather courage from the peaceful countryside outside Julien's window. I could do this. Once I explained everything to Paul, he would understand. And since the wedding was in a couple of days, he had to understand.

"On Sunday morning, when I was supposed to fly home, I woke up in the Plaza Athénée, and all of my things were stolen. My suitcase, my passport, everything. All that was left in the room was that red dress you saw me wearing in the photos, and obviously that dress does not belong to me."

"Someone broke into your room?"

I closed my eyes and willed my pulse to stop racing. I had to keep going. I had to tell him the truth.

"On my last night in Paris, I was having a drink at the hotel bar—a sparkling water—and I met a man named Claude Dubois. I can barely remember anything about the night, but I know that I agreed to have a glass of wine, and that he put something in my drink…because I let him come back up to the room. I don't remember it, though, and—"

"You brought him up to your room?"

"Yes, but like I said, I don't remember anything. I'm certain he put something in my drink. You know me, Paul. I barely even drink in the first place, and I would never cheat. You do know that, don't you?"

Silence traveled through the line, making my heart sink through my chest. "Paul?"

"I don't know what to believe anymore, Chloe. The police said you're under investigation for fraud. Claude was one of the brother's names they mentioned. They said they think you're working with him, and with his brother too. And now I'm all wrapped up in it because it involves our joint checking account."

"Paul, you *know* me. I don't break rules. I've never done anything bad in my life. I've never lied to anyone, ever!"

"Well what have you been doing to me for the past three days?"

"I know. I didn't want to freak you out. I thought I could get my passport back and get home without you ever knowing any of this mess had ever happened, and I just didn't want to ruin our wedding. Let me finish explaining everything, okay? It will make more sense once you've heard the whole story. I know you'll understand."

Paul let a sarcastic snort slide through the line, but I ignored him and charged ahead. I had to get it all out. Now that I knew for certain I was going to make it home in time for my wedding, I had to make sure the wedding actually happened.

So for the next half hour, I told him everything. Well, almost everything. I left out a few select details, like how Julien kissed me in the hallway of the Plaza Athénée, and how I had to pretend he was my husband on the Newlywed Romance Tour Bus, and how he'd seen me in that skimpy lingerie, and how we'd slept in the same bed for the past two nights, and would probably sleep in the same bed again tonight.

Those details were completely irrelevant. And none of that would matter once I was home with Paul and walking down the aisle to marry him on Saturday. I would forget all about Julien and this whole insane trip.

I was sure I would.

After I'd finished telling Paul everything he needed to know to fully understand what had happened over the past few days, and why I hadn't told him anything until now, I waited for a response. I waited for him to tell me he loved me and that he believed me, and that this was all just nonsense and that he couldn't wait for me to get home so he could marry me.

But life is never that simple, is it?

"Just tell me this. What were you planning on doing with Claude when you *voluntarily* brought him up to your hotel room?"

"I told you, Paul, I don't remember anything about that night. I know he got me to drink a glass of wine at the hotel bar, and I barely remember anything past that point. Julien told me that Claude put something in my drink, which would explain me allowing him to come to my room and not remembering any of it."

"How convenient."

"Paul, I'm telling you the truth."

"Like I said before, Chloe, I don't know what to believe anymore, and now it looks as though I'm all wrapped up in some kind of legal mess. This could be a disaster for my career. How could you do this?"

"Paul, I told you. My name has been cleared from the investigation, which means you're in the clear too. They're done checking us out. They know I was just another innocent victim of one of Claude's cons, and they're after him now. Like they should've been all along."

"How do we really know they're letting you, and *me*, off the hook? How can you trust this Julien guy so much? You've only known him for a couple days, and he's an ex-con himself! How was he able to just make a few phone calls and get you off the hook? It doesn't add up."

"I'm coming home tomorrow and I'm all set to go. You are not in any kind of legal trouble. This isn't going to ruin your career. Everything will be fine."

"If you really want to marry me on Saturday, Chloe, why didn't you just tell me everything from the beginning? If you knew you'd been drugged, or whatever, by this Claude guy, why wouldn't you just tell me the truth right from the start? I mean, I'm a good lawyer, and I'm your fiancé. I obviously could've helped."

"I...well, I just didn't think you'd understand. And I thought I could work it all out on my own, without ever having to worry you or the rest of my family."

"It's too late for that. Your sisters are out of control. Calling the house, screeching into the phone at me. Sophie was ready to get on the next plane to France and come find you last night after the detectives came by. She was convinced you'd been kidnapped. I told her she was nuts."

"Well, in a way..."

"Chloe, you weren't kidnapped. You *voluntarily* took that man up to your room. You *voluntarily* followed his brother all over the damn country. You weren't fucking kidnapped."

I flinched. Paul never cursed at me.

It hit me then, that in this entire conversation, Paul had never once asked if I was okay. He'd never expressed anger at Claude for doing this to me, or at Julien for whisking me away on this wild chase through France. He didn't seem jealous or worried or any mixture of the feelings that I would hope my fiancé would feel after hearing what had happened.

Sophie knew me the best out of my three sisters. She knew what a straight-edged rule follower I was. It made sense that she would think I was kidnapped. That would be the only logical explanation for anyone who truly knew who I was.

But Paul was concerned about his career. About his reputation.

"I have to get ready for work." Paul's voice came hard and cool over the line.

"Are we okay?" I asked.

"Define *okay*."

"Are we still getting married this Saturday?" I held my breath, not sure I wanted to hear his response. Whether he said yes *or* no, I wasn't sure I wanted to hear it.

"Just come home tomorrow and we'll talk some more. I need to go to work now and make sure no one at the firm has gotten wind of this disaster."

"Right. Okay, then. I'll see you tomorrow night. I'll e-mail with my flight details."

"Sophie will come pick you up because she'll already be in the car picking up the rest of your crazy family."

I flinched again, Paul's stinging tone like nails down a chalkboard. "Okay, I'll see you when I get home then."

"Bye."

"Bye, Paul."

I hung up the phone and stared at it for what felt like hours, my eyes glazed over with tears, my heart not sure what it was feeling anymore.

NINETEEN

I wasn't sure where I was going, or when I would stop walking. All I knew was that I needed to clear my head. I needed to find a way to believe that things were going to turn out okay. But the fact that Paul had refused to confirm whether or not we were still getting married on Saturday made it a bit difficult to believe.

Rows of lush green vines encircled me as I treaded along a grassy path, the early afternoon sun beating down on my face. I reached out and brushed my hands against the soft leaves as they rustled in the warm summer breeze, and when I closed my eyes, there it was again. That same soothing scent—the scent of my mother.

I lifted my gaze to the sky, wondering where she was. If she was here, with me, or if she was up there somewhere, watching my mess of a life, wondering herself how it would all play out.

What would she tell me to do? What would she say to comfort me if she were here?

It had been so long since I'd seen her, since I'd held her soft hand, that I wasn't even sure anymore.

But as I continued to walk in between the endless rows of vines, the birds singing around me, the leaves cool on my fingertips, I found myself wishing I could just stay here forever. Because when I thought of the disaster that would be waiting for me when I arrived back in DC the next day, dread washed over me like a shot of ice water to the face.

Paul wasn't sure he wanted to marry me anymore. He didn't believe me that I had no intention of cheating on him. That I wasn't, in any way, involved in Claude's scam.

If he really knew me, and if he loved me unconditionally—the way I wanted my future husband to love me—wouldn't he trust me? After eight years with me, shouldn't he know that I would never purposefully enter into such a crazy situation?

When I thought of the way he'd kept using the word *voluntarily*, I shuddered.

And even worse, when I remembered the way he talked about his career, as if it were a person, as if losing *that* would be the worst thing to ever happen to him, I felt nauseated.

Shouldn't losing *me* be the worst thing that could happen?

At the same time, though, if I put myself in his shoes and thought about how I would react if things were the other way around, I couldn't say that I'd be quick to believe him either. From the standpoint of our stable, uneventful, working lives back in DC, this was complete insanity. And even though I hadn't *chosen* to be a part of Claude's scam, by choosing to follow Julien and choosing to evade the police, I had certainly participated. And, even worse, I'd lied to Paul about all of it.

I needed to cut Paul some major slack. He was freaked out and angry. That was normal, considering the circumstances. He would come around. I would go home tomorrow, we'd talk things out again, and by Saturday, we'd be saying our vows as if this had never happened.

But as I continued down the sun-kissed path, I tried to envision walking down the aisle to Paul, and yet again, I couldn't imagine his face.

Instead, the face that invaded my wedding daydream wasn't anything like Paul's. It was unshaven and rugged. It had messy hair and big brown eyes and a dimple in its right cheek.

I shook my head and walked faster. What was *he* doing in my head? No matter how hard I tried, though, I couldn't erase that face from my mind. As my mother's scent swam past me in one more gush of summer wind, I broke into a sprint. I ran blindly, sucking the air into my lungs, blinking back the tears that threatened to pour out and make me feel things I hadn't felt in years.

But I denied them and kept running. I ran so fast and so hard, my eyes boring into the grassy trail ahead of me, that I almost tripped when the path dead-ended into a small white cottage on a hill overlooking the entire vineyard.

Stopping at the front porch, I rested my hands on my knees to catch my breath. As the dizziness and exhaustion set in, I realized I hadn't eaten or drunk anything all day.

In true con-lady fashion, I didn't bother knocking as I twisted the knob to the bright-red door and let myself into someone else's quaint little home.

"Anybody here?" I called out. Before the unsuspecting tenant could answer me, my foot caught on a dusty easel, and I toppled to the floor, a massive painting crashing down right next to me. "Dammit."

From my new vantage point on the paint-splattered floors, I peeked around the small cottage, taking in the striking artwork strung over every spare inch of wall space, sprawled atop the kitchen table, propped up on easels. The artist had painted warm sunsets blanketing the Seine River, astonishing views of the Eiffel Tower, the Louvre, the Champs-Élysées. Each image showcased a different Paris sight in a completely unique and breathtaking style, but there was one common thread that accompanied every single painting—a young couple locked in a sexy, passionate kiss. The heat of their embrace sizzled up off the canvas and settled in my tired bones.

I blinked the tears from my eyes, refusing to acknowledge the thought that coursed through me at the sight of these fictional couples kissing in Paris—that there was only *one* time a man had kissed me and I'd felt that same scorching passion.

And it *wasn't* with Paul.

Scrambling to my feet, I headed straight to the kitchen, not caring if the artist came home. Damn these stupid paintings. I needed to eat or I was going to pass out. I poured myself a glass of water, downed it, then found a wheel of camembert cheese and a basket of bread, which I immediately began devouring.

After eating close to half the wheel and drinking another full glass of water, my head started to feel a little more normal, and the dizziness subsided.

But the confusion remained. And while the face of the man I'd been with for eight years seemed to be somehow permanently erased from my mind, the man I'd known for only two days had now etched himself in there and was stubbornly refusing to leave.

As I set the basket of bread back where I'd found it, I spotted a full bottle of Beaujolais wine already uncorked on the dusty countertop. I grabbed the bottle, sat back down at the kitchen table, and poured a huge gulp of fruity alcohol down my throat.

And after a few more swigs, like magic, my confusion was swept away, along with my memory of the awful conversation I'd just had with Paul.

The one thing that remained was Julien's face.

I leveled my gaze with the bottle and decided I would keep going until he disappeared.

"Chloe, wake up." A distant, deep voice called out to me. I must've been dreaming.

"Chloe!" he said again, his voice stronger this time.

A warm hand cupped my cheek, then another one behind my neck. My eyelids fluttered open, then shut again, and finally back open.

Scruffy cheeks, worried brown eyes, and a rustled head of chestnut hair met my gaze.

"What's going on?" I asked as Julien propped my head up onto a pillow.

"I came back from the hospital and couldn't find you in the house. I thought something had happened. I thought Claude had come back and...never mind." He shook his head, the worry disappearing from his eyes. "I see that you just took a walk." He waved an empty bottle in front of my face. "And you found some wine."

Ugh. My stomach curled as the smell of alcohol wafted past my face.

"Get that away from me."

Julien held back a grin. "So you are a drinker now? I never thought I would see the day."

"I'm not a drinker."

"Of course not," he said as he pulled me up to a sitting position.

"What time is it?" I asked, squeezing my eyes closed to stop the spinning.

"Three o'clock."

My head swayed slowly from side to side and as I turned to focus on Julien's face, I noticed his head was swaying too.

Damn, I was still drunk.

Julien placed his hands on my shoulders. "You are a little wobbly, no? Do you feel okay?"

"Mm-hmm. I'm fine. Just a little…"

"Drunk?" he finished for me.

"If that's what you want to call it, fine."

"You need to eat something," he said as he leaned me back against the couch cushions and stood up.

"I did eat. I ate that cheese. That camenamburt stuff."

"You mean the camembert?"

"That's what I said."

"Is that all you've eaten today? Some cheese?"

I nodded.

Julien swiveled around on his heel and headed toward the kitchen, mumbling something under his breath. I closed my eyes as I heard him banging around in there, when suddenly a thought came to me.

I shot up from the couch and charged into the kitchen.

"We have to get out of here!" I gripped the counter as I felt myself toppling over. Maybe I'd stood up too fast.

He turned, an amused expression on his face. "What are you talking about?"

"This isn't our place," I hissed. "I broke into some artist's cottage. We can't just take their food. We have to leave. *Now.*"

Julien laughed, then turned back to the refrigerator. "You are the one who broke in first and stole the wine and the cheese. If anyone gets in trouble, it will be you."

A sinking feeling seized my stomach as the room swirled in circles around me. "I'm not getting in any more trouble. We have to go."

"Relax," he called over his shoulder. "This cottage belongs to me."

"What?"

"It's mine. I bought it from my father when I moved back to the vineyard two years ago. I've only been staying in the house with my mother since my father died."

"Oh," I said, a hiccup escaping from my lips.

"So you broke into *my* cottage and stole *my* food and wine. I should have you arrested, you know."

"Very f-funny," I stuttered, once again taking in the paintings of Paris, of the kissing couples, adorning every bare surface of the cottage. "Wait a second, so *you're* the artist? *You* painted all of these?"

"Yes, as a matter of fact I did. And I was not very happy to see that *someone* had run in here and knocked over my latest work in progress." Julien raised a brow at me as he set a plate of fruit, vegetables, and bread on the table, then filled up a tall glass of water. "In case you are worried, which you do not seem to be, the painting you flung to the floor is not damaged. Now sit. You need to eat."

Dumbfounded, I plopped into the kitchen chair. "I didn't *throw* your painting onto the floor. I tripped over it. And how come you never told me you were an artist anyway? Where did you learn to paint like this? Is there anything else I should know about you?" I grabbed a sliced carrot and stuffed it into my mouth.

Julien sat across from me and watched me nibble. He leaned back in his chair and sighed. "You women are very dramatic, you know that? All I ask is to have a simple life. To live in my nice little cottage, paint my paintings, drink some wine, and of course help the police arrest other con men like me. But as long as there are women in my life, such a simple existence is never possible."

I glared at him from across the table, while secretly feeling relieved that he'd fixed me this plate of food. Raw veggies had never tasted so delicious.

"I think you like the drama," I told him.

"That is ridiculous. No man likes drama."

"Even French men?"

"Even French men."

"Well, I'm just about the *least* dramatic woman you'll ever meet, so if *I'm* too dramatic for you, then you might as well…" I trailed off, losing track of where I was going with that. The giant strawberry in my mouth was making it hard for me to remember.

"Might as well what?" Julien asked.

"I don't know. You get the point."

He laughed, the lines around his eyes crinkling. "So finally, I get to see the *relaxed* version of Chloe. It took quite a lot to get to this point, you know?"

"I'm *not* relaxed," I told him through a mouthful of strawberry.

"Oh?" he arched an eyebrow. "But you are free and clear. The police do not care about you anymore. And you are going home tomorrow. How could you not be even a little bit relaxed?"

"That's all true. And thank you, for, you know"—I waved my hand back and forth in front of me—"dealing with all of that. But there is still a problem. A *huge* problem. My fiancé doesn't even know if he wants to marry me this Saturday."

Julien's smile disappeared. "That is a problem."

"Two detectives came to our house to question him and now my family knows everything, and it's going to be horrible when I go home tomorrow. Horrrrrible," I slurred as I closed my eyes and plopped my forehead into my hands.

"The wine is making a little more sense now."

"You'd be drinking too if you were me." I lifted my eyes to his. "I'm sorry. I'm talking all about myself, as if my problems are the only ones that matter. How's your mom doing?"

"She is doing a little better. She will be released from the hospital in a couple hours."

I smiled. "That's great news. Why did you come home then? You could've stayed there with her."

Julien's eyes darted down to the table, then back up to mine. "I wanted to make sure you were okay."

"Oh," I said, feeling my cheeks flush. "Thanks." All of a sudden, I remembered yelling at Julien earlier that morning, telling him that he deserved whatever was coming to him. That he deserved to lose this vineyard. That I didn't care if he ever found the painting.

"You know," I said softly, as I pushed a stack of carrots around on my plate, "I'm sorry about what I said to you this morning. About you deserving to lose your home. I didn't mean that. Well, okay, at the time, I might've meant it. But that was just because I was angry because I found out about your whole con-man past. I don't really want you or your family to lose the vineyard. It's so amazing here."

Julien's brown eyes flickered. "It is okay. You were right, after everything I have done, I do not deserve to have good things happen to me anymore."

"That's not true."

"Maybe it is not enough to change. Maybe the wrongs I have committed in the past will always follow me."

I shook my head. "I don't think so. I think everyone deserves a second chance."

"That is just your American optimism speaking."

"But you're doing a good thing now. You're taking care of your mother. You're trying to help your family. And trust me, I know *all* about helping crazy families. That's what I've done my entire life. Well, ever since my mom died anyway."

"I am sorry about your mother. When did she die?"

"It was a long time ago, when I was twelve. She died giving birth to my youngest sister."

"That must've been tough at such a young age. I know how hard it has been to lose my father, and I am a grown man."

I plopped another strawberry on my tongue and chewed. "Tough doesn't even begin to describe it. But it's okay…well, it wasn't okay for a long time. My dad's anxiety was through the roof trying to raise three little girls and a newborn by himself, so I stepped up to the plate and took over where my mom left off. Every time my dad or one of the girls went off the deep end, I handled it. I made *sure* it was okay. And I still do. Which Paul doesn't like all that much because then I don't have as much time to take care of *him*. And it doesn't help that my sisters are totally crazy when they're all together, and he really can't tolerate women in large doses. But whatever, he just has to deal with it because he doesn't have a choice. Because he's marrying Just in Case Chloe. The one who's prepared for whatever disaster they throw my way."

Julien looked thoughtfully into my eyes. "Who takes care of you, then? Who cleans up your disasters?"

"I don't have disasters."

"No? What would you call your trip to France, then? An adventure?"

"Fine. With the exception of the last few days, I don't have disasters. What about you? It seems like you're the one who handles everything around here."

"I am a man. I am supposed to take care of my family. That is what men do."

"That's a little old-fashioned, don't you think?"

Julien ran his hand along the smooth wood until his fingers brushed over mine. He opened his mouth to say something, then closed it abruptly.

"What were you going to say?"

He shook his head. "Nothing."

"Sometimes you're just as bad of a liar as me. What were you going to say? Tell me."

"If I was your fiancé, I would take care of you. Not the other way around."

My drunk mind zipped back to the wedding daydream I'd had in the vineyard a few hours earlier. And how I hadn't been able to erase Julien's face from the place up at the altar where Paul should've been standing.

No. *No.* That was ridiculous.

"Paul takes care of me," I said, trying to sound confident. "It's just…he's just different. We have more of a modern relationship. You know, where both of us are equal. I have my own career. I don't need him to provide for me."

"What if you go to Pennsylvania?" he prodded. "He will not provide for you there?"

I'd almost forgotten about Pennsylvania. "Paul knows I don't want to go there."

"Does he?"

I didn't want to talk about this anymore. "So what are you going to do about the painting?"

"I'm working on it."

"Looks like we both have some pretty shit problems right now, huh."

"Looks like it." Julien held my gaze for several seconds before breaking away and staring past me out the window. "I better go back to the hospital. My mom and Camille will be waiting, and Guillaume should be on his way there too."

"Of course." I stood up from the table, feeling a little more stable now that I had food in my stomach, but when another hiccup sounded from my mouth, I knew I was still kind of drunk.

Julien laughed, and I whipped my head around to face him. "What's so funny?"

"When you go home, I think you should start drinking more wine. It is good for you, you know?"

"Whatever," I said as I plowed my hip into the corner of the kitchen table. "Ouch."

"Come. I will walk you back to the house. You can sleep off the alcohol while I am at the hospital."

"Okay."

I may have been drunk, but not drunk enough to ignore the way Julien rested his palm on the small of my back as he walked me past painting upon painting of kissing Parisian couples, and out into the fresh, warm air. I also couldn't ignore the way he kept his hand on me for our entire walk through the vineyard. What I did choose to overlook, though, was the fact that I liked it.

TWENTY

"So this is Julien's new American girlfriend! Finally, she is awake!" bellowed a plump old man with a black beret barely covering the top of his bald head and a gray mustache hovering over his lips.

I stood in a state of confusion in the back doorway of Julien's house, still groggy from my four-hour drunken siesta. A slew of French people sitting at a long table, which appeared to be set for a feast, turned around to look at me—*Julien's new American girlfriend.*

Oh, God.

The old man smiled a toothy grin before standing from the table, the view of the sun setting over the vineyard just beyond his beret. Then he waddled up to me, leaned in, and kissed both of my cheeks. "I am Pierre-François, Julien's uncle." He leaned closer and whispered gruffly in my ear. "Julien said you were a beautiful girl, but I did not expect you to be quite this beautiful!"

Julien had told his uncle that I was beautiful? Obviously it was just part of the act since apparently we were now telling not only his mother, but his entire family, that we were an item.

My cheeks flushed all the same as I smiled back at Pierre-François and glanced out at the others, who were still eyeing me curiously, tossing hushed whispers across the table.

"Come," Pierre-François instructed as he placed a firm hand on my shoulder. "I introduce you to the rest of Julien's family." He leaned in and whispered again, softer this time. "They are a crazy bunch, so do not get scared and run away. Julien will take care of you—he is the most normal one of us all."

If an ex-con who worked undercover for the government *and* secretly painted portraits of couples kissing all over Paris was the most normal one of them all, this family had some serious issues.

As we walked over to the table, I scanned the relatives for Julien or Camille or their mother, but instead found a mixture of their traits in the faces that waited to greet me—deep-brown eyes and dark shades of hair, from chestnut brown to black. A few of them even carried the same high cheekbones as Julien and his siblings.

Pierre-François started at the left and worked his way around the table to the right, introducing me to all twelve of Julien's relatives who'd come by for dinner out on the tree-covered terrace. "This is Julien's aunt Caroline; his cousin Aurélien; his uncle Manu; Manu's wife, Coralie..."

I lost track after Coralie, so I just smiled politely at each of them and twisted the diamond on my left ring finger around so they wouldn't see it. I'd forgotten to take it off before I came downstairs. But then again, Julien hadn't informed me that I would be meeting his entire extended family.

Just as the family took their focus off me and began passing around one of the five bottles of Beaujolais wine that sat uncorked on the table, I felt a familiar hand on my lower back.

Heat flooded up my spine as I turned to find Julien with a wide grin spread across his face, his other hand holding a steaming platter of chicken, rice, and vegetables. "I see you have met my family."

I nodded as Aunt Caroline, or was it Aunt Coralie?—well, whatever—thrust a glass of wine into my hands. "*Merci*," I said with a smile, thinking that I would be hit with a wave of nausea at the smell of it. But as the fruity scent passed under my nose, my stomach growled.

Julien set the dish down on the table in between his relatives, then leaned into my ear. "You don't have to drink that. I will get you some water."

"It's okay," I told him.

He gave me a funny look then led me over to an empty seat in the middle of the table. "Here, have a seat. Camille and I will be out with the rest of the food in a minute, after we wake *Maman* up. I made a quiche for you, and a salad." He winked at me before crossing the terrace and disappearing into the house, leaving me amid a group of jolly, babbling French people.

Why was Julien including me in his family dinner? Wouldn't it have been easier to just tell me to stay upstairs for the evening?

"Chloe, are you *végétarienne*?" one of the aunts asked me from across the table, interrupting my silent questions.

I nodded as I took a sip of water, making sure to keep my left hand under the table.

"How interesting. That is a very American way of life, no?"

"Actually, I don't have many friends at home who are vegetarians. I suppose in France there are even less of them."

Julien's uncle Manu groaned. "A life without meat! I cannot imagine!"

They all laughed as they passed a baguette around and tore pieces off, not caring about the crumbs spilling all over the table. As their warm laughter traveled with the gentle evening breeze, I couldn't help but laugh with them.

"So, tell us, Chloe," one of the female cousins said, once the laughter had died down a bit, "How did you meet Julien? He tells us you have only known each other for a short time, but I can tell by the way he spoke of you, he is already in love."

I choked on my water and began coughing furiously, tears springing to my eyes. What was the matter with me? Julien was just a really great liar. He had to pretend that I was his girlfriend since we'd already told his mother, so whatever he'd told them about me, it was all just for show.

When my coughing fit finally calmed down, I peered around the table to find that everyone's eyes were still glued on me in anticipation. I opened my mouth to respond, not sure what the hell would come out. But suddenly the crowd's attention shifted to the back door of the house, where Julien and Camille stood with their mother.

Whew.

All of the family members exchanged worried glances around the table as Julien and Camille each held on to one of their mother's arms and guided her to a seat at the head of the table. Her skin was pale, her hair matted down from being in bed all day, and her eyes weary.

As everyone quieted down, Julien's mother looked up, smiled a weak smile, and said something in French, which got everyone laughing and talking again. Then she stole a glance at me from across the table and winked.

I smiled back at her then watched as Julien and Camille ran back into the house and reappeared seconds later with four huge plates of food.

"*Oh là là!*" squealed one of the aunts as she took a whiff of the quiche, its crust just lightly browned, melted cheese drizzled over top. "*Ça sent bon!*"

"*Julien, t'es le meilleur chef de cuisine, tu sais!*" Cousin Aurélie whooped as she dished a slice of the quiche onto her plate.

I thought she'd said Julien was the best chef, but I wasn't quite sure. They were all speaking so fast it was hard to keep up.

"*Mais bien sûr il le sait! Il est vaniteux, mon frère!*" Camille called at her brother before taking a big gulp of wine and losing herself in laughter.

Okay, I was totally lost on that one. Julien made his way around the table, his smile the biggest and most relaxed I'd seen since I met him, then took a seat next to me. He wore a white-collared shirt with the sleeves rolled up, his tan, muscular forearms reaching to the center of the table to pass the food around.

He stretched his arm around my chair and whispered into my ear. "I owe you."

My stomach fluttered as his hand rested on my shoulder, the skin on his forearm brushing against the back of my neck. "It's okay. I *did* wreck your car. Do they know about that yet?" I whispered back.

"*Maman* hated that car. She will be happy it is gone. But no, she does not know yet. I will tell her Claude stole it." He chuckled as he poured himself a tall glass of red wine.

"I didn't know there was a family gathering tonight," I said softly through my smile.

The rest of the family was chattering up a storm, forks clanking against plates, glasses clinking with each other, so Julien raised his voice. "You see, we missed our traditional family dinner on Sunday. On our way home from the hospital today, *Maman* told me she wanted to be in the company of her family. That only food and family would make her feel better. So I cook dinner, and here we are."

"Did you make all of this?"

Julien nodded. "Camille never liked to cook, so my mother taught me instead. I love to create dishes, to throw things together and see how they taste. Kind of like a painting, you know?"

"Wow. So you're a closet artist *and* a cook. Unbelievable." I gazed around at the chicken, the buttery vegetables, the colorful salad, and the steaming-hot quiche, my sour stomach eager to fill up with some of this amazing cuisine. I couldn't believe that Julien had made all of this himself. I was used to late-night takeout since Paul and I were both horrible cooks and never had the energy to whip something together at the end of a long workday.

"My mother loved to cook too," I told him. "She started to teach me when I was younger, but after she passed, my dad opted for microwave dinners and macaroni and cheese instead."

"Macaroni and cheese?" he echoed, his brow furrowing.

"You don't really do the whole processed food thing in France, do you?"

Julien shook his head. "I picked some of the vegetables for this dinner over there in that garden." He nodded to his right. "The *poulet*...euh, I mean the chicken, I buy from a farm down the street, and the wine, well, it is obvious where that comes from. So no, the French are not big fans of food that is not fresh."

"That's probably why you're all so thin."

"Oh, so you agree with me now? That French people are healthier than Americans?"

"I didn't say that."

"I kid," Julien said as he broke off a piece of bread, handed me the baguette, then gestured around the table. "You see, I love big, crazy families. I do not understand how people live without them. It is what keeps life interesting."

"I thought you didn't like the *drama*."

"Mmm, yes. I did say this earlier, didn't I?" He shot me a sly grin. "I was lying. I love it."

The laughter and joking didn't cease as bottles of wine were consumed at record speed and every last bit of food disappeared off the serving dishes. As most of the chatter was in French, it was lost on me, but Julien stopped to translate as often as he could.

I didn't mind sitting there in a haze of my inability to understand French. Even though I'd slept off most of the alcohol from my depressive binge earlier in the day, I was still feeling more than a little off, knowing that in less than twenty-four hours I would be home, running damage control on my family, on my engagement, on my life. And I was secretly hoping the French chitchat would carry all the way through dinner so I wouldn't have to answer any more questions about my *new relationship* with Julien.

But, about halfway through the meal, the mood suddenly turned somber. Pierre-François stood and walked over to the head of the table, where Julien's mother was wiping a tear from under her eye. He placed a hand on her shoulder, then lifted his glass.

"*À Jacques*," he said, his eyes suddenly red rimmed and sad.

"*À Jacques*," everyone else echoed with a lift of their glass.

I realized then that they were talking about Julien's dad. I raised my glass with the others and took a sip, the berry-flavored wine rushing down my throat. I stole a sideways glance at Julien, his brown eyes soft and full of warmth as he gazed over at his mother.

I felt my heart pull as I watched him turn to his sister, who was also wiping a few stray tears off her cheeks. He smiled, clinked his glass with hers, then took a gulp.

"*À papa*," he said.

"*À papa*," Camille repeated.

Julien cleared his throat, then turned to me. "From what you have heard about my father, you probably think he wasn't such a good man. But for all of his faults, he was the happiest man I knew, and he kept my mother very happy. He would have liked you. It is too bad he is not here tonight to meet you."

I glanced up at the sky. "Maybe he's up there somewhere with my mom."

Julien smiled. "I hope so. I am sure your mother was a beautiful woman, if she was anything like her daughter."

I fidgeted in my seat, dropping my gaze to the table and wondering why Julien felt the urge to say all of these sweet things to me when his family wasn't even paying attention.

"I see that you are drinking the wine," Julien said, nodding toward my glass. "After today, I thought for sure you would never drink again." His devious grin was back.

Just as I was about to respond, a female voice called my name from across the table. I turned to find Julien's mother gazing over at me, a weak smile etched onto her pale face. "I am sure you did not come all the way to France to hear a bunch of old French people crying. And besides, my husband would not have wanted us to be sad. He would be happy that our Julien has *finally* found such a nice woman. *Alors, racontez-nous l'histoire!* How did you meet my son?"

I glanced over at Julien for rescue, hoping he didn't expect me to answer this question. *He* was the more experienced liar, after all. To my astonishment, though, Julien's cheeks were a shade pinker than normal, and his mouth, for once, was out of words.

Julien's mother raised an eyebrow at us. "Maybe it is not a story for the dinner table. Am I right?"

Oh, God. She thought we'd had a one-night stand. I turned to Julien once more, hoping he'd figure out something believable to say to them. But then I remembered how he'd told the newlyweds that we'd met on a nude beach. *Merde.*

"No, *Maman*, it is nothing like that," Julien assured her. "I was in Paris, on…euh…business, and I saw Chloe walking out of her hotel, and…" Julien trailed off as his eyes locked with mine. "And the moment I saw her, I knew she was someone I would be spending a lot of time with. So I kissed her."

"Is this true, Chloe? My son walks up to you on the street in Paris and kisses you?"

My stomach flip-flopped as I remembered Julien's lips on mine in the lobby of the Plaza Athénée. A burst of nervous laughter escaped from my lips. "Yes, that's exactly what happened, actually."

"*Oh là là.* This story is just like one of Julien's paintings, no? I cannot believe you are still here. You must be a very special girl, Chloe."

The rest of the family giggled, not tearing their eyes from me and Julien.

Julien's mother clapped her hands together as an ornery grin and a bit more color peppered her cheeks. "You know, this makes me think of a song."

"*Maman,*" Camille said in a tone reminiscent of a two-year-old girl stomping her feet.

"*Tais-toi, ma fille. Va chercher mon disque de Charles Trenet.*"

Camille stood and stomped toward the house, not masking her disapproval of whatever her mother had just said.

"What's going on?" I whispered to Julien.

"I hope you like to dance."

"What?"

Before he could explain, an old French song traveled from the kitchen window out into the balmy summer evening.

Julien's mother set her laughing gaze on us, the weariness now wiped clean from her eyes. "*Dansez!*" she ordered, nodding toward the tree-covered patio next to the table.

With a chuckle, Julien took my hand and led me over to the patio.

"We're not seriously doing this, are we?" I hissed through my smile as I trailed along behind him.

Julien didn't answer. Instead he slid his right arm around my waist and pulled me in to his chest.

"*Quelle chanson, Maman?*" Camille screeched out the window, irritation ringing through her voice.

"'*La Romance de Paris*,'" Julien's mother called out as she sipped her wine and watched us expectantly.

"Don't worry, I will lead you," Julien's voice carried over the upbeat tune that flooded the warm summer night.

Before I had another second to protest, Julien spun me around, then pulled me back in to his chest, his breath hot on my cheeks, his hand gripping my waist. I swayed with him to the fast-paced music, aware of everyone's eyes on us—this new *couple* who seemed to be bringing a spark of happiness to a family who'd just experienced a monumental loss.

And I tried *not* to enjoy it. I tried to tell myself that this was all just a part of the act. That I wasn't in any way having an incredibly nice time with Julien or his huge, fun-loving French family. That I was simply doing him this favor because he'd figured out a way to get me home in time for my wedding.

But I couldn't ignore the comfort I felt in his arms, the rush I felt from spinning around on the patio with him, and the gnawing thought in the back of my mind that maybe this *wasn't* for show.

Julien held his rugged face close to mine as he sang along to the old French song, the short verses rolling off his tongue, the tune reminding me of the black-and-white films my mother used to love.

"What do the lyrics mean?" I asked after he'd spun me around again and pulled me back into his embrace.

Julien held me tighter, a sultry gaze passing through his eyes. "They have loved each other for barely two days. There is sometimes happiness to be found in pain. But now that they are in love, their destiny—or their *fate*—is no longer unlucky. *That* is the romance of Paris."

Suddenly I forgot about our audience, their chatter fading into the background, and I all heard were the song lyrics, replaying themselves over and over in my head.

The romance of Paris. Barely two days. Happiness in pain. A fate that is no longer unlucky.

All traces of the turbulent few days we'd spent together were wiped away as Julien's hands led me around this magical slice of paradise where orange and pink hues swirled in the sky overhead, casting golden beams down on the rolling hills of the vineyard.

In that moment, I forgot about Paul too. About my wedding. About Claude stealing my passport. About Julien's past. And about the fact that this dance was just an act we were playing in front of his family.

Because for those brief seconds, as I relaxed into Julien's arms and let him twirl me around the patio, it felt real.

It felt as if *this* was supposed to be my life…my *destiny.*

But as the song carried on and each verse brought us closer to the time when this dance would end, when we would go to bed, when I would wake up in the morning and leave this vineyard never to see Julien or his family ever again, I realized I didn't want it to end.

Not the song. Not this moment. Not my time here.

Julien nudged his scruffy cheek against mine. "What are you thinking about?"

I shook my head in an attempt to cast off the feelings that had, in an instant, lodged themselves deep into my being, refusing to leave. But with each sway of our hips, each squeeze of Julien's hands on my waist, each lustful gaze he threw my way, the layers upon layers of armor I'd wrapped myself up in since the death of my mother began to peel away. And all that was left was the truth.

Instead of being messy, Julien's five o'clock shadow was suddenly sexy. His strong arms wrapped around me were comforting, and I knew that if I slipped, his arms would catch me. He would make sure I didn't fall.

It's what he'd always done for his family. And it's what he'd done for me for the past three days. He'd made sure I was okay. Made sure I didn't fall. And he hadn't even known me.

"Chloe?" he asked again, jolting me from my thoughts.

"Yes?" I whispered, noticing that the rest of the family had paired up and joined us for a dance on the patio, and that they were no longer watching us.

"What were you thinking about?"

"Nothing. I mean, just that...nothing," I bumbled, my eyes avoiding his gaze, my heart plummeting to a place I didn't want it to go.

He laughed, then gave me a smile that melted my insides, right down to the core. "You know, I am going to miss you when you leave tomorrow."

Heat slithered through my body as he tightened his arms around my waist, pulling me in until our noses touched.

I couldn't respond. I couldn't move. I just swayed back and forth in his arms, his penetrating brown eyes burning right through me, our lips so close I could've fainted.

Julien cupped my chin in his palm, then lifted my face to meet his.

And before I had a chance to reason or to rationalize, Julien's soft, full lips were on mine.

I closed my eyes as I leaned into his kiss, the stubble on his face brushing against my skin, his breath hot and heavy, his hands now gripping my waist. And just when I expected him to pull away and to whisper in my ear that this was all for show, that he didn't really mean it, his lips pressed harder, more forcefully into mine. His hands trailed up from my waist to my shoulders, and finally he laced them around the back of my neck as he pushed his firm body into my pulsating chest, making me throb, making me ache in places I hadn't felt in years...or maybe ever.

Our lips parted, but he kept his hands intertwined around my neck, our noses still touching, his gaze buried in mine.

"Are you still thinking?" Julien whispered.

I shook my head, unable to speak.

But I *was* thinking. I was thinking about how that had been the most electrifying kiss I'd ever had. And that when I flew home the next day to commit to a lifetime with Paul, I would never experience anything like this ever again.

But to be more specific, that I would never experience any*one* like Julien again. Because for all of the reasons I'd loved Paul, he was Julien's polar opposite.

Julien opened his mouth to say something but I lifted my fingers to his lips. "Shhh." I pressed my cheek into his, our bodies still moving in synch as a slow song now filled our ears. I didn't want to hear whatever he had to say. Because whatever it was, I knew I couldn't handle it right now.

We danced in silence amid the company of Julien's family, the swirly pink sky fading to a deep night blue, clusters of twinkling stars surrounding the boasting full moon overhead. And there it was again—the lavender and the rosemary.

I wondered if my mom was here, with me, right at that moment. And if she was, would she tell me to fly home the next day and marry Paul?

Or would she tell me to trust this overwhelming feeling in my gut that I didn't quite understand yet, and stay here, in Julien's arms, for as long as I could?

TWENTY-ONE

The dance had ended, Julien's family members had left, and the wind had picked up, bringing with it a chill that snapped me back to reality.

What had I just done? I was *engaged.* I'd been with Paul for eight years, and before I'd arrived in France three days ago, I'd never so much as flirted with another guy. Now here I was, dancing with this ex-con and kissing him. *Kissing him!* And in front of his entire family, no less.

Engaged or not, though, I couldn't deny the fact that I felt something brewing inside of me. Something I'd never felt before, not in all my years with Paul, or ever. Something that I hoped I could ignore when I flew home the next day and attempted to salvage my future marriage.

But as I walked into the kitchen and watched the way Julien's broad shoulders flexed as he picked up a gigantic pot and scrubbed it clean, then felt my insides melting when he flipped around and looked at me with that heavy, lust-filled daze still swimming around in his massive brown eyes, I knew *he* wasn't going to be easy to forget.

"Can I help?" I offered.

"Camille and I will take care of everything. Go relax."

"Are you sure?"

Julien shooed me toward the doorway, resting his hand on my lower back and sending tingles up my spine. "Go," he said. "Relax."

Just as I was turning around to leave, trying to calm my nerves and act normal after everything that had just happened, I caught

Camille glaring at me. She didn't say a word, but instead narrowed her eyes, then swiveled around and began scrubbing a platter so furiously I thought it would break in half.

I shuddered. Camille knew the truth. She knew I was engaged. She knew Julien and I weren't really together and that we'd just lied to her entire family. And she clearly wasn't happy about it. I couldn't blame her. If someone did this to my family, I'd be furious too.

She *didn't* know that I'd called the police and given them Claude's license-plate number, *or* that Julien had used his last favor from Guillaume on me. And as I walked out of the kitchen and headed toward the stairs, I realized Julien had been right about not telling Camille or his mother about my run-in with the law today. No need to complicate the already insane situation any further.

Just as I was halfway up the creaky staircase, Julien's mother called my name. "Chloe, is that you?"

I turned back around and found her resting on the couch in the living room, sipping a glass of water and looking through a dusty photo album.

"Come sit with me," she instructed, patting the cushion next to her.

She had such a kind air about her with those warm, brown eyes and that sweet, light voice that I couldn't help but feel a massive pang of guilt for lying to her. I reminded myself that I would be gone the next day, and that Julien would handle everything with his family. It wasn't my job.

But still, I'd lied to her. And just because I'd spent the past three days lying didn't make me any happier to be doing it.

She smiled gently as I sat down beside her. "Since I first saw you last night, I thought to myself, *There is something about this girl.* Something familiar. I could not figure it out, but I knew it right here." She placed her hand over her heart. "Do you ever get this feeling?"

I nodded and smiled, having no clue where she was going with this.

"So, I thought about it all day. Even at the hospital, I was thinking about this, about you. Wondering why I feel as though I have seen you before. But when I watched you dancing with Julien tonight, it came to me. Here, look." She tapped her finger on one of the photographs in the album that rested on her lap.

I leaned forward, wondering what Julien's mother was getting at. But my breath refused to exhale when I saw *her*.

Her green eyes danced for the camera. Her long, wavy, auburn hair blew in the breeze, the rolling hills of the vineyard just beyond her. She smiled blissfully, looking young and happy, as if life was hers to capture. As if nothing could stop her.

She was my mother, just as I remembered her when I was a little girl.

And when I noticed the woman standing next to my mom in the photograph—her short frame, wispy dark hair, big brown eyes, and a sweet grin on her face—I realized it was Julien's mother.

"The woman in the photograph is your mother, no?" Julien's mom asked, breaking me from my trance.

I lifted my eyes to hers, my breath still on hold, my heart speeding up. "Yes, that's my mom."

And then it all came flooding back to me. My mom's conversation with me right before she'd died giving birth to my youngest sister. Her trip to France. The woman she'd met, who she'd named my baby sister after.

"Is your name Magali?" I asked, still not able to wrap my head around the fact that my mother was standing in an old photograph with Julien's mother, at this very vineyard. That *this* could be the Magali she'd spoken of that day by the Potomac River, when she'd held my hand and told me that *sometimes a girl just needs to spread her wings*.

Julien's mother nodded. "Yes, I am Magali. Did she tell you about me?"

"Yes, she did. And she named my baby sister after you. Before she…"

Julien's mom covered my hand with hers. "I know, *chérie.* I know about your mother's passing."

"Oh," I said, feeling a couple of salty tears spring to my eyes. I glanced back down at the photograph. "I can't believe this is her. I can't believe she was *here*, at this vineyard, with you. That *you* are the Magali she told me about."

Julien's mother removed the photograph from the album and handed it to me. "This is for you."

"Thank you," I said as one of the tears rolled down my cheek. I continued staring at the photograph in disbelief, overwhelmed at the sight of my beautiful mother so long ago, at *Julien's home.*

"Your mother was one of the kindest, sweetest women I have ever met. We had an instant, how do you say? Connection? Yes, a connection. We became friends the minute she visited the vineyard. And she loved it here, you know. She said this vineyard was one of the most beautiful places she had ever been. She loved the wine too...yes, if I remember correctly, we drank a lot of wine during her stay here." She chuckled to herself.

"My mom stayed here, in this house?"

"Yes, at this time, Julien's father and I used to take guests. Your mother was the last person to stay with us before I had Julien."

I looked back down to the photo in my hand, and I hadn't noticed it before, but there it was. A tiny bump protruding from Magali's stomach. "You were pregnant with Julien when this photo was taken?"

"Yes." She patted her stomach. "It is hard to believe it has been over thirty-four years since this day at the vineyard. Your mother and I, we wrote letters to each other after she left France. I heard about her marriage to your father, and all about you." Her eyes lit up then as if she'd remembered something else. "You know, I still have them. The letters."

"Really?" My hands shook at the thought of touching a letter my mom had written so long ago.

"Yes, I had forgotten about them. About our letters. It has been so many years. But I think I know exactly where they are. Come, I will show you."

I followed Julien's mother back into a small office, where she opened up a rickety filing cabinet and pulled out an old shoebox. She sifted through it for a few moments, when finally she produced an old, folded piece of paper and smiled.

"*Voilà.*" She handed the letter over to me. "There are more in here, I know it." As she kept digging through the box, I took a deep breath and gazed down at the letter.

My mother's loopy handwriting popped right off the page, just as it always had, making me remember her soft, pale hands and her warm, bubbly personality.

Dear Magali,

Ça va? *Okay, I know I'm terrible, but that is still the extent of my French. I'm so glad you speak English, otherwise our beautiful friendship wouldn't be the same. I'm writing to tell you that just three weeks ago, I gave birth to my precious Chloe. I never knew I could love anyone so much until I set eyes on her. She is an angel, Magali. I hope you get to meet her someday. You were right, being a mother is the greatest gift I could ever imagine.*

I hope your little Julien is doing well, and I look forward to the day when I can bring my baby girl to your magical vineyard, my favorite place in all the world, and she and Julien can play together (while we enjoy a bottle of your amazing wine, of course!).

Bisous *to you and Jacques, and* à bientôt,

Claire

I blinked back more tears as I gazed down at my mother's words. This was unbelievable. Unfathomable.

My mother had wanted to bring me here, to this exact vineyard.

And here I stood, seventeen years after she'd gone.

I looked to Magali, my eyes glazed over, lost in thought, in memories, and in the gravity of what this all could mean.

Magali regarded me softly, then reached out and wiped a tear from under my eye before handing me the stack of letters. "Claire would have wanted you to have these." Then she took my hand in hers and squeezed it. "I have never seen my son happier than when he danced with you tonight. We have your mom to thank for bringing you to us."

My lips formed a shaky smile as I stood there with Julien's mother, suddenly feeling overwhelmed with gratitude for her kindness, for the way she'd brought me this gift from my mother so many years after she'd gone.

But then my stomach turned when I remembered I was lying to Magali, allowing her to believe that her son and I were a couple, that I would be staying in their lives.

And I couldn't do it anymore.

"Magali, there's something you need to know." I gripped the letters and wiped the lingering tears from my cheeks.

"Yes?" she said, her gaze still soft and warm, making my heart sink even further.

"I'm engaged to someone else back in the States. Julien and I… we aren't really a couple. I'm so sorry for not telling you the truth."

She arched her eyebrow, just like Julien always did, the kindness in her eyes dissipating. Then she reached for my hand and turned it over, revealing the diamond engagement ring I'd been hiding all evening. "I see." Her face drooped in disappointment. "I suppose Julien knows about this?"

I nodded and stared down at the floor, unable to face her a moment longer. "Yes, he knows."

"Who knows what?"

I turned around to find Julien staring at the old letters in my hands, the lines in his forehead revealing his confusion.

"I know that you have not been telling me the truth about your relationship with Chloe," Magali responded, her voice not as soft and warm as it had been just moments before.

"*Maman—*" Julien began, but Magali held a hand up to quiet him.

"I have no idea why you would lie to me about such a thing, but I am too tired and have been through too much this week to worry about it. Julien, if you have feelings for Chloe, like I suspect you do after watching you dance with her tonight, don't be a coward. And Chloe, my dear, engaged or not, there is a reason your mother brought you here. I do not believe in coincidences."

And with that, she let out a little huff and left us alone in the office.

I felt like a little girl who had just been caught kissing a boy in the coatroom at school. Except that I was an adult, and I'd lied to a woman who'd just lost her husband, who'd been friends with my mother no less, and I felt horrible.

"What are these?" Julien reached for the letters in my hand.

I didn't want to tell him what they were. I just wanted to let myself believe that my mother coming to the vineyard all those years ago *was* a big coincidence. One of those crazy, freak things that could never be explained, but that also carried no real significance.

"Chloe?" he prodded, taking the letters from me. "What are these?"

"They're…they're letters from my mom."

"To you?"

"No, they were written a long time ago, to *your* mother. It turns out our moms were friends." I handed him the photograph.

"She looks just like you." Julien was breathless, his eyes fixated on the photo. "Is this why you told my mom the truth about us?"

"I couldn't lie to her anymore. It felt wrong to let her believe that you and I were together, and that the fact that my mom visited the vineyard so long ago has anything to do with why I'm here now."

"Do you honestly believe this is just a coincidence?"

I thought of how I'd felt my mother's presence so strongly since I'd first stepped foot on this vineyard. How her unmistakable scent had come to me several times in the past twenty-four hours, when in all the time I'd lived just a stone's throw from where she'd raised me in DC, I'd never felt her in this way. But I couldn't admit that to Julien. Because if my mother really had brought me here, if it really had been her presence I'd felt, then what did that mean for my life back at home?

"I mean, sure, it's crazy that our mothers knew each other," I said, trying to sound convincing, trying to believe my own words, "but it doesn't mean anything."

Julien laid the letters down on the desk and took a step closer to me. I could smell his warm, musky scent, feel his hot breath on my lips. "Chloe, tonight, when we were dancing, when I kissed you, you cannot tell me you did not feel what I felt."

I avoided his sultry gaze and fidgeted with my hands, keeping a firm distance between us. "It was just an act, to make your family believe we were together. You didn't feel anything, and neither did I."

Julien stepped an inch closer, his chest meeting my nervous hands. "Stop lying, Chloe."

I lifted my eyes to his for a brief second, and something about the way he looked at me made my legs feel like they were going to collapse beneath me. I had to get out of here.

"I can't do this," I said, pushing past him.

I ran down the hallway and out the back door, letting it slam behind me. Sucking the balmy night air into my lungs, I skimmed over the grass toward the table where Julien's family had sat just hours before. I plopped down in one of the chairs to catch my breath, noticing how quiet and empty it seemed now without the passing of wine bottles, the incessant French chatter, the laughter that had filled up the night air like a song.

But before I had a chance to process the confusion swimming around in my head, to gather some sort of clarity from this inconceivable situation, the back door clattered behind me.

I didn't need to turn around. I knew it was Julien. I'd known he would come out here for me, that he wouldn't let me get away so easily. And while part of me wanted him to turn back around and leave me alone, I couldn't ignore the other part of me—the part that wanted him to be near me, to never leave my side.

Julien stood before me, his head blocking the iridescent moon that shone over the dark vineyard. "Walk with me," he instructed, nodding toward the vines.

And so I stood on wobbly legs and followed him down the path in silence, the night breeze whistling through the vines to either side of us. I wasn't sure why I stood. Why I followed him. But with my mind an eternal pool of unanswered questions, it was all I could do.

"Tonight was not fake." Julien's firm voice cut through the silence. "It was not, as you said, an *act*."

"Well then, what was it?" I asked, not sure I was strong enough to hear the answer.

"It was real, Chloe. I know this is fast, and it is not the way you are used to things happening, but I have feelings for you."

I swallowed hard and picked up my pace. "You're crazy, Julien. We've only known each other for a couple days. There's no possible way you could have real feelings for me. And even if you *think* you do, I'm getting married Saturday, so it doesn't matter anyway." I pulled away from him, my hands trembling, my cheeks as hot as a chili pepper.

"Chloe, this thing with your mother, it means something. You can't deny that. It's not a coincidence that we met. I know you think it is impossible to fall for someone so quickly, but you're all I can think about. And I don't want this to end."

I kept walking ahead of Julien, not sure what I felt, what I believed, or what I should say. This was all too crazy. My life wasn't like this. It was orderly, stable, planned. And Julien was the exact opposite of all of those things. He was unpredictable and dangerous. And being with him made me feel volatile and out of control, made me do things that just three days ago, I never would've dreamed of doing.

"Do you love him?" Julien called out to me, his footsteps following closely behind.

"What do you know about love?" I called over my shoulder. "You're an ex-con, for God's sake. You're an expert at fooling people, and apparently, you even know how to fool yourself!"

"I'm not fooling anyone," Julien said, falling into step next to me. "You are the one who is afraid to admit that you are about to marry a man you are not in love with."

"You have no idea what you're—"

But before I could finish my sentence, Julien's strong hands planted firmly on my shoulders. He flipped me around to face him, and the look in his eyes stopped me cold. It was the same look he'd given me earlier in the night, right after he'd kissed me—a mixture of passion, of lust, of need.

He moved closer, not giving me time to finish my sentence, to catch my breath, to list all the reasons why he needed to leave me alone this instant. He grabbed the sides of my face and pressed his firm, rock-hard body up against mine, making my breath plummet through my chest.

Then his thick, moist lips hovered over mine for a few seconds before he covered my mouth with his, a burst of passion so strong I couldn't have stopped it if I tried.

And as I found myself kissing him back, my fingers running through his hair, goose bumps forming on my skin as he ran his hands down the front of my chest, over my trembling stomach, and then stopping at my waist, I realized I didn't want to stop him.

Because nothing—and I mean *nothing*—in my life had ever felt so good and so *bad* all at the same time.

Julien pulled his lips from mine, our heavy, hot breath filling up the space between us. I gazed into his eyes, my head dizzy with desire. My body ached to let him take me, right here in this vineyard, to make me forget about the fact that I had to leave this house in less than twelve hours, that I was about to fly home and…oh, God, *get married*.

As Julien's hungry lips plunged down my neck and made their way to the top of my chest, his hands roaming down to my hips and eventually to that space in between my thighs, I felt my engagement ring on my left hand.

What was I doing?

I thought of Paul, back home. Of how angry he'd been on the phone with me earlier. Of how I'd been lying to him, deceiving him. It wasn't fair, not to Paul or to Julien.

I couldn't do this. I couldn't.

"We have to stop," I told Julien, a mixture of relief and regret engulfing me as the words escaped from my lips. But Julien kept kissing me, kept touching me, kept making me want to forget I had a life before I met him.

"Julien," I said more forcefully. "Stop."

He lifted his face to meet mine but kept his muscular arms wrapped around me, his breath fast, his eyes not hiding their disappointment.

"I'm sorry. I can't do this."

Julien stepped back, separating our heated bodies, then wiped his brow with his forearm, revealing a wrinkle of frustration. "No, I am the one who should be sorry."

He turned on his heel, but stopped and rushed back up to me. "No, I take it back. I am not sorry. I know I have made mistakes in the past. For many years I lived my life as a dishonest person. But this is the one thing in my life I am not sorry for. I'm not sorry for kissing you in the hotel when I first saw you, for spending all of these days with you, for dancing with you, and for kissing you tonight. There is nothing to be sorry for when what I feel is real. When you make me feel things I have never felt for any other woman."

I stood with my lips parted, unable to speak, unable to move. No one had ever said anything like that to me before. Not even Paul.

"So just answer the question," he said. "Do you love him?'

I wanted to tell him that yes, I loved my fiancé. And that kissing Julien earlier tonight and letting myself get carried away again just now was all just a big mistake. A fling we would both forget about as soon as I stepped foot on the train the next morning and left France for good.

But I couldn't bring myself to say it.

"I'm going home tomorrow. I don't have a choice."

"You always have a choice," he said.

"What? You want me to cancel my wedding? To break up with the man I've been with for eight years for someone I've only known for a couple days? For someone who has spent the majority of his life lying and stealing from people to make a living?" I regretted the words as soon as they'd left my lips. Julien wasn't that person anymore, and I knew that. But it didn't matter. I was engaged, and I was going home. I couldn't consider whatever it was Julien wanted me to do.

I forced myself to keep the coldness in my eyes, even though inside I was crumbling.

"I love Paul," I said, my voice shaking. "And I'm marrying him this weekend."

Julien flinched, his eyes searching mine.

But when I held firm and didn't take back what I'd just said, Julien's brown gaze turned bitter, the corners of his mouth falling.

"Fine," he said. He turned his back to me, leaving me alone among the vines, my hands trembling, blood coursing through my veins.

And as I watched his broad shoulders disappear from under the moonlight, I realized that Julien was right.

I did have a choice.

I just hoped I was making the right one.

TWENTY-TWO

I woke alone in Julien's bed the next morning. I'd lain awake for what felt like hours the night before, staring up at the ceiling, thinking about the things Julien had said to me, about my mother, about Paul. Hoping that when I arrived home, I would forget about everything that had happened at the vineyard, be able to salvage my engagement, and move on with the life I'd always planned for.

But as I climbed out of bed, my head throbbing from all the wine—and from all the drama—the day before, my stomach dropped as soon as I noticed that Julien's side of the bed still hadn't been touched.

I headed toward the shower, determined to wash off Julien's intoxicating scent, which still lingered on my skin, a reminder of his touch...and of how I'd enjoyed it. And as I stood underneath the stream of steaming-hot water, I closed my eyes and told myself that I was making the right choice. That Paul was the man I loved. That marrying him and keeping my life plan intact was the right thing to do. I just had to get through one last car ride with Julien, and then I would be free of everything that had happened over the past few days.

And relief would surely come after I said good-bye to Julien for good.

After toweling off, changing into the clothes Julien had bought for me, and using his thin black comb to work through my long, wavy hair, I opened the bathroom door to find Julien sitting shirtless on his bed, slamming his cell phone shut and mumbling furiously under his breath.

When our eyes met, he clamped his mouth shut, a heavy silence settling between us in the small bedroom. The passionate spark in his eyes had disappeared. All that remained was anger.

"Is everything okay?" I asked, immediately realizing what a stupid question that was. Of course things weren't okay. He probably wished I would walk the thirty miles to the train station so he didn't have to look at me for another second.

He stood and threw the phone onto the desk so hard I was surprised it didn't break. "Yes, everything is fine."

In silence, I packed up the shopping bag of items I'd collected over the past few days—new clothes, lingerie, letters, and the photograph of my mother. But when Julien slammed his closet door and muttered something under his breath, I stopped. "What's going on? Did something just happen?"

"It is nothing." He threw a dark-gray T-shirt over his head and grabbed his pack of cigarettes off the desk.

"Well, it's obviously something. What's going on?"

"It is nothing for you to worry about. Just get ready so we can leave for the train station." His voice was so cold and hard, I almost didn't recognize it.

"Does it have to do with me leaving today? With the passport or anything?"

"No," he snapped, his eyes full of rage. "Your passport is fine. Everything for you is fine. Guillaume called. Claude's been arrested."

My initial urge was to jump up and down—that heartless thief was finally going to get what he deserved. But when Julien's jaw tightened and I noticed the way his eyes weren't filled only with anger, but also with worry and sadness, I remembered the painting.

I sat down on the bed, letting the clothes fall into a heap at my feet. If I hadn't called the police with Claude's license-plate number, this wouldn't have happened. "I'm sorry," I said softly.

"Don't apologize," he snapped, pacing back and forth in front of the window, wringing his hands together. "You have nothing to do with this."

"Did Guillaume say anything about the painting? Are they looking for it?"

He stopped pacing and glared at me. "Like I said, you have nothing to do with this anymore. It is my problem to deal with. I will be waiting outside whenever you are ready."

Julien's harsh tone made me flinch. And as I sat alone on his bed, watching him storm out of the bedroom, my heart sank. If Julien didn't find that painting, his family was going to be ruined. And I'd always know *I* played a part in that.

And as if that wasn't enough, I'd hurt Julien. While three days ago, his feelings wouldn't have mattered to me in the least, now, after everything we'd been through together, and especially after yesterday, I did care. I cared more than I wanted to admit to myself, or to him.

But there was nothing I could do anymore. He was right—it wasn't any of my business. I'd chosen Paul, so what right did I have to probe into his family's problems? I'd done enough damage.

I finished packing up my bag, then walked outside, where Julien was sitting on the front stoop, smoking a cigarette.

"I'm ready," I said, wishing he wouldn't turn around. Wishing I didn't have to face him again.

He smashed his cigarette into an ashtray and stood without saying a word.

The only sounds accompanying our awkward walk to the car were the crunching of our shoes on the gravel, the birds singing their merry little tune, and the *whoosh*ing of the leaves overhead as the wind picked up.

With my hand on the car door, I took one last look at the vineyard. But before I allowed myself to feel all of the mixed emotions that threatened to engulf me as I left this gorgeous place, this place my own mother had loved, this place where I had officially cheated on my fiancé, I squeezed my eyes closed and reminded myself that it didn't matter what I was feeling or what had happened here, because it was time to go home and face the music. And things would feel right again when I arrived in DC and worked things out with Paul. I knew they would.

My stomach tightened as I climbed into the car with Julien, and as he started up the engine without looking at me, without saying a word, I rolled down the window and turned my head completely away from him. I didn't want to think about the way it made me feel to be sitting so close to him, not talking, not bickering, not seeing his dimple press into his scruffy cheek each time he smiled.

When I thought about the fact that this silent, uncomfortable car ride would be the last time I would ever see Julien, the last chance I'd ever have to speak to him, a knot the size of a golf ball formed in my throat. I didn't want to end it like this. But there was nothing left to say.

A half hour later, Julien swerved the car into a parking spot on a crowded street in Lyon. He pointed out the window. "There is the station. You are okay to go in on your own?"

I nodded, feeling my heart sink. "Thank you for finding a way to get me home." I searched his brown eyes for the warmth I'd found in them the night before.

But that warmth, that spark, that passion—it had all disappeared.

I rested my hand on the door handle and told myself to just get up and walk away. It was time to go home. Julien was finished with me, and rightfully so. I'd rejected him. And he had more important problems to deal with.

Plus he'd lied to me. Claude hadn't infiltrated the police. And Julien wasn't a government agent. He was an ex-con. A man who *used* to be exactly like Claude.

It was time for me to go home to my stable, anti-drama fiancé.

So I tore my eyes from Julien's, opened the door, and stepped out onto the bustling sidewalk, wishing I didn't feel like my heart was tearing in half. Because, after all, *I* was the one who was choosing to leave.

I stood at the car door, motionless, my feet like lead on concrete. "Good-bye, Julien," I said softly.

"Bye, Chloe," he said, the tone of his voice just gentle enough to make me want to tell him how much I knew I was going to miss him.

But I didn't tell him. I didn't say anything.

Instead, I closed the car door, turned around, and walked away from him, trying to convince myself that once I got home, once I saw Paul, I would know I'd made the right decision.

Later, as the train pulled away from the station, I watched a couple on the platform kissing each other good-bye until they became just specks through the window. Just like one of Julien's paintings.

When they finally disappeared from my sight, my stomach turned and my heart ached. I wanted to run to the front of the train and tell them to stop and go back.

As much as I knew I should want to go home right now, I couldn't deny the overwhelming feeling in my gut telling me that I didn't want to leave Julien. I didn't want my time in France to be over.

But whatever had begun with Julien back at the vineyard was over now.

And as the train rumbled down the tracks, speeding away from Julien so rapidly, so abruptly that I could hardly breathe, I closed my eyes and tried to focus on the next big thing—going home.

My breath failed me at the thought of seeing Paul, of trying to work things out with him after everything that had happened... after I'd let myself have feelings for and even *kiss* another man. Oh, God, just remembering Julien's lips, his hands, his...okay, I had to stop.

Focus, Chloe. Focus.

I needed a game plan. I needed to figure things out *before* my plane landed in DC, otherwise the chaos would surely spiral and end in complete disaster.

The problem was, I was so utterly confused—about Paul, about Julien, about my mother, about *everything*—that I didn't even know where to start.

So I just didn't. I didn't start. Instead I spent the entire two-hour train ride staring out the window, watching the sun rise higher in the sky, its rays beaming down on the lush, rolling French countryside. I didn't think about the fact that I didn't like where this train was taking me, that I felt sick at the thought of facing Paul, that I felt more worried about how Julien would get the painting back than how I was planning on handling things when I got home.

Instead I forced myself to think of nothing. Because I knew that in twelve hours, when Paul put the events of the past four days under a microscope and dissected them to the point of exhaustion—the way he always did with his cases at the firm—the peace and the calm that I'd found at Julien's vineyard, and in this French countryside just beyond my window, would be lost.

I just hoped it wouldn't be lost forever.

TWENTY-THREE

When the Washington monument came into view from my cramped seat on the plane, I felt as if I'd been transported into another world over the course of the past twelve hours.

Everything had gone just as Julien had promised—there'd been a man in a black suit waiting for me at the train station in Paris. He'd handed me an envelope containing a passport, which had gotten me straight through customs without so much as a second look.

But now, all of that felt light-years away. And as we flew over the place I'd called home for my entire life, the scary feeling that I was now in foreign territory planted itself in my psyche and refused to leave.

I can do this, I repeated to myself as I exited the baggage claim area and searched the crowd for a face I recognized. *It will all be okay. I will feel better the minute I'm back with my family, and back with Paul.*

"Chloe!"

I flipped around to see where Sophie's voice had come from, and there she was, with her long golden-brown hair stretching all the way down her back, but her usual breezy California smile was missing. Standing on either side of her were my two youngest sisters—Lily, the twenty-three-year-old blonde, blue-eyed beauty; and Magali, the only one who'd inherited my father's olive complexion and dark hair. And at seventeen years old, she still looked like a baby to me.

They waved at me in unison, their faces panicky and distraught.

Here we go.

"Oh, my God, Chloe," Lily started before I'd even had a chance to say hello. "What the *hell* is going on?"

"It's not true, is it?" Magali piped up. "That you were involved in some kind of…" She leaned forward and whispered loudly in my ear, so loud that everyone around us could surely hear. "Some kind of *scam*? With a pair of French *thieves*?"

"And that they stole all of your things? And that your bank account is screwed?" Lily added, her crystal-blue eyes widening in horror.

"Why didn't you tell me any of this when we talked?" Sophie demanded, her voice a pitch higher than normal. "Paul is losing his shit, and Dad is going out of his mind. And I've been worried sick! I told Paul you were probably kidnapped because you, of all people, would *never* get wrapped up in something so out of control, so crazy."

"Okay, okay!" I shouted over them to no avail as we headed toward the parking garage. "One question at a time."

But they didn't miss a beat. They trailed alongside me, bickering over each other and shooting questions at me like rapid fire, unable to comprehend that Chloe, their big sister, who'd basically acted as their mother—their responsible, understanding, grown-up mother—could ever have been involved in exactly what I'd been involved in.

I stopped abruptly and turned to face them. "Shut up!" I cried, registering the immediate shock on their faces. "Just shut up. You're all driving me crazy. How about instead of grilling me and acting like a bunch of maniacs, *you* be the calm ones for once! How about asking me if I'm okay?"

"Well, are you? Okay, I mean?" Lily asked as she spun one of her long blonde locks around her finger, the way she'd always done as a little girl when she was in trouble.

"Yes, I'm as okay as I can be after…never mind. Let's just get to the car."

Sophie pointed straight ahead at a black BMW.

I turned to her. "Paul let you take his car?"

Her eyes darted to the ground as she charged ahead. "Well, he wasn't exactly in the best mood today, and he was locked up in his office when I needed to leave to pick you and Lily up at the airport, so I just took the keys."

"Why didn't you take my car instead?"

She shrugged as she unlocked the doors.

"Hand me the keys." I thrust my open palm at her.

"Why? What's wrong with me driving?"

"Paul's already not going to be happy that you took his car without asking, so it's best if I drive it."

"At the moment, he's happier with me than he is with you, so you might as well let me drive."

"Sophie," I growled as I climbed into the driver's seat and threw my shopping bag at her feet in the passenger's side.

Sophie lifted the bag up onto her lap and peered inside. "Is this all you have with you?"

"So it's true then? They did steal your stuff?" Magali asked, her choppy dark hair swishing against my seat as she popped her head in between me and Sophie.

I sighed as I checked the rearview mirror and pulled out of the parking lot. "Yes, it's true. And it's not *they*. It was just one man who stole my things."

"Oh, my God. What is *this*?" Sophie screeched.

I glanced to the side, only to find Sophie dangling my raspberry bra and panty set in front of my face.

"Put that back!" I yelled.

"Is this even *yours*?" she asked. "You never wear stuff like this."

"How do you know?"

Giggles erupted from the backseat.

"What's so funny?" I asked as I sped away from the airport.

"Chloe, seriously. *You* wear something this sexy? Not in a million years," Sophie said.

When I didn't respond, she kept digging through the bag.

"Sophie, what are you, like ten years old? *Stop* looking through my things," I said, clenching the steering wheel so hard my knuckles turned white.

"How did you buy this if that thief stole your wallet?" she asked, her voice just a pitch too high for me to stand.

"Sophie, seriously, I'll tell you guys everything that happened. Just put my stuff back."

"Fine." She put the bra back in the bag and plopped it down at her feet. "So, answer the question. How did you buy the lingerie?"

"Someone gave it to me," I said, feeling my face flush as I remembered Julien pressed up against me in the dressing room of the lingerie store.

"Who?" Lily screeched, leaning over Sophie's shoulder.

"A guy named Julien."

"You let a random French man buy you lingerie?" Magali asked, her hazel eyes widening to the size of quarters in the rearview mirror.

"No, he wasn't a *random* French man. He was the brother of the guy who stole my things."

"Oh, my God," Lily said. "He's a thief too, though, isn't he? You let a French thief buy you lingerie?"

"Why are your cheeks turning red?" Magali asked as she stared me down in the mirror.

"They're not red," I replied as calmly as I could, feeling my skin heat up to the temperature of the broiling sun.

I floored the gas, wishing I could jump out of the car and avoid all of their questions. God, this was much worse than I'd thought it would be.

"They're totally red," Lily said.

"Did you *like* this guy?" Sophie asked.

"I needed some clean underwear," I snapped. "Remember? All of my things were stolen?"

"Is he cute?" Magali asked.

"Okay! Enough. Can you all just calm down and stop firing questions at me? I just got off a plane from France, I'm exhausted, my life is a mess, and the three of you aren't helping!"

Silence comforted me for about ten seconds before Magali piped up again from the backseat. "But we don't understand what's going on. Can you just explain it to us?"

With my head spinning and my eyes trying desperately to focus on the highway, I sighed. "Fine. But no more questions. Just listen, okay?"

"Okay," my sisters said in unison.

It didn't matter how old they were now, when they were all together, they still reminded me of the same little girls they were after my mom had died.

I told them the whole story, just as I'd told it to Paul, leaving out the details that were still reeling in the forefront of my mind—like the way Julien had kissed me the night before and the way I'd felt when I'd walked away from him this morning, as if I was leaving a part of myself in that car with him, and I wasn't sure if I'd ever get it back. I also left out the details about our mom, and thankfully Sophie had stopped looking through my shopping bag before she'd found the letters or the photo.

I focused on the facts. Claude stole my passport. I followed Julien—the *supposed* undercover agent—to get it back. I found out Julien was really Claude's brother and an ex-con himself, then I called the police after Claude showed up. Julien's other brother—the *real* government agent—got me off the hook, and now everything was going to be fine.

But as I pulled into my driveway, turned off the car, and swiveled around to look at my three sisters, they just stared at me, their eyes agog, their mouths hanging open.

"What?" I asked. "Stop looking at me like that. I told you all what happened. Now let's go inside and move on. We have a wedding to deal with."

"Move on?" Sophie's dark-blue eyes fixated on me. "Are you serious? You have a bag full of French lingerie from the guy you've just spent the past four days with, and just the mention of his name, *Julien*, makes your cheeks blush. You didn't give us any of the details. The *juicy* details. Come on, Chloe, this is the first time, like *ever*, that you've had something interesting happen to you."

"What do you mean by that?"

"Nothing. Just that your life is really...you know."

"Oh, just spit it out, Sophie," Lily chimed in from the backseat. "It's boring!"

I flipped my head around and glared at my pale, blonde sister, her blue eyes suddenly not so innocent.

"So give us the rest of the story," Sophie prodded.

"There is no rest of the story. I told you everything that happened, and now it's time to go inside, back to what you all apparently think is my *boring* life."

Sophie grabbed my arm. "You've always been a horrible liar. What happened with this guy?"

"Nothing happened, Sophie. Let go of me."

"Are you and Paul going to be okay?"

Before I had a chance to come up with an answer, her cell phone rang.

I snatched my bag from Sophie's hands and climbed out of the car, my feet heavy on the pavement, my body limp and exhausted from all of the arguing, all of the lying. Things were usually the other way around with my sisters and me. *They* were the ones calling *me* with their dramatic episodes, and I was the one asking the questions, offering advice, fixing whatever needed to be fixed.

They weren't used to being in the position of caretaker, because they'd never had to be. I'd taken over for my mom right where she left off, determined not to let our little family disintegrate into a million pieces after our lifeline, our strong post, our mother, was taken from us so suddenly.

I stopped on the walkway and stared up at the faded redbrick town house where I'd lived with Paul for the past year, watching as a massive black rain cloud loomed over the roof, threatening to heave pellets of cold water on the place I'd thought I would call home for a long time to come. Closing my eyes, I realized that I was right back where I'd been when I was twelve—on the cusp of another family disintegration. Except this time, even at twenty-nine years old, after years of counseling, fixing, and planning everyone else's lives, I hadn't a clue what to do to prevent *my life* from spiraling into oblivion.

"Chloe," Sophie called out just as I had convinced myself to unlock the front door. "It was Dad on the phone. He's at Maggiano's up on Wisconsin Avenue with Paul and his parents. They're waiting for us for dinner."

"Don't say a word about anything I told you in the car or about what you found in my bag," I instructed my sisters as the four of us bounded into Maggiano's, the massive, family-style Italian restaurant where Paul's parents always insisted on taking us each time they came into town.

"*Obviously.* We're not idiots, Chloe," Magali said. I could tell by her teenage, know-it-all tone that she'd probably just rolled her eyes at me, but I couldn't deal with her right now. I couldn't deal with any of them. I was about as hyped up as a cat being ported off to the vet for its yearly vaccinations, except that in this case, I'd rather take the needles. Anything would be better than facing Paul for the first time in this huge, sterile restaurant in front of my dad, my sisters, and much, much worse—in front of my future in-laws. Well, my potential future in-laws. Ugh.

The smell of lasagna and tomato sauce should've come as a comfort to my empty stomach, but instead it made me feel nauseous. We trailed behind the overly bubbly hostess as she weaved us through swarms of crowded tables, the laughing and the banter shooting through my ears like a car alarm in the middle of the night. I needed to talk to Paul in the quiet of our home. Alone. Not in this zoo of a restaurant.

And before I could stop it, there he was. There was Paul.

He stood when he saw us approaching and a generic, tight smile washed over his pale face. I tried to smile, tried to appear normal. But as Julien's warm, goofy grin, his dimple, and his smiling brown eyes flashed through my mind, the corners of my mouth just wouldn't budge.

Paul, being the polite, well-mannered man he'd always been, walked up to me and kissed me on the cheek, though I couldn't help but notice the way his chilly gaze avoided mine and the awkward manner in which he held his hands at his sides, not sure if he even wanted to touch me.

Julien's words from the night before made an unwelcome appearance in my already dizzy head as I circled the table to greet Paul's parents.

You always have a choice.

I'd made my choice. So why didn't this feel right?

"So how's our bride-to-be holding up?" Paul's father, James, bellowed above the restaurant clatter.

"Oh, just fine," I murmured, trying to keep my voice steady as I leaned down to hug Patricia, Paul's mother.

She gave me her usual air peck before smiling awkwardly, the way she always did when anyone, even her own son, embraced her.

I sat down in between Paul and my big bear of a father, his gray hair in desperate need of a haircut, his belly a little larger than the last time I saw him. "Hi, Dad," I said wearily, trying to ignore the way the lines on his forehead pressed together, a telltale sign of the anxiety he'd carried around with him ever since my mother had died, which was no doubt flaring up in full force this week.

He leaned toward me, the smell of his Old Spice aftershave too strong for my weak stomach. "Jesus, Chloe. Are you trying to give me a heart attack?" he whispered in my ear.

I placed my hand on his and squeezed it with a pleading smile. "It's great to see you too, Dad."

I prayed that both he and my sisters would be capable of acting normal and keeping their mouths shut for this one night in front of Paul's parents. I knew for certain that Paul would never have told them what was going on, so if we could just get through this dinner—

"So, Chloe, Paul was just telling us that your business trip to France was extended," James said as he cut off a slice of bread and slathered a knifeful of butter onto it.

"Mm-hmm." I nodded, hoping he and Patricia hadn't seen the nervous glances my sisters were exchanging across the table.

"Horrible timing with the wedding coming up this weekend," James said. "That boss of yours sounds like a real slave driver. Good thing you won't have to put up with her for much longer."

I was just about to change the subject when I realized what James had said. I turned to Paul to find his eyes darting around the table, looking anywhere but at me.

"You quit your job?" Sophie asked as three servers arrived at our table and began setting down giant platters of fresh mozzarella, pasta, and salad.

My eyes were still glued to Paul, my words caught in my throat. But finally, I willed them to come out. "Paul, what is your dad talking about?"

He turned to me, his eyes cold. "You know, Chloe. The Pennsylvania job." Then he reached forward and dished a heaping spoonful of spaghetti onto his plate.

"You took it?" I asked, certain he would tell me that no, of course he hadn't taken the job without waiting for me to come home and talk things through. That his dad was just jumping the gun, as usual.

But instead, he nodded.

"What Pennsylvania job?" Lily asked through a mouthful of salad.

"You're moving to *Pennsylvania*?" Magali added, not hiding the disgust in her voice.

"Why didn't you tell us this?" My dad's gruff voice overpowered the servers singing an obnoxious version of "Happy Birthday" at the table next to us.

And Paul just sat there, chewing his spaghetti and slurping his ice water, like nothing had happened. Like his fiancée hadn't just returned from an insane chase through France, like he hadn't just told me the day before that he wasn't sure if he still wanted to marry me, like I hadn't just found out through his *father* that he'd taken the job in that remote town in Pennsylvania.

Suddenly my sisters, my father, and Paul's parents all began talking at once—a firing squad of questions shooting straight at my head.

And for once in my life, I didn't have the answers. I couldn't fix the problem. It was all I could do to push myself up from that table and walk blindly through the dining room and down the hallway, knocking over a tall vase of red gladiolas on my way out the door, and not stopping to apologize.

I sucked the humid evening air into my lungs as I raced down the busy sidewalk, trying desperately to find that comforting scent of lavender and rosemary I'd smelled at the vineyard.

But I couldn't. It was gone.

TWENTY-FOUR

The cab dropped me off at the only place where I knew I could find her.

I ran my hands, wet from wiping the stream of tears off my cheeks, over the engraving.

Claire Marie Turner
Beloved Mother and Wife
March 20, 1953–September 1, 1993

My shaky fingers hovered over the date we lost her, and I realized that tomorrow of all days was the first of September. It was the anniversary of the day we'd lost my mother. I'd been so consumed with my own problems that I hadn't remembered.

I didn't even feel my legs folding beneath me until my hands met the cold, wet ground. I wished the earth would swallow me whole, take me to wherever my mom was, so I could see her again. So I could tell her I was sorry I'd forgotten.

And so I could ask her *why*.

Why had the life I'd planned out so perfectly, so precisely, flipped upside down in a matter of days?

And why didn't I know what to do about it?

My back collapsed to the ground, my weary eyes gazing up at the looming, dark clouds moving swiftly overhead, still threatening to unload their heavy rain, but not willing to give in quite yet.

Was I being stubborn like those clouds, holding on to something that it was time to let go of? Hovering over those closest to me, as if *I* knew what was best for all of them, when I clearly didn't even know what was best for myself?

A big, cool drop of rain splattered on my cheek, followed by another, and another, until the drops transformed into a full-on downpour.

My heavy body sank deeper into the earth above my mother, the water washing over my face, pooling in my eyes. And I knew then, deep down, that I *had* been holding on too tightly. I'd been planning, controlling, and fixing everyone else's lives for so long that I hadn't stopped to evaluate my own. Instead, my life plan was to play it safe. Never rock the boat. Stay in control.

Paul had been part of that plan. Even back in college, when we'd first started dating, he'd been the safe bet. He'd been there to comfort me when I'd found out my boyfriend of two years had been cheating on me, and from one look at Paul—the way he combed his jet-black hair neatly to the side and always carried a ballpoint pen in his front pocket—I knew *he* would never cheat. He was stable, and after the years I'd spent steering my family to shore after the loss of my mother, I needed stability. I craved it.

And suddenly there it was. The voice I needed to hear so badly, so desperately—the voice of my mother—asking me the one question I'd been avoiding all along. The same question Julien had asked me just one night and an ocean ago.

Do you love him?

I knew the answer to that question. I *used* to love Paul. I did.

But I also knew that I wasn't *in love* with him anymore.

With the rain drenching me, and my back sinking farther into the cold, wet ground, I gripped my mother's headstone and sat up.

I'd known for years that I hadn't been *in love* with Paul.

But he was stable. And I'd clung to that stability like a life vest, thinking that without it, I would drown.

But here I was, drowning anyway.

And it was time to swim back up to the surface.

I stood in the doorway of Paul's office back in our town house in DC, my hair and my clothes sopping wet as shivers wracked my body.

Paul sat alone at his desk, staring straight ahead at the wall, his framed degree from Georgetown Law perched just above his gaze.

"We need to talk," I said as I gingerly took a seat on the couch, my body still trembling with chills.

"Where were you?" He turned to me, his expression numb, his black eyes a deep, bottomless void.

"I had to get away to think. I went to see my mom."

When he didn't respond, didn't even acknowledge my words, I pressed on. "Paul, are you happy with the life we have together?" I knew it was a loaded question, but it was one that I desperately needed to hear a true answer to.

Paul shook his head at me, his passive expression turning to frustration as he slammed his fist down on the desk. "Not right now, I'm not. No. What the hell were you thinking, storming out of dinner on my parents like that? You know I didn't tell them anything about what happened this week. The least you and your family could've done was act normal and keep your mouths shut for one fucking night."

"I'm sorry my family isn't picture-perfect like yours," I snapped, unable to mask the bitterness in my voice. "And why exactly were we even having dinner with your parents on my first night back when there are obviously bigger things we need to be dealing with, like do you even want to marry me on Saturday?"

Paul crumpled up a piece of paper in his fist and threw it at the trash can, missing by about an inch. Then he lifted his eyes to mine, a mixture of anger, hurt, and sadness passing through them. But he didn't answer me.

"Before all of this happened, before this past week, were you happy with our life together?" I pushed.

"What exactly are you getting at?"

I wrapped my arms around my chilled body, goose bumps still prickling my skin, and summoned up the courage to keep going.

"Just answer me, Paul. Was this the life you've always wanted? The two of us working nonstop, doing project after project on this town house—"

"I thought you loved the town house."

"I do, Paul. But you're missing my point. I know we've been together eight years, and I know it's normal for some of the passion—or the romance, so to speak—to die down." I locked eyes with him then, wanting to be sure he really heard me. "But was it ever really there to begin with?"

"That's what this is about? Passion? Romance? What do you think this is, Chloe? A goddamn romance novel?"

"No, Paul. I don't think our lives are supposed to mirror a romance novel. I just think that…well, we've been living like we're business partners for years now! All we do is work, fix up the house, talk about work, and talk about fixing up the house."

"Don't forget the hours—or *years,* rather—you've spent fixing your family. Maybe if you didn't spend every waking minute on the phone with your sisters and your dad, counseling them through every single crisis that comes up, there would be more time left for us."

I wanted to slap him. Tell him he had no business judging what I'd been through with my family, and the way I'd chosen to handle it.

But there was truth to what he was saying. And I couldn't deny it any longer.

"I'm sorry for the way I've let their drama overflow into my life…into *our* lives. It's all I knew how to do, though, after losing my mom."

"Chloe, your mom died like twenty years ago. Don't you think your dad and your sisters should be able to manage their own lives by now?"

"It'll be eighteen years tomorrow. And yes, they should be able to run their own lives without my constant help, and that's something I need to work on. I know that. But I love them, Paul. They're my family. They're the most important people in my life. And if we're going to get married, they're going to be your family too. I guess I always thought you'd warm up to them. Maybe even become excited at having a big, crazy family since you grew up as an only child. But I see now that that's not the case."

"Whatever," Paul mumbled, his tone like a pouty little five-year-old.

"My crazy family isn't going anywhere, Paul. And I'm not going to distance myself from them just because things get a little chaotic sometimes."

Paul huffed out another angry breath and crossed his arms over his chest. The disdain he harbored for my dad and my sisters was yet one more glaring red flag that I'd chosen to ignore for years now.

"Just answer my original question," I snapped, unable to skirt the issue at hand for another second. "Are you happy with us? With this life?"

"Why do you think I took the Pennsylvania job?"

"You think moving to the suburbs and popping out kids is going to fix this? Fix us?"

"I didn't realize we were so broken," he said coolly. "But I'm seeing pretty clearly now, after this week, that apparently there were a lot of things I didn't know about you."

I hugged my legs to my chest and felt cold drops of water slipping off the ends of my hair and sliding down my back. "I'm sorry, Paul. I'm truly sorry for everything that happened this week. I should have never lied to you. I should've told you the truth right from the beginning instead of always trying to handle everything on my own."

Paul leaned back in his chair, his mouth drawn shut, his eyes tired.

"But I need you to be honest with me," I continued. "If I had told you what really happened, right from the start, do you think you would feel any differently than you do now?"

When Paul's cool gaze leveled with mine, I finally recognized the look I'd been seeing in those dark, black eyes for months, even years. And I'd just been so good at ignoring it, so skilled in seeing only what I wanted to see, that it was as if I was seeing it for the first time.

He wasn't in love with me either.

"What do you expect me to say, Chloe? That if you'd called me right away and said, 'Hey, listen, honey, I let some French guy get me drunk last night, then I *voluntarily* brought him up to my room and passed out while he stole my things. Can you help me?' that I would've been on the first plane to France? Is that what you want me to say?"

A cold tear stung the back of my eyelid. "I told you, Paul. I was drugged. I never would've taken him to my room unless I had no idea what I was doing." But as the words flew out of my mouth, a vision of Julien's lips pressed up against mine flashed through my mind. I'd known what I was doing then, and I'd done it anyway.

"It's all too far-fetched. Ever since this happened, I just don't feel like I know you anymore," Paul said, staring past me out the window.

When my mind refused to stop thinking of Julien, I looked to the ground. "Maybe you don't."

An excruciating silence hovered over us in the small office, until, a few moments later, Paul broke it. "Is that where this is coming from? Your sudden concern with the apparent lack of romance in our relationship? Did your stint running from the cops with that ex-con make you realize you needed more *passion* in your life? More excitement?"

Paul's dry, sarcastic tone stung me to the core. But, if I was honest with myself—and with him—that was exactly what had happened.

"Don't you ever wonder if we were headed down the wrong path? If we were just working and saving and working and saving for a life that we weren't really *living*?" I asked.

"No, that's not how I feel, Chloe, or how I've ever felt. I wanted to go to law school, so I did. I wanted to become a lawyer, so I did. I wanted to get that job at the firm in Pennsylvania and move to a smaller town, so that's what I'm doing."

I could almost hear Julien's voice in my head. *Boring, boring. Where's the passion?*

And now, thousands of miles away from Julien, from all of those conversations where he'd accused me of not really being in love, of having no passion, I realized I agreed with him. Where *was* the passion?

"Paul, think back to when we first started dating, back in college. Do you remember feeling like you just had to be with me? Like you couldn't live without me?"

Paul's eyebrows knitted together in confusion.

"Was there even a spark?" I asked.

"Not all relationships have to be like that, Chloe. Some relationships are stable."

There it was again. *Stability.* My life vest.

But I didn't want it anymore. I didn't need it.

"But to sustain a marriage, there needs to be more than just stability," I said.

"It doesn't matter anymore anyway. After this past week, whatever stability we had is gone now."

"So, your mind is made up? You're moving to Pennsylvania."

"Yes, I took the job because I want to go there!" he shouted, the veins in his forehead popping out. "I thought we wanted the same things. I thought you would realize what a great opportunity this could be for us. I thought you would want a bigger home and a family, just like I did. I mean, isn't that what you do after you've been together eight years?"

"I might want all of those things...one day. But I'm not ready yet. And I told you that. I've been telling you that all along."

"Or maybe you're just not ready for those things with *me*," Paul said, his face hanging, his eyes weary and beaten down.

One lone tear rolled down my cheek. And I knew that he was right.

"I'm sorry, Paul. I'm so sorry."

He rubbed his fingers along his brow line, hiding his eyes from view for a few seconds before lifting them up to meet mine.

"So this is it, then? All these years, and this is what it comes down to?"

I couldn't answer. I couldn't even look him in the eye. I felt like I was breaking in half, and once I let him go, I wasn't sure who would be there, if anyone, to sweep up the pieces.

"What should we do then, about the wedding?" he asked, his voice deflated.

"I'll take care of it," I said. I'd canceled weddings before in my event-planning career…just never my own.

He nodded and stood up. "I'll stay with my parents for the weekend, then I'll be back next week to move my things out." His voice had switched into the same formal tone I'd heard him use with his clients over the phone.

"Okay," I said as I watched him head toward the door, feeling the urge to say something else, to keep apologizing, but knowing in my heart that I'd said enough for one night.

He turned, gave me one last tired look, then left the office. Two minutes later, the front door slammed shut, its echo sounding through the empty house.

Paul was gone, and with him, all of the stability I'd stored up for the past eight years.

I sank back into the couch and gathered up a blanket sitting next to me. I pulled it tight around my shaking arms. I hoped with every fiber in my body that I'd made the right decision, and that somehow, after this rain had finished pouring down on me, I would find the strength to pick myself back up and move on to sunnier skies.

TWENTY-FIVE

Hushed whispers filled my ears. Was I dreaming?

I rolled to the side and peeked through the unwelcome slit in my eyelids. All three of my sisters stood over me, shooting worried glances at each other.

I shut my eyes again.

"Chloe, why are you sleeping in the office? And why are you all damp?"

Sophie knelt down beside me, removing a strand of hair that had been matted to my cheek. "We couldn't find Paul anywhere," she said softly. "Did you guys talk about things last night?"

Oh, God. Last night. How was I going to tell them that the one relationship they'd been able to count on for the past eight years was officially over? That their older sister had completely lost control of her life?

Had it all really happened?

But as I remembered watching Paul's thin frame walk out the office door and hearing the front door slam shut, I knew it was real.

I pushed myself up, the lack of food in my stomach making me dizzy. And I turned to face my sisters. There was no avoiding it. No running away.

"Paul's gone. The wedding's off," I said, unable to believe the words even as they walked, mechanically, right out of my own mouth.

"The wedding's off?" Lily screeched from behind Sophie.

"Lily," Sophie hissed. "Get it together."

"Sorry," she mumbled.

I braced myself for Sophie's typical hundred and one questions as she sat down next to me.

But instead, she wrapped her arms around me and pulled me into her chest. "I'm sorry, Chloe," she said, stroking the back of my head. "I'm so sorry."

And while my first instinct was to pull away and tell her I was fine, that I could handle this, I found myself collapsing in her arms, grateful for the strength they provided on a morning when mine had been zapped.

"It's going to be okay," she said in the most soothing voice I'd ever heard come from her lips.

I laid my cheek on her shoulder and sighed. "How? How is it going to be okay? The wedding was supposed to be in two days. My life is a mess."

Sophie laid her hands on my shoulders and squared her face in front of mine. "That's why you have us. You've cleaned up our messes our whole lives. Now it's our turn."

"But you can't possibly—"

"Chloe, just stop. We'll handle everything. All we need is the list of people to call, and it's done. You're not getting on that phone today."

"Really? But what about Dad? He's going to flip out. All that money he paid, there's no way we're going to be able to get it all back."

"He'll live," Lily said, taking a step toward me. "And we'll deal with him *and* his anxiety. It's not your job today."

"Okay," I said, wondering how my sisters had grown up so much without me noticing.

"Now, come on," Sophie said, grabbing my hand and pulling me up from the couch. "You need to take a shower because you stink. What were you doing last night? Rolling around in the mud?"

Well, maybe they hadn't grown up quite that much.

After showering and eating a big plate of fluffy pancakes drowned in maple syrup that Sophie had made for me, I gave the girls the guest list and phone numbers of all 184 people, the contact information for the photographer, the videographer, the florist, the DJ, and so on. They closed themselves in the office with their cell phones without so much as a peep.

I tossed and turned in my huge, lonely bed for about a half hour, unable to think of anything but the fact that, at that very moment, per my request, my sisters were dismantling my wedding, promising friends and family members that their gifts would be returned, saying things like, "They just weren't meant to be, you know?"

But then, after a little while, after I forced myself to stop worrying about my failed wedding, a new feeling crept into my chest.

I was free.

On the plane ride home, I'd told myself over and over again that I would feel relief when I saw Paul. That I would find comfort in the stability our relationship had always provided for me.

But I hadn't felt relief or comfort. Instead, sitting at that dinner table with his uptight mother, his overbearing father, and Paul not caring that he'd just taken a job in a place I never wanted to live, I'd known that if I sat there for one more second, I would suffocate.

And now, like a storm cloud that passed through in the night and was gone by morning, that suffocating feeling had disappeared. And in its place, I found freedom.

I'd been with Paul for *so* long, and before this week, I'd never examined our relationship. I'd never stopped to think about the fact that at times, it was exhausting—*he* was exhausting. His incessant need to clean, his perfectionism, his predictability, his stability. These characteristics were originally the reasons I'd chosen to be with Paul, but now, as I lay alone in my bed, with the future a blur of the unknown, I knew that they were the last things in the world that I wanted.

Suddenly, I felt an opening in my chest, like I could breathe again. I could fill my life with whatever I wanted now. I didn't have to be limited to the kind of life I was going to have with Paul.

Just as I began to ponder what I *did* want to include in this new, untouched future of mine, which lay ahead of me like a blank page waiting to be filled up, my bedroom door creaked open. My big, burly dad filled up the doorway, the worry etched into his brow like a tattoo.

He let himself in and sat down on the edge of the bed near my feet. And just as I expected him to start in on his usual diatribe about how all of us girls were going to give him a heart attack, the wrinkles in his forehead dissipated, then he softened his brown-bear eyes and smiled at me.

"I'm so proud of you, you know that?"

"Proud?" I asked, thinking my sisters must've drugged him. I'd never seen him this calm in the face of a crisis.

"Yes, proud. I never thought Paul was the right man for you. And I know your mother wouldn't have either."

"What do you mean?"

"He just didn't make you glow."

Okay, Sophie had definitely slipped Dad whatever she used to take in college. Where was my father?

"He didn't make me *glow*?"

"Yes. Like your mother did, when we were together."

And then, before I had a chance to say anything, my dad pulled me into one of his rare embraces, the scruff on his cheek scratching against my face, his massive arms swallowing me up.

"So you're not mad? About all the money? About telling the whole family that there isn't going to be a wedding?"

My father placed his warm hands on my shoulders and smiled at me.

"Chloe, you are the most caring, responsible young woman I've ever known, and after your mother died, you sacrificed your teenage years and your young adulthood to take care of this family. When your friends were out meeting boys, having their first drink, and getting into trouble, you were home with me, taking care of baby Magali, making sure I took my anxiety meds before bed every night, waiting up with me every time Lily was late for her curfew, and flushing Sophie's pot stash down the toilet before I could find it."

I chuckled at the memories, but also felt relieved that it was all over.

My dad's voice grew softer. "But it wasn't fair to you, Chloe. You grew up too fast. You missed out on all those years of being irresponsible. Of making mistakes. Of running around and getting into trouble. Instead you were at home, saving your family. And *this*...this is the first time something has happened that you couldn't fix. So no, sweetie, I'm not angry with you. I'm angry with myself for not being a better father. For not being there for you the way I should've been."

"Dad, I—"

"No, Chloe. It's true. I haven't been the best father to you and your sisters. And you've stepped in every time I wasn't pulling my weight. But you need to know now that we're all okay. I'm okay. Your sisters are okay." My dad reached up and tucked a strand of hair behind my ear, his eyes glazing over with tears. "And it's all because of you. Your mother would be so proud of the woman you've become. But she would also want you to live your life. And as your father, that's what I'm *ordering* you to do now. Live your life, sweetie, because God knows it goes by fast, and I don't want you to spend the rest of it worrying about me. Besides, don't you know your sisters at all?" A grin popped onto his big, burly face, causing a tear to bubble down his cheek. "They get everything they want. Getting most of the wedding money back will be no exception."

I giggled and wiped a tear from my own eye as my dad pulled me into another warm embrace. "Thank you, Dad. Thank you so much."

After the tightest bear hug ever, I asked, "Why didn't you say anything to me earlier about Paul?"

"It wasn't my place."

"But you're my dad."

"You know yourself, Chloe. You had to come to this realization on your own. I have no idea how in the hell it happened, but I'm just happy it wasn't too late."

I glanced past my father to the shopping bag I'd stuffed in the corner of the bedroom—the bag that still held my mother's letters and her beautiful photo. And I realized that I hadn't exactly come to this realization *solely* on my own.

"Dad, there's something I want to show you. It might help all of this make a little more sense."

"Oh?" He arched an eyebrow, reminding me of Julien.

I lifted my exhausted body from the bed, crossed the room, and picked up the one bag I'd managed to bring back from France, hoping that maybe, *just maybe*, it held a glimpse of those sunnier days I was so desperately hoping were on the horizon.

That night, after every last call had been made, after my family had, for once, helped *me* through a crisis, instead of it always being the other way around, I stretched out on my bed and spread my mother's letters out before me.

I'd let my father read them in privacy earlier that morning, but I hadn't yet summoned the courage to read through them myself. Tonight, though, on this eighteenth anniversary of the day we'd lost her, I knew it was time. My clever mom had found a way to come back to me through these words she'd written so long ago, and I knew that somehow, wherever she was, she'd led me to this point. I only hoped her letters would give me some clarity as to where I should go next.

And so, over the next hour, I pored over my mom's bubbly, cheerful handwriting—her words making me laugh, making me cry, making me feel alive again. My mom had only been around for forty years, but she hadn't played it safe. She'd lived—*really lived.* She loved my father more than I thought anyone could ever love another person, and when my sisters and I came along, she cherished every minute with us. It was all there in her letters to Magali—she traveled, she never passed up an opportunity to have a good glass of wine, she was adventurous, and most of all, she was never afraid to take a risk.

She wouldn't have wanted me to waste my entire life playing it safe while running everyone else's lives. And that's exactly what I'd spent the past eighteen years doing.

It was time to change, time to move on. And like my dad had ordered me to do, it was time to let my sisters and my father live their own lives and fight their own battles. And it was time for me to follow a new path, because the old one wasn't looking so great anymore.

Just as I was folding up my mom's letters, being careful not to tear the thin, yellowed paper, the bedroom door swished open. My three little sisters stood in the doorway, clad in T-shirts and baggy pajama bottoms, reminding me so much of the way they used come to me when they were little, looking for a hug, a bedtime story, and comfort after Mom had gone.

But that wasn't why they were knocking on my door. They were all grown up now, and tonight, they were here for me. I smiled at them, feeling overwhelmed with warmth at how much I loved them.

The three of them shuffled into the bedroom and climbed onto the bed with me.

"We just wanted to make sure you were okay," Magali squeaked, all traces of her teenage attitude gone as her innocent hazel eyes met mine.

I reached over and squeezed her hand. "Thanks, Mags." Then I looked to all of them. "Thank you, guys, for everything."

"Well, it's not every day that your big sister calls off her wedding," Lily said.

"Hopefully, this is the last time we ever have to call off a wedding," I responded with a sigh. "*Please* don't follow my example."

"Dude, no offense, but since when have we copied anything you've done with your life?" Lily retorted.

"Very true," I said, not minding her snarky attitude after everything she'd done for me today.

"What are those?" Sophie asked, nodding toward the stack of letters in my hand.

I gazed down at the old letters filled with my mom's words, a gift that had unbelievably found its way into my hands, and I knew it was time to tell my sisters. Time to tell them the details—*the juicy details*, as Sophie had put it—of what I was beginning to see as my French adventure.

An hour later, after I'd spilled it all—from Julien kissing me in the lobby of the Plaza Athénée, to the Newlywed Romance Tour Bus, to the lingerie store debacle, to the police interrogation, to me drinking my face off in Julien's cottage after finding his paintings of couples kissing all over Paris, to our dance and our kiss under the stars, to the late-night vineyard passion, and finally to our mother's connection to this whole crazy event—the girls sat wide-eyed and silent. Silent only because I'd made them promise to keep their mouths shut until I was finished, but still, by the stunned looks on their faces, I knew they couldn't believe what I'd just told them.

After laying out this unbelievable course of events, and for once, not holding back my feelings, I realized I now wholly believed it *hadn't* been a coincidence I'd ended up at Julien's vineyard—the very vineyard my mother had visited and loved so many years ago.

I also knew now, without a doubt, that if I didn't do something about it, if I didn't follow this overwhelming urge coming both from my mother and from my own intuition to be bold and step out onto this path of the unknown, I would always regret it.

"Are we allowed to open our mouths now?" Lily asked, her clear-blue eyes still widened in shock.

I leaned back against my pillow and braced myself for their questions. Except that this time, I was ready to answer them. "Shoot," I said.

"Oh, my God. You *kissed* a French con man, *three* times, while you were engaged to Paul?" Lily shrieked as she flipped a strand of her long blonde hair off her face. "No wonder you called the wedding off! Where is my big sister? I think someone stole her and sent this slut in her place!"

"Lily!" Sophie snapped.

"I'm not saying it's a bad thing! I like this new version of Chloe. I just can't believe it, that's all."

"Was he a good kisser?" Magali asked.

"Is he still, you know, a con man?" Sophie asked.

"I bet he's hot in bed," Lily said.

"Did his breath smell?" Magali asked.

"What the hell kind of question is that?" Lily said to Magali, slapping her on the knee.

"Okay, okay," I said, quieting them down. "Yes, he was a good kisser, no his breath didn't smell, and no, he's not a con man anymore. And I wouldn't know if he's *hot* in bed because I'm not as big of a slut as you, Lily."

"Hey!" she yelled, although I could see from the gleam in her eye that she'd taken it as a compliment.

Sophie snickered. "You know it's true," she said to Lily.

"Fine. But I've never slept with a French guy. I bet they're so sexy in bed."

"Ew, Lily. You're so disgusting," Magali said.

"Can it, you two," Sophie said, giving them each the evil eye. Then she turned her attention back to me. "I can't believe everything that happened with Julien, first of all, but Mom's connection to the vineyard is just…unbelievable. Those are really her letters?"

"Mm-hmm." I held them out for Sophie to see.

"Can we read them?" Magali asked.

"Of course. She wrote about all of us, even about when she was pregnant with you, Magali. And she talks about how much she loved Dad. And how much fun they had together."

Lily turned her face toward the wall, not meeting eyes with any of us, the way she always did when she was trying not to cry.

Sophie's eyes glazed over with tears as she took the letters. "And the picture?"

I reached over to the nightstand, picked up the photograph, and placed it in the center of our little circle for my sisters to see.

We peered over in unison, gazing at our mother, in all her youth, her beauty, and her love.

Then, one by one, the girls lifted their eyes to mine, their questions gone, their bickering over.

But one question remained.

"So what are you going to do?" Sophie asked.

I grasped the photo of my mom and smiled at them—the first genuine smile I'd had since I'd arrived back in DC. "I'm going back to France."

TWENTY-SIX

Last-minute plane tickets to France were *not* cheap. But at this point, with all the money we were losing from the wedding and with half of the money in my checking account still not replaced, who even cared?

It was five a.m., the morning after The Day I Called off My Wedding, and here I was, scouring the Internet for a ticket to France with no clue what I would actually do when I arrived. I didn't have Julien's cell phone number, and even if I did, would he want to talk to me? And what would I say to him?

"Hey, Julien. I just called off my wedding *yesterday* and I know I rejected you and made you feel small and insignificant, but now I can't stop thinking about you. Sorry I screwed your family's chances at getting the painting *and* the vineyard back, and sorry about crashing the Smart car. Can I come stay for a while? Assuming you even have a house?"

No, that wouldn't do.

What if Julien didn't even want to see me? Between trying to save the property, taking care of his mother, and grieving over the loss of his father, he had enough of his own problems to deal with. He didn't need an emotional American woman hunting him down.

But when I thought back to the things he'd said to me that night at the vineyard, the way he'd looked at me, the way he'd touched me and kissed me, I was certain he'd felt the same way I did. After the way I'd left things, though, I didn't know if he'd be willing to talk to me ever again, let alone give me a second chance.

I shook my head and refocused on the computer screen. I hadn't been able to plan or control anything that had happened in France, and this was no different. If I was going to go back to see what *could* happen with Julien, then I'd just have to get on a plane and let the rest come naturally. Even if that meant getting hurt in the process.

And after calling off my wedding and ending an eight-year relationship, I couldn't go much lower, so what did I have to lose?

After about a half hour of searching, I found a one-way flight to Lyon that was as reasonably priced as it was going to get. But before booking it, I pulled up a new tab and did an Internet search for Julien's family's vineyard. And once I found it, there, at the bottom of the page, I spotted a phone number.

I reached for my phone and without thinking, without planning, without worrying, I dialed the international number.

"*Allô?*" Magali's sweet voice came through the line, immediately making my heart beat faster.

"Magali? Hi, it's Chloe."

A moment of silence followed. I really hoped she wasn't going to hang up the phone. I wouldn't have blamed her if she did.

"I thought I might be hearing from you." Magali's voice was soft and knowing, not at all full of the rage I feared.

"I made a mistake, Magali. I'm coming back. I'm coming back for Julien."

"You did not get married?"

"No, I called it off. I know now that it wasn't a coincidence that I met Julien, that I came to the vineyard, and that my mother knew you."

A soft chuckle traveled through the line. "I'm glad you see now, *chérie*, that there are no such things as coincidences. When will you be arriving?"

The tension I'd been storing in my shoulders relaxed when I realized she wasn't going to tell me that she didn't want me within a thousand miles of her son. "I'm not sure of the date yet. Probably sometime this week. Will Julien be at the vineyard?"

"I'm afraid not."

"Where is he?"

"He left this morning for Annecy. He told you about the painting, I suppose?"

"Yes, did he find it?"

"Not yet. But he found out that it is in Annecy. Exactly *where* in Annecy, he is not sure, but if I know my son, he will figure it out."

"Would you mind giving me his cell phone number?"

"Not at all," she said, and I swore I heard her smiling through the phone.

"You know," she said, after relaying Julien's number, "you are a lot like your mother."

I smiled. "Thank you, Magali. I hope to see you soon."

"Me too."

And with that, I grabbed the replacement credit card that had just come in the mail and booked a flight to Lyon that was set to leave at four p.m. I didn't care that it cost triple the price I'd originally planned on paying.

And the reason I didn't care was because I suddenly knew *exactly* where Julien would find his painting. But he would need *me* to show him the way.

TWENTY-SEVEN

"*Allô?*"

My heart threatened to pound right through my chest at the sound of Julien's voice. "Julien, it's me, Chloe."

A long pause traveled through the line. "Chloe?"

"Listen, I don't have much time to talk. I'm just leaving the airport in Lyon to catch a train to Annecy in a half an hour. You're still there, right?"

Julien paused again. *Please don't hang up,* I begged silently.

"You are here? In France?" he asked.

Just hearing Julien's deep voice again made me smile, but I couldn't ignore the dread that had coated my butterfly-filled stomach. What if I arrived in Annecy and he didn't want to see me?

I couldn't worry about that right now, though. I had to help him find the painting.

"Yes, Julien. I'm here, and I know where the painting is."

"Yes, we already know it is in Annecy, but—"

"No, I know *exactly* where it is. I need you to trust me. I'll be at the train station in Annecy at ten a.m. Can you meet me there?"

He paused again, his heavy breath traveling through the line. "Yes, I will be there."

"Okay, I'll see you at ten."

I hung up my new international cell phone and exhaled the giant breath I'd been holding in during that phone call. I didn't know if Julien would be happy to see me again, but at least I could help him find the painting.

I closed my eyes as I settled back in my seat on the shuttle bus, unable to believe that I was actually here. That on the same morning I would've been walking down the aisle, instead, I was traveling through France to find a stolen painting…and to see an ex-con man who I couldn't stop thinking about *and* who may never want to look at me again.

Maybe Lily had been right. Maybe someone really had stolen me and replaced me with a new, crazier version.

But I had to admit, even if this was all for nothing, I was liking this version more and more each day.

Carrying only a purse and a small duffel bag, I stepped off the train in Annecy and breathed in that crisp mountain air, hoping it would relieve the bundle of nerves that had seized my gut.

No such luck.

I gripped my stomach as I followed the herd of passengers down the stairs, scanning the platform below for Julien.

And when I spotted a pair of deep-brown eyes, a five o'clock shadow covering a set of defined cheekbones, and a hint of a dimple that made me melt right there on the stairs, I couldn't help but smile.

The minute our eyes met, he set off toward me, and there, in the middle of a crowded train station, we found each other.

Standing face-to-face with Julien, all words evaporated from my tongue. And as I saw the look in his eyes, I immediately knew that I'd made the right decision in coming back. I didn't know what would happen, how long I would stay in France, or where any of this would lead me, but it didn't matter. For once in my life, I'd followed my heart instead of my head, and as Julien took my hands in his and brushed my cheeks with his soft lips, I felt as if the weight of the world had been lifted off my shoulders.

"I cannot believe it is you." Julien's eyes combed my face, his mouth forming a hesitant smile. "What are you doing here? What happened with your wedding?"

"We called it off," I said. "In the end, you were right. I wasn't in love with Paul. And as it turns out, I have feelings for someone else."

Julien arched an eyebrow. "Oh? And who might this someone else be?"

I poked him in the ribs and laughed. "I think you probably have an idea."

He grinned, his eyes still wide, his breath fast. "How long are you here for?"

I shrugged and shot him a flirty smile. "That depends."

"On what? When you must return to work?"

"I'm not worried about work," I said.

"*You* not worried about your job?"

"No, for once, I'm not. It *depends* on how long you can put up with me. I bought a one-way ticket."

Julien finally broke into his sweet, goofy grin, then slid his arms around my waist, picked me up, and kissed me smack on the lips right in the middle of the bustling train station.

"You are here to stay?" he asked after he'd pulled his lips from mine, his electrifying touch still lingering on my skin.

"Yes, I'm here to stay."

He squeezed me one more time and kissed me again on the cheek. "I *am* sorry about the wedding. You are okay, though?"

"Let's not pretend like you're *that* sorry."

"I am trying to be sensitive and see if you are okay, and here you go again assuming I have bad intentions," Julien said, stifling a laugh.

"You're impossible." I shook my head, still unable to wipe the smile from my face. "But we can argue later. We have a painting to find."

Julien took my bag from me and slung it over his shoulder as we set off in the same direction we had just days before, yet things were now so, *so* different.

"Tell me," he said as we left the station and waited at a crosswalk. "*How* do you know where the painting is? And *where* is it?

Because I have been here for one day now, and I know who has it, but I still cannot find it."

"You know who has it?" I asked as we wound through the familiar cobblestoned streets and past all of the charming sidewalk cafés, where just days before we'd been running from the police.

"Yes. You obviously remember the man with the tattoos and his girlfriend in the lingerie store?"

I didn't miss the glimpse of flirtatiousness dancing around Julien's eyes. "How could I forget?" I said.

"I have not forgotten about it either. In fact, I have thought about it many times."

I smacked him in the arm. "Of course you have. Just get on with the story."

He snickered. "Okay, okay." Julien looked to either side of us, then lowered his voice. "I went to the prison and threatened…I mean, *talked* to my brother. He told me that he gave *them* the painting because he knew the police were close to catching him. The plan was that Ralph—the man with the tattoos—and his girlfriend, Sara, would take the painting abroad and sell it to a museum, and then they would split the money three ways. And you remember Ralph's sister, Marie? The woman with the long, black hair?"

"Mm-hmm," I mumbled. How could I have forgotten *her*?

"Marie was telling the truth that day. She does not know anything about the painting. It appears that they are hiding it from her. So it is not in her apartment, and over the past day, I have been trying to get into Ralph's apartment too, but either he or his girlfriend has always been home. And I found out through Marie that Ralph and Sara are leaving the country tonight. Marie just thinks they are going on vacation, though. She has no idea."

"Is Ralph's girlfriend extremely short? With long, blonde hair?" I asked.

"Yes, but how do you know that? You did not see her that day in the lingerie store, did you?"

"No, I didn't see her that day. But I saw her the night before."

When Julien's expression remained a giant question mark, I stopped walking and turned to him. "This is probably going to sound really strange to you, but I need you to trust me, okay?"

He nodded. "Okay. So how do you know her?"

"The night that we arrived in Annecy, when I followed you to the apartment?"

"Yes, when you should *not* have followed me?" he interjected, stepping to the side to allow the throngs of tourists to pass by.

"Right. Well, after I watched you sneak into the apartment, I saw this woman with long red hair, just like mine. And when she turned her head, her face looked exactly like my mom. I don't know what came over me, but I had to follow her. It was like I couldn't control myself. But she was going too fast and I couldn't keep up that well, and then finally, when I followed her around a corner, she was gone. Like she'd disappeared into thin air or something. So I was standing there, feeling like an idiot, because at that point I had no idea where I was or how I would find my way back, when this really tiny girl with long, blonde hair came out of a garage, checked all around to make sure no one was looking, and locked it up. Then she saw me when she was walking away, and she jumped. Like she was hiding something."

Julien's eyes widened. "Where is this garage?"

I shifted my weight, feeling a stab of nerves in my chest. "That's the thing. I can't tell you street names or anything, but if you can take me back to Marie's apartment, to the red door, I'm hoping I'll remember the way."

Julien smiled, but I could still detect a hint of doubt in his eyes.

"I know this sounds insane," I said again, desperate for him to believe me, "but you're saying that the girlfriend is really short with long, blonde hair. There aren't that many people in France with long, blonde hair. Almost everyone here is a brunette. And when I say short, I mean like not more than five feet tall."

He scratched his chin and nodded, the doubt leaving his eyes. "Yes, I think we are talking about the same woman."

"I'm telling you, I just have this feeling that I'm right. Because seeing that woman who looked like my mom…well, it was like she was leading me there for a reason. At the time, I didn't think anything of it. I just thought I was losing my mind, but now…"

"I trust you, Chloe," Julien said, placing his hands on my shoulders. "I will take you to the red door. We must not waste any more time, though. *On y va?*"

I smiled. "*On y va.*"

Julien took my hand and led me back to the bubbling stream that ran through the center of town, where once again I glimpsed the sparkling blue lake and those amazing mountains. And now, with the weather a little cooler, a white layer of snow capped a few of the highest peaks, making them all the more stunning.

We made our way down the cobblestoned streets, underneath that same stone archway I remembered from before, and there it was. The red door.

"Okay, this is it," Julien announced as he peered both ways down the road. "But we must move quickly and be discreet. We do not want to run into Ralph or Sara until we have a plan. Do you remember which way you went from here?"

I closed my eyes and mentally transported myself back to that night, when I'd seen my mother's face so clearly. I'd been trying to recreate that image for the past day, hoping that when I arrived back at this spot, my mom would reappear or that somehow she would guide me back to that place.

But when I opened my eyes, I realized I didn't need her to show me the way. I already knew it.

I pulled Julien's hand and sped down the same path I'd gone before, but this time with certainty and confidence. After winding through a maze of streets, all of the stone buildings looking the same, goose bumps suddenly prickled the back of my neck, and I knew we were close.

I led Julien around a corner, the last corner where I was sure I'd seen the woman with the auburn hair.

But my heart dropped as we gazed across the street. What I hadn't noticed the first time I'd stood here was that the entire road was lined with small garages, all of them with the same silvery-gray door, the same padded lock on the bottom.

"Are we here?" Julien asked, his eyes combing what must've been at least ten gray doors, all clones of each other.

I nodded, the disappointment setting in. "Yes, but I don't know which one. I only remembered seeing one that night, not all of these. What are we going to do? Break into each one?"

But before Julien had a chance to respond, one of the doors began to open.

Julien pulled me off to the side of a building where we hid in the shadows, waiting to see who would emerge from the garage.

The door was completely raised now, but there were no lights inside the space, so we couldn't see who or what was lurking on the other side.

We've come so far, please let it be the right one, I pleaded silently, hoping that if my mom had led us to this point, she wouldn't stop now.

A bulging, tattooed arm appeared. My breath quickened, and I noticed that Julien's did too.

This was it. This was so it. *Thank you, Mom!*

And just as Ralph's head popped out of the dark space, a miniature blue car sped up the skinny road and screeched to a halt right in front of him, a wisp of long, blonde hair blowing out the open window.

Julien pulled his cell phone out of his pocket, typed something on the keypad, then thrust it into my hands. "Type in the street name and press Send," he whispered. "And no matter what, don't move. Okay?"

"Got it." Adrenaline surged through me as I craned my neck to see the blue street sign tacked onto the building across the road.

Trying to steady my trembling hands, I typed the name and pushed the Send button.

When I lifted my gaze, I spotted Ralph and his girlfriend lugging a large rectangular object wrapped in a blue blanket into the backseat of the car, but I didn't see Julien anywhere.

Before I had a chance to worry about where Julien had gone or how he was planning on stopping them from driving away with his painting, a cool cylinder pushed against my temple and a sweaty arm wrapped around my neck. My heart thudded in my chest and tears immediately sprang to my eyes.

"Don't say a fucking word," a female voice whispered in my ear as she pushed me forward toward the car. I recognized her accent immediately—it was Marie, the Australian Seductress.

She kept the gun pressed to my head as she walked us both forward into the street so that we were now clearly visible to Ralph and his girlfriend, but as my eyes frantically darted from side to side, I couldn't find Julien.

Oh, God. Where is he?

Marie peeled the barrel of the gun off my temple and pointed it straight ahead at Ralph's tiny girlfriend.

"Marie, what the fuck are you doing?" Ralph shouted, his deep voice booming through the alley.

I plastered my arms and hands at my sides, trying to calm the trembling, trying to tell myself that this would all work out. But with Marie's arm squeezing my neck so tightly I could barely breathe, and Julien nowhere in sight, panic overtook me.

"Just shut up!" Marie screeched at him, making me jump. "If either of you move an inch, I'll shoot both of you, and I'll shoot her."

"Who the fuck is she?" Ralph barked, clearly not fazed that his lunatic sister was pointing a gun at them.

"Don't you remember? Julien's little American girlfriend? Which reminds me. Julien!" she called out, her voice shaky and wild. "Where did you go, Julien? I just saw you a minute ago. If you come out now, your precious little *Américaine* won't get hurt."

Julien!

But when Julien didn't appear, Marie walked forward, taking me with her, until the barrel of the gun was just a few feet away from Sara's nose. The look in Sara's cool blue eyes morphed from panic to complete dread.

Marie's frantic, desperate voice shrieked in my ear again as she waved the gun toward Ralph. "You dirty bastard of a brother! I know you're planning on leaving me here and never coming back. And after everything I've done for you, the least you could've done is cut me some of the money you're going to make off this painting. You know I have nothing. *Nothing!*"

"Marie, just put the gun down," Ralph said in a steady voice, his fists still clenched at his sides.

Just as I noticed Ralph's eyes flicker suddenly, their focus changing from Marie's face to something just past her head, Marie tightened her grip around my neck. She squeezed and squeezed, making me gasp for air. The last thing I saw as blackness closed in around me was Sara's tiny face contorted in fear. But then, as my body went limp, Sara's face disappeared.

A loud *bang* startled me awake. I rolled my head to the side as a violent cough rocked through my chest, and there was Julien, just a few feet away from me, wrestling the gun from Marie's hands.

When he managed to steal it from her death grip, she smacked his arm, causing the gun to fly from his hands in my direction. I pushed myself up off the rough cobblestones, which were jabbing into my back, and coughed again, my neck and lungs screaming in pain. I blinked my eyes and peeked up to find Ralph shoving the painting in the backseat of the car and Sara climbing into the passenger side.

Lunging forward, I grabbed the gun off the ground, stumbled to my feet, and ran toward the car. Just as Ralph and his girlfriend slammed their car doors shut and the engine revved up, I raced to the side of the car, aimed the gun at the front tire, and fired.

The force of the gunshot propelled me backward, but I quickly gained my bearings, aimed at the back tire, and let another shot rip through the quiet alley.

And just as Ralph's eyes turned to fire and he lunged out of the car toward me, a piercing siren stopped him in his tracks. Two police cars barreled down either side of the street, blocking us in.

I dropped the gun and jumped backward as it clattered to the ground. Julien had pinned Marie's arms behind her back, and she finally stopped struggling as she watched the police officers jump out of their cars.

Before I had a chance to process what was happening, a familiar face appeared amid the uniformed officers running toward us. It was Guillaume—Julien's special-agent brother.

"Fuck," Ralph muttered under his breath as Guillaume slammed him against the car and cuffed his wrists behind his back.

Another officer rounded the car and cuffed the girlfriend, and a third took Marie from Julien's grasp and arrested her too.

I shook my head, still trying to digest what had just gone down when Julien appeared in front of me, his huge brown eyes full of concern. He took my face in both of his hands. "Are you okay?"

I nodded. "I think so."

"How did you know how to use the gun?" he asked, a look of pure astonishment washing over his face.

A grin slid over my lips. "I asked my dad to teach me when I was a teenager...*just in case* something ever happened when I was home alone with the girls."

His eyes lit up as they poured into mine. "Chloe, you are incredible."

My cheeks flushed from the feel of his strong hands on my skin, my heart overflowing with warmth from the way he looked at me as if he'd never felt this way for anyone in his entire life.

Then he leaned down and pressed his lips against mine, his kiss a violent burst of passion and desire, his hands weaving through my hair, his firm arms wrapping me up and holding me tight.

I relaxed into his kiss, my brain unable to think as his masculine, sexy scent engulfed me.

After our lips had parted and I'd caught my breath, I looked deep into Julien's eyes. "So, what now?"

He slid his arms around my waist and pulled me in even tighter, his mouth meeting the skin on my neck and trailing down to my collarbone, making me forget all about my aching neck and my short breath.

"I am thinking I will take you to a nice dinner to celebrate, and then we will stay in Annecy for the night. I will book us a room at the Splendid Hôtel. How does that sound?"

I laughed as I ran my fingers through his soft, chestnut hair. "Splendid."

But as Julien's curious hands continued roaming over the curves in my back, only stopping once they reached my hips, I leaned in and whispered in his ear, "Maybe we should just skip dinner…I'm not that hungry after all."

A deep, throaty laugh rumbled out of his chest and he kissed me again on the cheek. We watched two of the policemen unload his family painting from Ralph's car and haul the criminals off to jail, where I hoped they stayed for a long, long time.

Guillaume appeared by our side, patted Julien on the shoulder, then raised a brow in my direction. "I see you have decided to return to France already."

A full-blown laugh bubbled from my lips, my nerves finally releasing.

"It was Chloe who knew where to find the painting," Julien said, his face beaming with pride.

Guillaume's curious gaze landed on me once more. "My older brother has finally met his match. And let me tell you, Miss Turner, there is no more loyal man than Julien. I promise you that."

"You can call me Chloe," I said with a grin.

He laughed. "Come, I will drive you both wherever you need to go, and I will arrange for the painting to be driven back to the vineyard. I am sure *Maman* will be very happy."

Julien patted his younger brother on the back and thanked him as we walked toward the police car.

But just as I was about to take Julien's hand and climb into the backseat, a flash of wavy, auburn hair caught my eye. I whipped my head around to where I'd seen it…but she was gone.

I raised my eyes toward the bright-blue sky, the puffy white clouds sailing softly overhead, and the sun's warm rays beating down on my face, and I knew in that moment that I would never again have to feel like I had no one to look out for me.

My mother had been here with me all along, watching over me, guiding me, and giving me the courage to step out on a limb and take a risk, to really *live* my life.

So I said a silent *thank-you* to my beautiful mother for leading me down this unpredictable and sometimes crazy path. I tossed my rationalizations out the window, took the hand that was stretched out before me, and rode off toward a future full of adventure and passion, a magical life that even in my wildest dreams, I never could've imagined.

EPILOGUE

From: Angela Kelly
To: Chloe Turner
Sent: Saturday, October 8 at 1:00 a.m.
Subject: Former boss desperately seeking French lover

Chloe,

Heard through grapevine that wedding has relocated to France and a sexy, French ex-con has taken the groom's place.

Two pressing questions for you:

1. Where is my invitation?

2. Does this sexy, French ex-con man of yours have any brothers? If he does, I don't care if you invite me or not. I'm on the next flight to France.

Angela Kelly
Kelly and Rain Premier Event Planning
Washington, DC

P.S. Does he talk dirty French to you in bed? Do you know what he's saying? Do you even care? Vive la France, sister!

The End

Read on for an excerpt from

SLEEPING WITH PARIS

by

Juliette Sobanet

www.juliettesobanet.com

ONE

vendredi, le 24 septembre

Just because lawyers know how to lie doesn't mean they're good at it.

"Keep in touch," I called, waving a not-so-tearful good-bye to my coworkers for the last time. I stepped out into the muggy DC heat and was so happy to be done with that hellhole that I felt like ripping off my little black suit and skipping down M Street in my underwear.

After seven years of practice, both as a student, then as a poor college graduate, I'd become quite the expert at strutting in heels down the brick sidewalks of Georgetown. Today, as I glided along in a state of total disbelief that this day had finally arrived, my normally uncomfortable heels effortlessly carried me away from my boring part-time translating job—make that my *ex*-translating job—down to Wisconsin Avenue, where my fiancé was wrapping up his last day at his Georgetown law firm.

Unable to hide the enormous grin spreading across my face, I reached into my purse and pulled out my flight itinerary just to make sure, for the hundredth time that day, that this was, in fact, my life. I scanned the piece of paper for our names.

Charlotte Summers and Jeff Dillon. One-way flight departing from Washington Dulles International en route to Paris Charles de Gaulle. In two days. *Two freaking days!*

After stopping at the liquor store and splurging on a fancy bottle of champagne, I bounced into Jeff's posh office. His bubbly administrative assistant, Tara—a former hometown beauty queen—greeted me with her pearly-white smile.

"Hey, Charlotte," she said, her gum popping like miniature firecrackers in her mouth. "You getting excited for Paris?"

"Well, I just put in my last few hours at the office otherwise known as hell, so excited would be an understatement."

Her platinum-blonde ponytail bobbed as she giggled. "Jeff sent me the pics of your new apartment over there. Oh, my God, it's gorgeous!"

I beamed. "I know. Can you believe it? This firm doesn't mess around."

"Girl, you two are going to have so much fun. But don't forget about us back here. We're going to miss you so much."

"We're going to miss you too. But don't worry, we'll be back in the spring for our friend's wedding, and *technically* we'll be moving back in a year…unless I can convince Jeff to stay longer." I winked at her. "Hey, is Jeff in his office?"

"No, he just stepped out for a minute, but you can go on in and wait for him. He should be right back."

"Thanks, Tara."

"No prob, dear."

I walked down the long corridor, let myself into Jeff's secluded corner office, and ran my finger around his immaculate desk. Over my new ruby-colored bra and thong set, I was sporting a sexy black skirt coupled with a silky violet tank in the hope that we could relive the steamy sex we'd had the last time I wore this hot little number to his office…which was also when I gained a new appreciation for his extra-cushy swiveling office chair.

I plopped the bottle of champagne onto a neat stack of papers on Jeff's desk as I took a seat in the swivel chair. After I jiggled the mouse to bring his computer out of sleep mode, I signed into my e-mail account and clicked on a message Jeff had sent me the week before so that I could, once again, gaze at the pictures of the charming Parisian apartment that awaited us. In his e-mail, Jeff had written:

Welcome home, babe. Can't wait.

xoxoxo,

Jeff

My heart melted all over again, just like it had the first time I opened his e-mail. God, I loved this man.

Just as I was opening the first picture, an instant message popped up on the bottom right-hand side of Jeff's computer. I wasn't a nosy fiancée; I trusted Jeff. I couldn't help but read the bubble on his computer screen, though. It read:

Brooke: You there?

Brooke who? Must be a colleague, I reasoned. But then another message popped up:

Brooke: Give me a call when you have a minute…

I racked my brain trying to remember if Jeff had ever mentioned anyone at work named Brooke. Nothing came to mind. I considered responding to her and pretending to be Jeff to see what she would say, but then I thought better of it. I had nothing to worry about. I had faith in Jeff and in our relationship—so much so that I'd decided to pack up my life in DC, quit my French teaching position (which, by the way, I loved) *and* my summer translating job (didn't care for that one so much), and move to Paris with him. So, whoever this Brooke person was, she was probably harmless.

But then, another message popped up.

Brooke: I really want to talk to you…xxx.

A sickening feeling took hold in the pit of my stomach as I stared at the *xxx*. Who *was* this girl?

Closing my eyes, I took a deep breath and told myself to relax. She was probably just an old law school friend who was still hung up on Jeff. She obviously didn't know that he was engaged now, that we were moving to Paris together, and that he was in love with *me*.

But then I thought about my college boyfriend who'd been cheating on me for the entire last year of our three-year relationship. I remembered how blindsided I'd been. Wondering how I could've missed his infidelity when all along, it was right there under my nose.

Jeff wasn't like my college boyfriend, though. He'd fallen for me so quickly, so completely. He was sweet and honest. He wore his heart on his sleeve. He was different from all the rest. Which was why I'd fallen head over heels in love with him and why I hadn't hesitated to say yes when he'd proposed only six months after we met.

But when I opened my eyes and read Brooke's messages again, especially the *xxx* part, I couldn't ignore that nagging gut instinct telling me something wasn't right.

Hoping Jeff stayed out of the office longer than a few minutes, I launched into detective mode. With our impending move only days away, I figured a little investigation couldn't hurt. And besides, I was *sure* it would turn out to be nothing.

I pulled up the Internet history on Jeff's computer, scrolled through the most recent websites visited, and let out a sigh of relief. Nothing alarming.

But then, at the bottom of the list, my heart dropped.

Match.com popped out at me first. Then I saw Yahoo! Personals. And last, but definitely not least, eHarmony. As my stomach began doing flip-flops—*not* the good kind—and the blood rose to my head, I clicked on the Yahoo! Personals link.

There I saw a picture of Jeff, a picture I had taken on our engagement night, posted next to a caption that read:

Successful lawyer looking for fun in the nation's capital.

My hand trembled over the mouse as I blinked my eyes to make sure what I was seeing was real. This had to be a joke. There was no way, no way in hell, that my fiancé, Jeff, the love of my life, would ever do something so deceitful. He wouldn't hurt me like this. He just wouldn't.

I desperately skimmed the page for some glimmer of hope.

Member since April.

It was now September.

My hands continued shaking as if I was holding a loaded gun and wasn't sure if I should pull the trigger or let it drop.

As I scrolled farther down the page, though, I saw it. The clincher. The mother of all blows. A message from a redheaded, big-busted girl named…Brooke. It read:

I've had such a wonderful time with you this week, Jeff, I can't wait to come visit you in Paris…xoxoxo, Brooke.

Brooke. All I could see were her giant boobs bursting out of her porn-starish, shiny, blue tube top. Red hair. Boobs. xoxoxo. Brooke.

My vision blurred, refusing to see what was staring me in the face. I shook my head in an attempt to regain composure. This could not actually be happening two days before we were moving to Paris together. And less than six months after Jeff had proposed.

It had to be a mistake.

I clicked on the instant message from Brooke and without thinking, I responded.

Jeff: Hey.

Brooke: There you are, sexy. Busy day at the firm?

My hands quivered over the keyboard as I continued, not caring in the least that Jeff could be coming back at any second.

Jeff: Crazy busy. You?

Brooke: Feeling a little tired after last night…

What the hell happened last night? Who did she think she was?

Jeff: What happened last night?

Brooke: LOL. Like you don't remember.

Jeff: How could I forget? I love hearing you talk about it, though…

Brooke: You kept me up all night!

Stupid whore. I was going to kill her. Just as soon as I killed Jeff. Filthy, scum-of-the-earth bastard.

Jeff: Tell me more. I love it when you talk naughty.

Brooke: You really want me to give you the details?

Jeff: Work is really boring today…throw me a bone.

Brooke: Well, I remember your naked body on top of mine…Does that jog your memory?

I could feel my breakfast making its way back up through my stomach. But I had to get it straight. I couldn't lose Jeff without knowing for sure.

Jeff: Yes, but I want to hear you tell me the full story. All the details.

It took a few seconds. But then I got more clarification than I had ever wanted.

Brooke: LOL. Well, first there was the time in your office last night, and then all night long at your place, and oh yeah, this morning in the shower. And, that's right, one last time on the kitchen counter before you left for work.

A fiery-hot, uncontrollable rage boiled up inside of me as I remembered Jeff calling me the night before to cancel our dinner plans. He'd said he had to stay late at the firm. It had become the routine for the past few months. *Staying late. Lots of work to do. Can't make dinner. Sorry, babe, I love you.*

God, I was such a fool.

Just then, Jeff burst through the office door.

"Hey, babe, no more summer days in a cubicle! And you brought champagne, how sweet."

I stared up at Jeff in disbelief, at a complete loss for words. There he was—my six-foot-three, blond, blue-eyed, gorgeously built fiancé. The man I had trusted with all my heart, with every fiber of my body. The man I was going to build a life with. How could he have done this to me?

As my eyes darted from Jeff to the screen and back to Jeff, a stray tear fought its way down my cheek.

"Babe, what's the matter? What's going on?" he asked as he rounded his desk to comfort me.

I rose with more force than I knew I had in me at the time and glared at him. "*You* tell *me* what the hell is going on."

"Charlotte, what are you talking about?" he asked defensively as a hint of panic passed through his eyes. "Are you okay?"

"No, Jeff, I'm not okay." I wiped the tear from my face, determined not to let any more of them fall. "Tell me what's going on. Who's Brooke?" I demanded as I pointed a trembling finger at his computer screen.

He glanced at the screen long enough to see the nasty sex talk from Brooke, and then looked back at me with desperate, pleading eyes. "I can explain, it's not what it looks like—"

"Then what the hell is it?" I rounded the desk to get away from him and that revolting computer screen. "You're sick. How could you do this to me? To us?"

Jeff ran a shaky hand through his wavy blond hair and shook his head. He didn't have an excuse. Because there was no damn excuse.

"How long? How long have you been seeing her?"

"Charlotte, don't—"

"Stop lying to me. Just tell me how long it's been." My legs felt like they might give way, but I forced myself to stay standing.

"About a month," he mumbled as he locked eyes with the floor.

"And these websites? All of your online profiles? How long have you been doing that?"

Jeff shook his head in silence, his eyes darting frantically around the room as if he was desperate to escape. Desperate to jump out of his skin and be anywhere but here.

"Answer me."

"Charlotte, I love you. I didn't mean to hurt you, really," he pleaded as a couple of stray beads of sweat rolled down his forehead.

"You sure have a sick way of showing your love." I couldn't take any more. I had to get out of there. I pivoted on my wobbly legs and bolted for the door.

"Charlotte, don't go. We're leaving in two days. We can work this out. We can get through this!" Jeff grabbed hold of my arm, but I yanked it back and smacked the champagne bottle in the process. The tall bottle of Veuve Clicquot flew through the air in slow motion, then shattered all over the shiny hardwood floors. I stared at the shards of glass and fizzy bubbles that circled our feet, my heart aching for what should've been a celebration of our love, but what had now become the aftermath of Jeff's deception.

I lifted my eyes to his, knowing that this was it. No matter how much I loved Jeff, I couldn't stay. "*We* are not leaving in two days. I'm not going anywhere with you. I'm not marrying you, and I'm not moving to Paris with you."

With that, I left him bewildered in his office, and I stormed outside into the stifling DC heat.

ACKNOWLEDGMENTS

I would like to thank my editor, Kelli Martin, and the entire Montlake team for your support and expertise. Kelli, your enthusiasm for my stories puts a smile on my face every day. Special thanks to my amazing agent, Kevan Lyon, for your insight and guidance. I would not be here without your support.

To Leslie, thank you for your continuous encouragement and belief in me. I appreciate it more than you know. Amanda, thank you for devouring my book on your iPhone and for being such a wonderful cousin and friend. Huge thanks to Kelly for reading my debut novel in its earliest stages, and to James and Zack for being the first male readers to test the waters.

I'm incredibly grateful for the fabulous support network I've made through blogging, Twitter, and Facebook this past year. I didn't realize it was possible to make lasting friendships online, but you've proved me wrong.

Mom, thank you for always telling me that I could be anything I wanted to be. And to Sean, thank you for listening to all of my "what ifs," even when you don't have a clue what I'm talking about.

Finally, I'd like to thank every single reader who has given my books a chance, and especially those who've written to me with words of support and encouragement. It makes me happier than a love-struck woman in Paris to know that you're enjoying my stories!

ABOUT THE AUTHOR

Juliette Sobanet is the Amazon.com bestselling author of *Sleeping with Paris.* A former French professor, Juliette is a graduate of Georgetown University and New York University in France, and she has lived and studied in both Paris and Lyon. Juliette recently relocated to sunny San Diego, where she lives with her husband and their two massive cats. When she's not writing, she's eating chocolate, practicing yoga, or scheming on when she can travel back to France. Visit Juliette's website at www.juliettesobanet.com.